MW01485960

CLOSING TIME

Also in the Michael Gannon series

Stop at Nothing
Run for Cover
Hard to Break
No Safe Place

Also by Michael Ledwidge

The Girl in the Vault
Beach Wedding
The Narrowback
Bad Connection
Before the Devil Knows You're Dead

Cowritten with James Patterson

The Quickie
Now You See Her
Zoo
Step on a Crack
Run for Your Life
Worst Case
Tick Tock
I, Michael Bennett
Gone
Burn
Alert
Bullseye
Chase
The Dangerous Days of Daniel X

CLOSING TIME

A THRILLER

MICHAEL LEDWIDGE

HANOVER
SQUARE
PRESS

HANOVER
SQUARE
PRESS™

Recycling programs
for this product may
not exist in your area.

ISBN-13: 978-1-335-09052-2

Closing Time

Copyright © 2025 by Michael Ledwidge

All rights reserved. No part of this book may be used or reproduced in any manner what-
soever without written permission.

Without limiting the exclusive rights of any author, contributor or the publisher of
this publication, any unauthorized use of this publication to train generative artificial
intelligence (AI) technologies is expressly prohibited. Harlequin also exercises their rights
under Article 4(3) of the Digital Single Market Directive 2019/790 and expressly reserves
this publication from the text and data mining exception.

This is a work of fiction. Names, characters, places and incidents are either the product of
the author's imagination or are used fictitiously. Any resemblance to actual persons, living
or dead, businesses, companies, events or locales is entirely coincidental.

TM and ® are trademarks of Harlequin Enterprises ULC.

Hanover Square Press
22 Adelaide St. West, 41st Floor
Toronto, Ontario M5H 4E3, Canada
HanoverSqPress.com

HarperCollins Publishers
Macken House, 39/40 Mayor Street Upper,
Dublin 1, D01 C9W8, Ireland
www.HarperCollins.com

Printed in U.S.A.

For Travis and Francis

PROLOGUE

PARTNERS IN CRIME

1

Andrew Paxton definitely wasn't one of your hopeless romantics, but when he saw the extraordinary color of the sky, even he couldn't help but open the sliders on the back deck of the beach bungalow to step out into the sunset glow.

The crystal glass sitting on the patio side table gave off a bell-like chime as it collided with the two-thousand-dollar bottle of Courvoisier L'Essence he clutched in his well-manicured hand.

Paxton gently swirled the cognac in the blood-orange light, wondering what to drink to. He drew a complete blank.

That's where I'm at, he thought, taking a smooth sip as he eased himself back into the chaise.

Out of everything, he thought.

He ran a hand through his shower-wet hair.

No ideas. No prospects. All tapped out.

A salt-tinged sea breeze blew in steadily through the king palms before him, and between their gently swaying green trunks he watched a cruise ship at sea coming around the far side of some land in the distance. A sharp pang of homesickness hit him from out of nowhere as he stared at it.

He suddenly wished he was on the ship, heading out of here, heading home.

Here was the Pansea Beach Club in Phuket, Thailand, in one of its Sunset Suites, to be precise. Besides the deep blue seawater view before him, there was an infinity pool, and beyond it, a football-field-long runway of manicured grass that led to a private beach.

Luxurious privacy, Paxton thought, remembering the website copy. He needed—no, he *deserved*—some luxurious privacy. As well as some rest and relaxation after all the fruitless meetings he'd just had.

He'd been led to believe that he could find a buyer for the very unique item he was trying to sell. That's why he had traveled from his hometown of Sydney, Australia, to the famous Coin Universe convention here in Phuket where the who's who in the Asian block-chain industry convened every year.

Well, that wasn't the only reason he'd come this far, was it? he thought, turning his glass in his hands.

He needed some distance from home, some discretion. The crux of the matter was that the provenance of the object in question had not exactly been completely legally nailed down. Paxton certainly had a claim to it as it had been left with his company and unclaimed for over the prescribed period. Finders keepers and all that.

But there were other things to consider.

Like the fact that his business partner, John Hayden, also had a claim.

He had not consulted Hayden about his plan to sell the item. The one time he had alluded to a sale, Hayden had told him that they should wait, not be too hasty.

But sometimes Hayden could be too cautious, Paxton thought, biting at his lip. Sometimes one needed to strike while the iron was hot, right? That's what he thought, anyway. Which was why he was here.

But as it turned out, he didn't need to worry about any ethical or professional violations, did he?

Because so far, the iron was about as hot as a witch's tit.

Among the angel and venture capital investors and other assorted grifters gathered at the confab, he had yet to come across even one serious player.

He looked out at the cruise ship again wistfully.

Please don't tell me I've taken a forty-five-hundred-mile trip for nothing, Paxton thought as he pressed his glass to his artificially smooth brow.

He'd finished his first drink and was pouring his next when he spotted a figure in the distance.

Up the grass runway off the beach with the ocean breeze came a young white woman, one with a salon-perfect updo, a smiling gold-tanned pixie face, and a body that just didn't quit wrapped in remarkably tight yoga wear.

"My, my," he mumbled, sitting up straight.

Paxton watched, riveted, as the pricey escort he'd ordered came up the teak steps. At the exorbitant price, he hadn't exactly been expecting something fresh off the interstate.

But this was a happy surprise, wasn't it? Paxton thought.

She could have been an American football cheerleader straight from the plains of Texas in search of her lost pom-poms.

"Hope you're ready, boss man," she said in greeting as she took the glass from his hand.

He watched as her beautiful eyes went big as cupcakes as she drained his cognac in one shot.

"We probably need to get started before wifey gets back," she said.

"Wifey is back in Australia," Paxton said truthfully in his Sydney accent.

The high-end hooker licked greedily at the rim of the glass.

"Well, well, then," she said. "When the cat's away . . ."

2

The escort was in the master bathroom getting things together and Paxton had just popped two blue pills and was about to drop his robe when he heard the creak of the bedroom door behind him.

The two men who had entered the room were burly Mediterraneans with dark hair and pockmarked olive skin. As Paxton stood gaping, a fair-haired man with broad shoulders stepped in from behind them.

"Who are you? Get the hell out of here! Out!" Paxton yelled as he looked around for a blunt object. There was nothing and no damn room. He was cornered and without his bloody pants!

He was still panicking when the bathroom door suddenly opened. Without a glance in Paxton's direction, the escort, still completely dressed, stepped out.

Paxton realized it then as the two dark thugs stepped aside to let her leave.

"You set me up, you bitch!" Paxton screamed at her back. "I'll get you back! Count on it!"

Paxton turned to the other man who chuckled softly at this. The crooked smile he gave him was somewhere between charming and unsettling.

"What is this?" Paxton said, turning his attention to the

thugs. "Who are you? Her pimps? You want my wallet? What do you want?"

Then as they stood there silently just staring at him, it came to him.

They were professional kidnappers, Paxton suddenly thought with a dry swallow.

Shit! He tried to remember his training. He'd paid for a damn course on executive kidnapping a year before. Nothing was coming to mind. It had been too long ago.

What happens next? he thought. A blindfold and a car trunk? Fingers snipped off with pruning shears? He was screwed.

Deep panic hit him then. The light in the room seemed to waver as if a dimmer switch had been turned. He was coming close to fainting. He was free-falling inside.

"Bring it, you bastards!" Paxton suddenly screamed, balling his hands into fists. "Who wants to bleed first?"

"Andrew, Andrew, stop working yourself up. Please. There's no need for all that," the other man said softly in a British accent.

When Paxton looked at him, he suddenly noticed how remarkably well-dressed the man was. The thugs were dressed like workmen, but this man was wearing a summery single-breasted sky-blue suit jacket with white skinny jeans. The subtly textured jacket looked like it was made of silk, and the tight tailoring screamed Savile Row. He looked like he was on his way to a cocktail party on a yacht.

"Who . . . who are you?" Paxton said.

"My name is Birch," he said. "And I am so very sorry to barge in like this, unannounced. I know it must be a bit of a shock. Unfortunately, it was unavoidable as you haven't been answering your phone."

Paxton squinted at him for a moment.

Then he figured it out.

And let out a breath of blessed relief.

3

Because it wasn't a professional kidnapping gang.

It was a client.

Thank you, thank you, thank you, Paxton thought, resisting the urge to clasp his hands together in prayer.

It was just a pissed-off customer from his bank.

Back in Sydney, Paxton and John Hayden ran a bank called Northdale Standard.

In some respects, Northdale Standard was a normal bank with real physical branches throughout Sydney and New South Wales.

But in other respects, there was nothing standard about Northdale Standard at all.

There were many clients in Australia and Asia who needed banking discretion, access to offshore accounts as well as access to the banks of Switzerland known for their famous dedication to financial privacy.

Northdale Standard provided such access by creating complex financial transactions and shell companies. These financial mazes, as Paxton liked to think of them, were designed to obscure the true nature of the funds and thereby to avoid detection by regulators. This maze-making generated a tidy profit for him and Hayden, which was usually a very good thing.

But lately there had been a problem.

A glitch.

They had been involved with another international bank in facilitating a state bond investment fund right here in Thailand. Unfortunately, a significant amount of money had disappeared from this fund, siphoned off by corrupt government officials, leading to a scandal. Their bank's exposure was minimal, but it had led to some significant losses among some of their clients.

And now some of those clients were claiming they had been deceived about the level of risk involved in their investment and were blaming Northdale Standard, which was legally laughable.

The only problem was these weren't the kind of clients who sent lawyers or threatened civil suits to resolve business disputes.

So he and Hayden had decided to leave Sydney for a while.

Their mission was to put in some face time with their international contacts and to pump them for a boost of some liquid capital to create a gesture of goodwill and to satisfy their more hotheaded clients.

Paxton wasn't particularly concerned. It had happened before with a firm out of Shanghai, and they had figured it out.

Just a glitch, Paxton thought, looking into the reasonable face of the Brit.

If push came to shove, Paxton could square this account with another in two clicks, he thought with relief.

What had Hayden called him once? *The Michelangelo of creative bookkeeping?*

Of course, he was. Changing deck chairs on the *Titanic* was his forte. He was a born juggler when it came to distracting the customers from realizing Northdale Standard had issued many more hat checks than they had hats. Which was why he had done so well in the finance biz.

"I said, I apologize for barging in," the Brit repeated.

Paxton finally managed a smile.

"Not at all. Mr. Birch, is it?"

"It is," Birch said, the weathered skin around his eyes crinkling as he smiled.

"So," Paxton said, tightening the fluffy belt, "I can see you represent a client perhaps?

"A client?" Birch said.

Now the puzzled look was on the Brit's face.

"No, no," Birch laughed. "I represent . . . someone else entirely, Mr. Paxton."

"Who, may I ask?"

Birch's mouth became a curt line. The instant coldness in his expression was as if Paxton had just implied something nasty about his mother.

"You may not," Birch said.

4

"Oh, yes, discretion, of course," Paxton said, managing a polite laugh. "Are you looking for a . . . redemption?"

"In a way," Birch said, tilting his head slightly.

"What way would that be?" said Paxton.

Birch held up a hand as he took something out of his suit coat.

It was a cigar. Paxton watched as Birch bit off an end. Then he frowned as he watched the man spit the end onto the bedspread.

There was a slightly musical clink in the silence of the room as he lit it with a Zippo lighter. Paxton stared at the lighter. It was made of solid gold. The man's hands, Paxton noted as he tucked the lighter away, were enormous.

The Brit puffed. The scent of the cigar smoke in the tight room was spicy, fragrant. It suddenly jogged a long-ago memory, Paxton as a twelve-year-old altar boy holding the chains of a thurible, the incense burner, at Christmas Mass.

"We heard you were looking to sell a certain item," Birch said, blowing a smoke ring up at the ceiling.

Paxton glanced at him, at his dark thugs.

So that was it, he thought.

Not a kidnapping.

Not a client.

This was a robbery.

Give it to them, Paxton thought. No ifs, ands, or buts. These men were obviously very dangerous, and it was finders keepers anyway, right?

Let it pass to another keeper, he thought. *Live and learn.* Flexibility was key to living to fight another day.

"It's in my bag in the closet there," Paxton said, immediately pointing.

One of the thugs opened the closet door and came out with the overnighter. He brought it over and dropped it at Paxton's feet.

Paxton lifted it onto the bed. He zipped it open and found the shockproof case and pulled it out.

Behind the case's glass, the motherboard array was the size and shape of a large index card. The chip in its center was larger than a regular one and rectangular instead of circular. The processor was about the size of a credit card, but instead of being wafer-thin it was almost as thick as a chocolate bar. It had a strange matte nickel finish that didn't make it seem like a computer chip at all. The green substrate of the motherboard that held it was much thicker than a regular one, with a much more elaborate filigree of copper tracings.

"Open the case on the desk," Birch said.

Paxton did as he was told.

The oscilloscope Birch took from his suit coat looked like a small walkie-talkie. He placed the tips of its leads to the opposite sides of the motherboard and pressed a button. Then he pressed another button and squinted at the screen through the smoke of his cigar.

Then he turned to Paxton and shook his head.

"Sorry, Andrew," Birch said. "Nice try. Where is the real one?"

"What? There is no other one," Paxton said. "That's it."

Birch studied his face. Or seemed to. It was hard to tell with the smoke.

"I guess your partner, Hayden, has it then," he said. "He must have left this as a decoy for you. Did the old switcheroo."

"Hayden? No, no, no. He wouldn't have done that," Paxton said, beginning to lose his composure.

"He was the only other person who knew about it, right?" Birch said. "And the only other one with unlimited access to your bank's vaults?"

"Yes, but I—I don't . . . believe it. Hayden's not like that."

And how do you know all of these things? Paxton wondered, but was too afraid to ask.

"He'd never do such a thing," Paxton insisted.

Birch tucked the oscilloscope away and removed the cigar from his mouth with his huge sausage-fingered hand.

"For a small matter of trillions of dollars, Mr. Paxton—" Birch spit some more tobacco onto the bedspread "—you would be surprised what men will do."

"I can't believe this," Paxton said.

"Nevertheless," Birch said as he puffed at his cigar, "your partner has it. Where is Hayden now?"

"He's on his way to a meeting in Germany with one of our biggest clients there. In Duren."

"Is he on the plane right now, or has he landed?" Birch said.

"Still on the plane," Paxton said.

Birch replaced the cigar in the corner of his mouth and held up his hands. His calloused palms looked as hard as the surface of a cast-iron pan.

"That was all we wanted to know, Mr. Paxton. Again, sorry for the interruption."

The sighing breath Paxton let out was long in ending.

"Actually, there is one last thing," Birch said.

He removed the cigar from his mouth.

"As it turns out, I'll have to take that redemption now after all."

Birch nodded at the thug who had gotten the bag. Paxton

noticed that the man already had something out and down by his leg.

"Wait," Paxton said.

But there was no waiting.

The gun, a silenced SIG Sauer P322, went off with two soft *pffts*.

There was nothing soft in the way Paxton fell.

Twice shot through the forehead above his left eye, the slim banker went down like a sledgehammered bull in a slaughterhouse.

Right down through the glass bedside table, headfirst Paxton went, sending the lamp sailing across the room.

5

The room was very silent now.

Sniffing at the air, Birch shuddered with pleasure at the scent.

Good cigar smoke mixed with cordite, he thought, closing his eyes. Nothing like the smell of another job well-done.

And it was a job well-done. Birch had been tasked with finding the chip, and for the first month there had been nothing.

But now, though he had not found the chip itself, he had found something almost as good.

He had finally found a solid lead.

"I need to go out to the patio to make a phone call," he said to his men as he turned.

As he was leaving the room, Birch watched as one of the men respectfully tightened the dead banker's robe before he seized his ankles.

He smiled. You had to appreciate men who were circumspect about their work.

In the living room, he found the remote and switched on the flat-screen. He had a great deal of money on his beloved Arsenal over Tottenham Hotspur, and he wanted to see if he could find the match.

But the only sports channel he could find was an American one that was televising a women's basketball game.

"Helena Upton drains another from the top of the key," said the female announcer excitedly. A deafening, flatulent fog horn blast sounded from the arena as the camera panned to some grinning, sweaty, horsefaced young woman.

Birch shook his head as he shut off the set.

"Americans," he mumbled as he pulled at the slider and stepped out onto the teak deck. "We may never understand."

He puffed at the cigar as he took out his phone and thumbed a number. As it rang, out at sea beyond the private beach, he could see the lights of a cruise ship against the darkening sky.

"Control," said a voice in his ear.

"It was a decoy. The other one must have it. Hayden," Birch said.

"Hayden," Control said. "Let's see. Yes. John Hayden. I have his file up. So Hayden is the target now?"

"Yes. He's headed to Duren. The plane probably hasn't landed yet, so you'll have to ring up the Jerries."

"I'll let them know," Control said. "Anything else?"

"Yes. Did Arsenal–Tottenham start?"

"Not yet. In about an hour."

"Cheers," Birch said.

As he hung up, he imagined his Gunners in the dressing room getting up for it.

"Right, then, lads, don't bottle this. I've got ten thousand quid on the line," Birch said.

Birch removed the E. P. Carillo from his mouth and looked at it. A damn fine cigar. He gazed at the gold-hued festival lights on the water.

He'd just tucked his phone away and stuck the cigar back in his mouth when he noticed the bottle.

"Now what," he said, smiling as he lifted the bottle of Courvoisier, "do we have here?"

He turned at the sound of the slider opening behind him.

"You want us to get started, Mr. Birch?" said Arben.

The machetes and loppers and the rest of the gardening tools inside the gym bag they had brought clanged and clattered together almost musically as the heavily muscled Albanian lifted it off the deck.

"Yes, Arben. Please proceed," Birch said, dipping his nose to the cognac as he lay back on the chaise. "I shall leave it in your ever capable hands."

6

Past customs, the rental desk gave Hayden a silver Mercedes-Benz C 300. Twenty minutes later, he pulled it out of the Köln Bonn Airport lot in the predawn dark and followed the signs to the A4.

He yawned as he pulled into the light traffic near Kreuz Köln–Gremberg interchange. He hadn't slept well on the way in and needed coffee badly. But it was only forty minutes to the hotel in Düren, and he decided he'd just get it there.

Hayden went through his schedule in his head as he drove. It was packed. He had a critical lunch meeting with a German multinational about their next big investment project in Australia, and then there was an afternoon session with a prominent exporter. The client owned a chemical company that specialized in cement additives, and they had to go over all the new EU cross-border regulatory checks on things like letters of credit and payment terms.

He'd also have to squeeze in a quick workout right after he hit the hotel, he realized.

He yawned again.

He had to be at the top of his game today to ensure a successful injection of badly needed liquidity for his bank. An afternoon spent with German finance sharks and cement executives was not for the weak or weary.

Off the highway exit thirty minutes later, there was a strip mall where he passed a gas station, a chain pharmacy, then the golden arches of a McDonald's. Many towns in the area had medieval architecture, Hayden knew, but most of Duren's oldest structures were from the 1950s because almost the entire city had been completely obliterated by Allied bombing in World War II.

As he passed the McDonald's, a memory came to him of stopping there with his daughter years ago when he had taken her to Europe for the first time with him on a business trip.

Josephine was a wonderfully silly and precocious seven-year-old at the time who had declared herself vegetarian. So when she asked for her standard McDonald's order of pies and fries, the German woman behind the counter was caught off guard to say the least. The baffled and somewhat offended expression on her face was nothing short of hilarious.

"Apfeltaschen *und* pommes frittes?" had been an ongoing inside joke between them ever since.

Hayden sighed as he looked at the empty seat beside him.

Where did the time go? he wondered.

The hotel on Bismarkstrasse that he arrived at ten minutes later was a modern white three-story building in the city center next to a park. He slid the Mercedes into one of the forty-five-degree-angle spots and cut the engine. Circling the park were a group of Muslim children on the way to school, chasing each other.

He grabbed his overnight bag and got out. He had just passed a young strawberry-blonde mother pushing a baby stroller alongside the park benches when he saw it.

He immediately stopped in his tracks and stared off beyond the park as his blood ran cold.

7

Parked in the small lot of the hotel was a green van.

He knew the van. He'd seen it before, almost four years ago, when he had come in for another meeting. Right before he was bludgeoned across the back of his head and dragged into it. Then he'd spent some rough days in Berlin in a windowless concrete room with a drain in the floor.

He considered what it meant. His thoughts turned then to his business partner, Andrew Paxton, and his standoffish attitude at the airport when they were going their separate ways.

What had Paxton done? Hayden thought.

He had done exactly what Hayden had told him not to, he realized.

Paxton had tried to sell the chip.

Hayden thought about calling him. Then he thought about who might be tipped off if he tried.

So, run then? he thought, passing a hand over his mouth.

No. He had planned for this. It just meant things were a tad ahead of schedule. He could get it rolling now and adjust on the fly. He was good at this game. He knew how hard it would be for them to find him, even now, if he just kept moving.

No, he thought.

He hurried forward and pushed through the glass doors of the hotel, smiling at the young female clerk behind the desk.

He was done running now.

His room was on the third floor, but he got off the elevator on the second and went into the stairwell and grabbed the fire extinguisher off the wall. He thumbed its hard aluminum edge as he headed back out to the elevator with it.

Room 324 was the last one to the right down the hallway. Hayden dropped his overnighter and stood before the door for a moment, looking down at the floor. The electronic card made the door click. He opened it slowly. Then he surged forward and heard an *umph* in the dimness as he smashed the first man dead center in the face with the extinguisher.

As his shoulder hit the light switch on the wall, Hayden saw the face full of blood and then he leaped past the man into the tight room, toward the second man.

The silenced gun went off with a soft *pfft* into the ceiling as Hayden, slamming into him, knocked the shooter's extended arm upward. Then Hayden was on the short and stocky assailant and got him around the neck with a forward hammerlock. A split second later, he cinched and twisted with his hip the way he'd been taught, and the man's neck snapped like peanut brittle under his elbow.

The one with the broken face was now reaching for the dropped gun when Hayden turned. The scream he let out as Hayden smashed all the metacarpal bones in his left hand with a hard stomp with the heel of his Florsheim wing tip was high, almost feminine. He knelt on his neck and frisked him as he pressed the gun's silencer hard against the blowhole at the back of his head.

"Halt den Mund," Hayden said.

The thug's cries turned into a whimper.

He fished out the man's handcuffs and phone. He dumped the phone on the carpet beside his head.

"Sprichst du Englisch?"

"Yes."

"Open your phone and bring up your contact."

The man paused. When he felt him tense, Hayden shifted the barrel to the back of the man's left knee and pulled the trigger twice.

The man howled like a hound dog in heat.

"You'll have a crutch now," Hayden said in the man's ear. "Next wrong move you make puts you in a wheelchair."

The man fumbled for the phone. With his free uninjured hand, he pressed some buttons and offered it.

"Leave it on the floor," Hayden said as he raised the cuffs.

When he had gotten the cuffs tight around the man's chicken-winged wrists, he lifted the phone.

Wir haben ihn, he typed.

We have him.

Hayden tossed the phone behind him. Then the handcuffed man screamed as Hayden shot him twice more through the back of his other knee.

"Heul doch," he said down to him.

Cry me a river.

This bastard deserved some payback, Hayden thought. These were the same two ruthless thugs who had mercilessly beaten him in Berlin to get a client's Swiss bank account number.

After Hayden gagged the still-crying man with his partner's socks and the belt, he fell back onto the desk, wiping sweat from his stinging eyes as he looked at the mess.

He turned to take a glance in the mirror behind him.

Look, Ma. No blood, he thought, scanning his clothes.

He'd wanted to go out with a bang, right?

"Bang, bang," Hayden said to himself, and he turned on his heel, picked up his overnight bag and opened the door on his way back to the elevator.

PART ONE

STROKE OF LUCK

8

Hammond Stadium, the spring training home of the Minnesota Twins in Fort Myers, Florida, could seat about eight or nine thousand. But there were only about a thousand people in the stands that Thursday night in early April to watch the Single-A Fort Myers Mighty Mussels second home game.

The game hadn't been off the Richter scale in terms of exciting. It had been pretty much a slowgoing pitchers' duel until the eighth when one of the Mighty Mussels hit a wall scraper of a home run to the shorter porch of right field.

Then in the ninth inning, with the Mussels up one to nothing over the Palm Beach Cardinals, the Cardinals put one on before the Mussels' closing pitcher struck out the next two batters.

I was standing where I always stood for each of the Mussels' home and away games, in the front row by the first base line up on my feet with my arms crossed. I was staring intently through the safety net at the Mussels' closing pitcher as if I had a great deal of money on the game.

I had far more than money on the line.

The pitcher just happened to be my favorite—and only— son, Declan.

Dec looked nervous as the Cardinals' best hitter, some phenom beast of a kid from Oregon, took his warm-up swings.

I didn't just *look* nervous, I *was* nervous. About as nervous as I had ever been in my son's up-and-down baseball career.

Some people think when a kid hits eighteen or twenty-one, you can stop worrying as you go off and buy a vineyard in retired Daddyland where there aren't any more troubles or at least very few.

There goes that theory, I thought as I stood there thumbing beads of sweat off my forehead.

I swallowed as Paul Bunyan 2.0 dug into the batter's box and spit some tobacco juice onto the infield.

Not good, I thought, crossing my fingers as he reared back with the bat.

I watched Declan wind up and held my breath as I followed the white blur of his fastball. Then I felt it, low and deep like a punch in my already churning guts, as the batter swung and I heard the crack.

No, I pleaded silently, tracking the ball heading toward the palm trees behind the scoreboard in center field. *Please, no. Say it ain't so.*

Glory be! I thought a moment later as my prayers were answered.

The beast hadn't gotten all of it after all.

"Yes!" I cried as I watched the ball die, the center fielder easily running it down just before the warning track.

Then I just stood there stunned. As the crowd burst into cheers and whistles and applause, my son turned and looked over to where I stood. He looked pretty stunned, too.

And why not?

My son had just closed out his first game as a genuine and official MLB Minor League pitcher.

9

I couldn't stop shaking my head as I watched Declan's team-mates emerge from the dugout to high-five him. Soon they had surrounded him excitedly and one of them flicked off his purple hat to tousle his hair.

What was especially awesome about this team celebration was how nervous Declan had been about fitting in with the guys. The team was a mix of both domestic college grads and inter-national talent, two cliques Dec didn't exactly fit into as he was basically a young walk-on. Many of them were three or four years older than he was.

There goes that obstacle, I thought, watching as his manager went over to give him an attaboy.

I smiled as the team mascot, the Mighty Mussel, shot past me and ran over, jumping up and down. Then in front of the mound, the silly character belly flopped, and everyone laughed as he started doing the worm.

I, too, felt like doing the worm as my girlfriend, Colleen Doherty, ran up from behind me and threw her arms around me, knocking off my hat. Like me, she was fully geared up, wearing a Mussels hat and jersey.

Colleen was a doll, I thought, bear-hugging her to me.

One swell doll, as they used to say in the old movies.

Having her share this moment with me was so incredible, I realized. It made it about a hundred times cooler.

"Congratulations, Mike! He did it!" she said when we came back up for air.

I picked up my Mussels hat and looked at it.

"Life is . . . incredible," I said as I squared it back on. "Five seconds ago, he was twelve, burning up the travel leagues, being a wise guy, asking me what kind of house we wanted when he got his signing bonus. Then he got hurt. Then his arm came back. Never dreamed it could actually happen. Never. I can't believe it."

"You're crying, you know," Colleen said, smiling at me.

"How do you like that," I said, laughing, as I touched my wet cheeks.

Then Declan was there by the rail and I had my arms around him.

I pushed him back by his shoulders and just looked at him. With his Florida heat-dampened hair matted to his head, he looked exhausted and exhilarated and more than just a little overwhelmed.

I suddenly realized how much he looked like his mother, my wife, Anna, who had died when he was fourteen. Of the three of us, Anna had been the real baseball fan.

I suddenly thought about her. She had always said one day this would happen. *Only a matter of time*, she used to say.

Right again, babe, I thought.

My son and I just shook our heads at each other, still trying to soak it all in and failing. We didn't need to say anything. We both just knew.

"It was the glove, Dad! All you!" Declan suddenly said, raising up the new Rawlings Pro I had gifted him with at the beginning of the season.

I laughed.

"Well, there you go," I said. "That's your lucky glove, then, son. Don't lose it, now."

Then I tousled his hair, too, and just stood watching as he headed into the dugout.

After wiping the embarrassing evidence of that little Hallmark moment off my cheeks as quickly as possible, I looked around and saw Colleen up the stairs by the midway tunnel on her phone.

She'd come down here to Florida with me on what was supposed to be just a vacation. But one thing had led to another, and she took a leave of absence from her job back up in New York, and here we were, still on vacation.

And it really was a vacation, truly something special. I wasn't sure when I'd been this relaxed and content since my wife had died. I'd certainly never laughed so hard in years.

We played golf together in the morning and read books in the afternoon. Colleen also liked to swim, it turned out. She was really good at the butterfly. Almost as fast as I was. Almost every other day we'd go to the beach or rent a boat like a couple of silly kids.

The one thing she wasn't into *yet* was my affinity for fishing. I could see her eyes glaze over every time I tried to take her out and teach her the finer points of a good cast. But she did seem to get a laugh at my collection of T-shirts that said things like *Good Things Come to Those Who Bait*. I took that as a sign that it was only a matter of time before she would come around.

I'm sure she was hoping the same thing about me once I had discovered her love of plays, especially musicals. For some reason that cannot be fathomed, Colleen's music playlist was filled with not just the soundtrack for *RENT* but also things like *Show Boat* and *Yankee Doodle Dandy*.

But what was really amazing was that Colleen didn't seem to mind the crazy situation I was in.

Not long before she and I had reconnected, when I was still living in the Bahamas, I had run afoul of the corrupt wing of the global intelligence services. I had inadvertently uncovered an international crime those alphabet-soup types were trying to pull off, and they had come to kill me to cover things up.

But because I was a former Navy SEAL and NYPD cop, this turned out to be a bad idea on their end, considering I had killed a bunch of them instead. Since then, I'd been pretty much in hiding in my own country. But even with my paranoid domestic skulduggery, wherever I went I always seemed to kick over a rock, and lo and behold, a new branch of this corrupt intel syndicate would be staring at me.

That's how Colleen and I ended up together. She had been investigating the suspicious death of a student at a ritzy college in Connecticut and asked me to help. Now, she knew the score. She knew I wasn't being paranoid, as the same crew after me had come after her as well.

No doubt about it, this woman was a real catch, I thought, as I topped the stairs to the midway. Colleen just got me, which was truly saying something. And crazy as that seemed, she didn't just get me, she seemed to like me.

Or maybe even something more than that.

10

Colleen was still on her phone by the turnstiles, and even at twenty feet, I could see on her hollowed-out face that something was deeply wrong.

"Okay. Okay. Thanks," she said as I stepped up. "I'll let you know."

"What is it?" I said as she hung up.

"My dad," she said, her eyes teared-up and face white as a sheet. "He's had a stroke."

"No," I said, immediately embracing her. "Oh, Colleen, I'm so sorry."

She took a deep breath.

"That was my cousin, Jimmy. He said he's at Montefiore Medical Center. They had to get an ambulance. My dad's awake, but it's not good."

"That's awful. I'm sorry," I said again.

I actually had known Colleen's father. I had been best friends since childhood with her brother, Connor, who had been one of the FDNY firemen who died on 9/11.

Mr. Doherty always had a joke ready when I came over on Friday nights to hang out with Connor. He was a kind man who had been like a father to me.

I also knew why Colleen was dazed, in total shock.

Her father was her remaining parent, I realized. Her mom had died ten years before. That's what happens when the last one dies: It hits you like a ton of bricks that your childhood is erased, officially over. She hadn't been expecting this.

"I need to go to him, Mike," she said.

"Of course. We'll both go," I said.

She looked at me, still bewildered. Then she looked down at the concrete. We both turned as a mother and her little boy eating an ice-cream cone clicked through the turnstile.

"No, Mike," she said, pushing at me. "You have to be here for Declan. He needs you now. You have to stay with him to support him. You said so yourself. This is do-or-die for him. This is his one shot."

"But—"

She shook her head.

"I just need to get a flight, Mike. The next one possible."

I looked at her, not knowing what to say.

I felt a stab of panic somewhere as I saw her beautiful gray eyes look off at the empty ball field behind us.

I don't know why, but something told me if she went back to New York, there was a good chance I would never see her again. I definitely didn't want that.

"I need to go," she said, finally looking me in the eye. "We'll just have to figure out the rest."

11

The next available flight back to New York was a Delta out of Key West International Airport, so after we made a stop back at our rental to grab her stuff, we took the ferry out of Fort Myers Beach. It was about a thirty-minute drive south, and we were lucky to just barely make it as the boat was about to pull out.

It wasn't the first time we'd been on the catamaran speed ferry. We'd visited Key West before to go fishing. The last time, we'd made a weekend out of it and sat topside with drinks, laughing, the sea breeze blowing.

But there was none of that now, I thought as I looked around where we sat inside on the plastic chairs with all the retirees.

I watched poor Colleen text back and forth with her cousin and her aunt, who were at the hospital back in the Bronx. Her father, a former ironworker now in his mid-seventies, had been sharp as a tack, but now he was having trouble remembering who they were. It didn't sound good.

The ferry landed in Key West a little late, so I had phoned ahead and had a guy waiting with a moped for us in the street just off the terminal entrance.

After I got Colleen's overnight bag strapped onto the back, she snuggled in behind me, and I zipped us around a tourist tram, tearing off down Grinnell Street, heading for the airport on the island's east side.

I knew the area quite well. Early in my career, I'd spent about a year at the nearby Naval Air Station Key West and when I wasn't at the base, like the rest of the guys I was busy handing over my meager pay to the Margaritaville bars.

When we reached the airport, I left the moped at the curb and helped Colleen inside. I saw right away on the screen above the check-in kiosk that her flight was on time.

I frowned.

The whole way over—even with all of the bad news—I was wishing it had been canceled. That a hurricane warning would suddenly be called into effect and Colleen would have to stay.

"Do you want something? You should eat. We didn't eat," I said as we came past the airport's seafood place.

"No. I'm okay. They're about to board. Let's just go to the gate," she said.

When we arrived, people were already lined up. For a few minutes, we stood there at the end of the line, saying nothing. I knew Colleen was upset about her dad, of course, but I was suddenly worried that she might be upset with me.

Now with something as serious as this suddenly in our lap, I guess it was making us look at what we were doing here pretending to be on spring break like a couple of college kids.

This bad news had burst that bubble. We weren't teenagers. We were adults. Ones with real adult issues and real adult feelings that we obviously hadn't been dealing with because we were having such a good time. Always something else to do. Another restaurant to try, another trip to go fishing or swimming, another golf course to play.

Bottom line, we were playing house, and we were both seasoned enough to know how it *didn't* work. At some point, playtime was over.

Just then, the line started to move.

"Colleen, I . . ."

I stood staring at her. She was so beautiful with her gray eyes and black hair, and whenever she smiled I couldn't look away. It was a perfect smile. Of course, she would disagree, lamenting that one of her eye teeth wasn't perfectly straight. But that was just it, I knew. I had read once that true beauty has to have something like that, some little unique thing that brings the house down. And that was it for me, her less-than-perfect tooth.

Why am I letting this woman leave? I thought. *You do not let a woman like this go.*

She looked me right in the eye as if pleading for me to not let this happen.

"I . . . I'm sorry," I found myself saying.

"I know," she said and kind of tilted away from me when I hugged her goodbye.

"Call me when you land," I said.

And then she was out the door walking across the tarmac for the stairs of the plane.

12

Somewhere over the North Irish Sea near the coast of Galway, there was a slight flash between two clouds as the Airbus ACJ319neo Infinito reached its cruising altitude of forty thousand feet.

Birch, in one of its mid-cabin seats, looked around at the incredible surroundings, the bird's-eye maple paneling, the butter-soft leather seats.

The Jerries had cocked it up in Germany, so Birch had been called back into service.

Lucky, lucky me, Birch thought, looking around at the Criterion Group's boss-level aircraft that had picked him up from Thailand. That it was to be his for the remainder of the mission was still hard to wrap his mind around.

If ever there was a reason to milk a job, Birch thought, smiling, spinning the captain's chair toward the puffy-cloud-filled porthole.

Birch had been from a poor working-class family in London. If they had stood out at all in their neighborhood, it was because his useless drunk of an old man had been a waiter at some of London's great restaurants like The Ivy and Le Caprice.

The only thing the old bastard had ever done for him was get him his first job at fourteen at The Grill. He'd only been scrubbing pots, but how his eyes went wide as he caught glimpses of the high life out through the swinging doors of that grimy back kitchen.

What luxury, what privilege he had seen! The Savile Row–bespoke men, the long-legged, beautiful women draped in silk and jewels. Princess Margaret herself had come in one night, and the American movie star Robert De Niro.

There he was like a starved, whipped dog salivating as the master carved off slices of rare roast beef that he could smell but never, ever taste.

Until now, Birch thought, brushing the baby-soft leather with the back of his hand.

He was finally getting his taste now, wasn't he? Birch thought.

And he was going to savor every morsel.

What was perhaps the most remarkable thing about the aircraft, he thought, was the elaborate aquarium in the stateroom behind him. It was a small swimming pool of a saltwater tank with reefs and sea horses and dozens of fish. It was hard to say how many gallons it was, except that it was insanely heavy, which in terms of flying was so incredibly, fuel-burningly expensive.

Just the idea of a school of fish in an aquarium flying the friendly skies was quite the puzzler. What was this? Noah's ark?

He was still looking back at the tank when Gabriella, the attractive flight attendant, arrived and placed a lacquer tray before him. The tray was lined with a bamboo mat, and on the mat arranged perfectly were six pieces of the most delicious-looking Edomae sushi Birch had ever laid eyes on in his life.

"Dassai 23?" she said, offering the black-and-blue sake bottle she lifted from the cart.

Birch smiled at the attendant, at the hundred-quid-a-bottle sake.

"I'd love some," Birch said, smiling.

He just had a fruity floral sip of it and was lifting some fresh New Zealand salmon to his mouth when his phone beside the tray rang.

"Hello, Control," he said merrily, placing the chopsticks beside the pickled ginger.

"He's on flight 564 to Atlanta like you said."

"Where does the computer say he is bound for? Key West?"

"Right again," Control said. "Sixty-three percent probability for Key West."

Criterion Group and their famous AI computer, Birch thought, rolling his eyes.

It seemed quite useless to him to keep it in the loop all the time when you hired professionals like himself. But the Criterion Group people seemed to worship the thing like a god, so *Whatevs,* as the kids said.

He sipped some more of the delicate and fragrant rice wine.

When in Rome, Birch thought.

He knew Hayden was heading for Key West because Northdale Standard used to have a bank branch there. Hayden would feel safe there. He needed to feel safe after the botched snatch job the Germans had pulled. They'd cocked it up, all right. Hayden now knew he was a wanted man, so he would be running for his life.

"He's looking for help," Birch said, looking at his notes. "Has the computer come up with any names and addresses of former employees yet?"

"I'll check," Control said, and there was a pause. "Nothing yet."

Do you check with the computer to see if you have to take a piss? he thought.

Instead, he said, "Who is in charge of Key West on our side? An American team out of Miami?"

"Yes, a lobo squad."

Lobo squad. *Interesting,* Birch thought. The CIA's blackest of black baggers. The poor bastard. He almost felt sorry for Hayden.

"They're on their way to the airport now," Control said. "They'll be there a half hour after his plane lands. But they also said they have eyes inside the airport. You are to head to Naval

Air Station Key West. And as usual, if it comes up, you of course will say you work for MI6. I will send your American CIA contacts on the ground when I get them."

"Splendid. Be in touch," Birch said and hung up.

Key West, he thought, remembering his file. He imagined Hayden out on the street, scurrying like a mouse looking for a familiar hole.

But Hayden was no mouse, was he? he thought as he recalled the blood-splattered photo of the two Germans in the hotel room in Duren. The shorter one's neck snapped, the head staring backward like an owl.

Hayden certainly wasn't your typical banker. He had Special Forces training from his time in Australia's Special Air Services Regiment. Plus some intel work. The hardcore kind. There was even some wet work in his file.

Birch thought about the way Hayden had made the German operative text that all was well. How it had bought him several hours more than if he had just run. Also, the neat way he had tied him up, leaving him alive after shooting him cleanly through the kneecaps.

They were dealing with a pretty dangerous, clever, and meticulous bastard, weren't they?

That was okay, Birch thought as he lifted the chopsticks and dug in.

As it turned out, he was one himself.

"More sake, sir?" the attendant said with a warm smile as she arrived at his seat.

"No, Gabriella. But if you would be a love and please tell the captain that plans have changed. Instead of New York, we are to head to Naval Air Station Key West."

13

When I arrived in Mallory Square half an hour after Colleen's plane took off, I could see that a full cast of characters for the famous Key West sunset celebration had already taken their places.

There were buskers, and people sipping watery rum-and-Cokes, and a guy on a unicycle juggling fire sticks, some kind of a magician.

It was a glorious evening. It had been hot all day, but a breeze had come up after sunset, and it was really was something to stand there staring out at the rose-gold wash of the setting Florida sun kissing the water of the gulf and the tops of the palm trees.

As I stood there, taking all of this in, sipping my own watery rum-and-Coke, a very smiley Jamaican guy with dreads arrived with a guitar. He got set up about ten feet away with a little speaker and then started doing an acoustic version of Bob Marley's classic, "Three Little Birds."

"*Don't worry about a thing,*" he crooned.

"I'm not so sure about that," I mumbled as I suddenly remembered how quiet Colleen had been as she left.

I took out my phone and quickly texted her.

Hey, can you see the sunset?

I waited. Even after a minute, there was nothing.

Maybe her phone was on Airplane Mode, I thought.

A second later, my face lit up as I saw the bubbles indicating she was about to respond.

But she didn't respond. The bubbling ceased.

I was still staring at the lack of bubbles as when my phone suddenly rang.

It wasn't Colleen.

"Dad?" said Declan. "Where are you? Jamaica?"

"Kind of. Still here in Key West, son," I said, sticking my finger in my ear. "I missed the last ferry back."

"That stinks. What now?"

"It's fine. I'll have to stay over and catch the nine o'clock tomorrow. I'll get a hotel room or something."

"How's Colleen's dad?"

"It's pretty serious, it seems. I'll know more once Colleen has a chance to see him in person," I said.

"How's she doing?"

I wished I knew the answer to that.

"Could be better, son, but don't worry."

"*About a thing*," my wiseacre son said, hearing the music.

"What are you up to after that win, Mr. Sandman? Better put that fire-hurler on ice."

"Ha ha. Yeah, for sure," he said. "The guys are actually taking me to dinner now. The hitting coach has a friend who owns some hot wings place in St. Pete's."

"How's Stephanie? Was she pumped? Is she still coming out?"

Stephanie was my son's fiancée who was back in Utah in nursing school.

"Oh, yeah. She was super psyched. She'll be coming as soon as the semester ends."

"That's awesome," I said. "Well, enjoy, son. I'm sorry I'm not there to tip a few back with you. I'm so proud of you. You know that, right? I know how . . . rough it's all been ever since

Mom died. You know I wish that I . . . I don't know . . . I wish I could have done a better job."

"Oh, shut up already, Dad," Declan said. "It's been rough for you, too, and I didn't help myself, did I? Shit, I did just the opposite after Mom died. I didn't care anymore, I guess. Hell, you did help me. Remember how hard you tried to stop me when I started hanging out with that maniac kid, Jared? Hello? Handcuffing me to the radiator that night? That's love right there."

I laughed.

"That I remember," I said. "That Jared was a bum. You know that he—"

"I know, I know, he said. "He ended up in prison. You told me a million times. You couldn't have been more right."

"I'm sorry, what was that?" I said. "Hold up. Let me get a tape recorder."

"You were right, Dad!" Declan said, laughing. "And thank you for handcuffing me."

"You're welcome," I said. "Handcuffing your teenage children is the epitome of a father's true dedication to tough love. When you have your first son, you'll see. I'll save the handcuffs for you."

"All joking aside, we did it. You and me. And Mom, too. You think she was watching?"

"Are you kidding, Dec?" I said. "Who do you think knocked that bomb out of the sky?"

Declan laughed.

"Well, I hope Mom sticks around. I'm going to need some angels in the outfield to get through the season. These hitters are for real. That last guy was a monster."

"And you took him downtown. Don't forget that. You belong there. You are an MLB pitcher now. Own it! Now, what time is the game tomorrow?"

"Seven-oh-five."

"Okay. Don't stay out too late. After I get back tomorrow, I'll come by your place for a late lunch. I'll bring sandwiches from that new Italian place. Chicken parm sound good? Say three?"

"Sounds awesome. See you then. Oh, and Dad?"

"Yes, son?"

"You get to bed early, too, *mon*," he said over the reggae.

14

Over the rim of his second pint of Guinness, Hayden looked around at the inside of the bar. He had always loved Key West. Until recently, they'd had a branch of their bank here, and visiting for annual meetings had been the highlight of his year.

Those were some meetings, he remembered. Meetings on fishing boats, meetings in the bars, private meetings in his hotel room after the bars closed down.

It actually wasn't just the sunny mayhem. He'd made some great friends back then.

Because it had been the good side of the business, he knew. The legit side with real customers and real employees. Normal people who had a wife and kids and a yard with a grill. Guys who checked their watch and said *Sorry, not tonight* when the rest of the high-finance scum pushed back the steak plates and suggested maybe they hit a strip club.

Men who probably went to church on Sunday, Hayden thought. Got down on their knees and prayed for God to forgive them, even though the worst thing they did was pay their bills, cut their lawn, and suck up the drudgery.

Men who probably knew all the prayers by heart the way his own father had, Hayden thought.

He shook his head. He himself had known them once upon a time, hadn't he?

But that was one hell of a long time ago, he thought as he tipped back his glass.

Whistles and cheers rose up then as a band came onstage up near the front of the place. He spotted an electric guitar, a mandolin. It looked like a bluegrass setup.

As he watched, a woman began playing the Pachelbel wedding song on a violin, and then the drunk crowd went nuts as the drummer and the bassist turned it reggae somehow. A couple got up, the woman in a white dress, and everyone clapped.

You've got to be kidding me, Hayden thought, laughing. Seemed like he'd walked into some kind of half-baked wedding reception.

The bar was called the Bartholomew Roberts, and it resembled a pirate ship. There were the requisite captain's wheels and anchors and exposed beams, of course. But then, inexplicably, there was a huge stained-glass window along the back wall opposite the bar that gave it the feel of a belowdeck chapel.

Had this actually been a church at one time? Hayden wondered as he sat, taking it all in. Maybe that was why the bride and groom had chosen the place for their reception. He shook his head. Hard to say. It was Key West, after all.

The best part about the place, he thought, was all the little seating nooks. Everywhere there were tucked-away booths where no one could see you. The one he was in now was tiny, about the size of an old phone booth. It was nestled beside the pool table on the way to the men's room.

He glanced at the wall of photographs beside it. Fishermen on docks beside swordfish hanging upside down, men working in a cigar factory, US naval aviators standing beside their gleaming jets.

In one of the photos that looked like it was from the 1950s, a woman in a bikini was standing inside a fake cake.

Ah, Hayden thought as he hoisted his warm Guinness, *a woman's touch.*

He checked his watch.

"Red, where are you, brother?" he mumbled.

Hayden wasn't there for the music or the wedding. The bar's owner, Red Callahan, was an old friend, and he needed his help. He needed someone to watch his back, and at six foot seven, Red, a former Navy SEAL and Special Forces Tier One Operator, was an expert back-watcher.

He'd hired Red many times before to do corporate security when the bank brought in heavy hitters. He was a good man to know when you were in a tough spot, and as this was about the toughest spot Hayden had ever found himself in, looking the man up was a no-brainer.

Problem was Red wasn't in, according to the bartender. But he was due back tonight. Whatever that meant. Hayden hadn't pressed the bartender about it. At least not yet. He still had time for the soft touch, but the clock was definitely ticking.

Because they were after him now. Of that he could be certain. He'd changed passports, but that would only slow them down a bit. Staying on the move was a vital step to this process if he wanted to get it done.

This process, he thought, twisting at his pub glass as if trying to screw it down into the table. It was quite a task, all right, and he needed to call in every chit and favor he could in order to get it done.

This was his last chance, he knew.

He looked at the stained-glass window.

To make up for all the wrong he'd done.

In the beginning, it had been easy. *Water under the bridge*, he used to say. But then the water started getting darker.

Because the memories started coming back, the faces. The ghosts were coming around now.

He hadn't banked on that, had he? No. No one ever did.

If what he had planned actually worked, it would make up for all of it. He knew that, at least. He looked down at the knapsack between his feet.

Boy, would it ever.

He sipped his Guinness and sighed.

He just wondered if he still had it in him to get to the finish line.

15

"What?" the bartender screamed over the Kenny Chesney cover band.

"I was wondering if you could help me," I screamed back. "I'm looking for Red Callahan."

"Who?"

"Red Callahan," I said. "He used to own the bar across the street when it was called the Sea Glass. Big redheaded dude, six foot seven."

I'd gone to a steak place for dinner, and while I was there I'd seen a photo by my booth. It was of some kind of Key West 5K from the year before, and as fate would have it, the face of the big man breaking the tape was my old buddy and mentor, Red Callahan.

I hadn't thought of old Red in years. Red Callahan had been one of the old-timers in the first SEAL team unit I was in. Like me, he was a narrowback, an American-born son of Irish immigrants from NYC, so he'd taken me under his wing. After I left the SEALs, he'd given me a job bouncing with him for a few months, back in the summer before I became a cop. Then he had retired, bought a Key West bar, and become a local hero.

"Oh, yeah. Red," the bartender said. "I know who you're talking about, I think. That was, like, ten years ago, right?"

"Yeah," I said. "I asked over there, but they never heard of him. Did Red sell the bar?"

The bartender, a salty old dog, smiled.

"Why all the interest? He owe you money?" he said.

"Owe me money? Definitely," I said, smiling back. "But that's not why I'm looking for him. He's an old friend. I was in town. Just wanted to see if he's around."

I wasn't lying about that. It would be fun to catch up with him.

Hell, I thought as I looked across the crowded dance floor, with Colleen gone there wasn't anything else to do.

"Yeah, I see him around. Let me get Sarina. She's been here forever. Maybe she knows where he is."

As I waited, I turned and looked across the street where there was another bar. It was a two-story number with the second-story balcony packed to the rafters. As I watched, a beer bottle fell from a railing and exploded off the curb.

Key West coming on midnight, I thought, looking at my watch, hadn't changed a bit.

An even saltier bartender showed up, a hippie sun-bleached woman of about sixty with gray dreads and John Lennon glasses.

"You a friend of Red's, huh?"

"Yeah. We were in the service together."

"Prove it," she said.

I showed her my frog man tattoo under my right bicep.

"Hubba-hubba," she said. "Now show me the other one."

I laughed.

"The other bicep?"

"No," she said, leering at me. "The other tattoo."

I laughed again. She was good at leering.

"Can't. Not in here. I'd get arrested."

"Wouldn't be the first time in here," she said.

"So do you know where Red is?"

She nodded.

"Red's a silent partner in a brand-spanking-new place, the

Bartholomew Roberts. Never been there, but I hear it's about a mile south down Duval across the street. Can't miss it."

"Thanks," I said with a wave as I turned.

"Wait," she said.

She cracked open a beer in a big blue can. It was a Foster's, the Australian beer. An *oil can*, I think they called it. She handed it to me.

"You'll need this," she said. "It's about a one-beer walk south."

I went for my wallet.

"Nah, put that away," she said. "A friend of Red's is a friend of mine. Plus, you earned it with the beefcake show."

I laughed as I flexed a few more times for her.

"You think I could go pro?" I said. "Chippendales hiring, you think?"

She gave me a *maybe* wave of her hand.

"Now, now," she said. "Don't get ahead of yourself, sunshine. You have to keep your feet on the ground when you reach for those stars."

16

When I finally found the Bartholomew Roberts, it was really late.

I didn't know if the hippie bartender was playing tricks on me or was high as a kite, but her directions were flat wrong. There was no Bartholomew Roberts on Duval. I'd spent the last hours in and out of about a dozen bars on Duval, asking around. I even tried to look it up on my phone, but I guess the place was so new it wasn't even on the Tripadvisor sites.

I was about to give up on my quest when, in a burst of inspiration, I headed over to a bar where I used to drink with Red on the other Key West strip, Truman Avenue. I'd just arrived to find that the old place was a now pharmacy, when I spotted something, a faint glow coming from a single neon palm tree beckoning from a dark little side street called Howe.

Bingo, I thought as I approached and saw the Bartholomew Roberts sign over the door.

The place looked like an old Victorian bungalow that had been airdropped into the middle of a forest of palm trees. I went up the sun-bleached creaky wooden steps and pushed through the door.

Besides the bartender, there were about a dozen people in it. Bob Marley's "Jamming" was playing from somewhere, but as the door closed behind me with a clunk, it was clear that no one was jammin' in here. All I could see was a drunk man and woman on the dance floor doing their best to simply hold each other up.

I looked behind the bar for Red. No luck. It was a stocky Black guy in a Hawaiian shirt.

"Red around?" I said.

"No," he said. "What are you drinking?"

"Corona," I said. "This is his place, though, right?"

He nodded vaguely as he uncapped a cerveza mas fina.

"Eight bucks," he said.

I'd paid and was just putting the bottle to my lips when there was an earwax-clearing clang.

It was the bartender, I saw. He was by the cash register, ringing what seemed to be a round prizefight bell that was attached to the wall.

"Last call!" he cried.

Suddenly, the lights went on. The blinking faces all around were like masks off at a ball, some overheated, some somber.

I looked into my own in the mirror behind the bar.

Some all alone, I thought.

I watched as the bartender took to his phone, and Sinatra's last-call anthem to drunken self-pity, "My Way," began to play.

As I was looking out at the couple sway to this, a guy arrived next to me at the bar. He looked to be around my age, very fit, nicely dressed with brown hair. He had a sharp, nice-looking face and clear blue eyes.

Still in my Mussels gear and camo cargo shorts, I looked like I belonged in a joint like this, but he looked out of place. Tan and trim and neat in his navy polo shirt and khakis, he struck me as corporate, probably sold yachts or Learjets or something. There was a palpable confidence to the guy, an easy, laid-back competence.

At second glance, he seemed kind of downcast. He looked

like he was maybe drinking his troubles away after a blown million-dollar deal, I thought.

"What's your last?" the stocky bartender said to him.

"Tequila sunrise," the guy said in an Australian accent. "Light on the sunrise," the Aussie added.

"And you?" the bartender said to me.

I smiled.

"The same."

"A sunny optimist, too, huh?" said the Aussie as the bartender left.

"Always," I said. "Why wait for the sun to come out tomorrow?"

We looked out at the couple rocking back and forth to Sinatra.

The bartender brought our drinks.

"So, no Red tonight?" the guy said, throwing down some bills. "No calls? No nothing?"

The bartender shrugged as he took his money. Then he turned to me.

"Fifteen bucks," he said.

"Wait, you know Red?" I said as I fished for my wallet.

"Yes," the Aussie said, peering at me. "What's it to you?"

"He's an old friend," I said, still trying to figure out which pocket I'd put my wallet in. "I was looking for him, too. Only reason I came here."

The Aussie seemed to instantly sober as he continued to stare at me.

"Friend, you're not putting me on, are you?"

"No," I said.

"I got this," the guy said to the bartender, laying down a twenty. "Let's have a seat."

17

"Thanks for the drink," I said as I sat across from him in a booth.

"My pleasure. Tell me, what kind of old friend of Red's are you?" he said. "From the service?"

I nodded.

"You?"

"He used to work for me," the Aussie said.

"In Australia?" I said.

"No, right here in Margaritaville. He did security for me for my . . . Anyway, you have any idea where he is?"

I shook my head. "Not the foggiest clue. I missed my ferry, and I'm stuck here till morning. Thought I'd catch up with him."

He peered at me. Then he offered his hand.

"Name's John Hayden."

"Mike Gannon," I said.

"You're not looking for work, are you, Mike?"

"Work?" I said.

"You ever do any security work?" he said.

"I guess," I said, nodding vaguely.

"I thought so. You remind me of Red. Anyway, I'm in town,

and I need someone to watch my back, and I'm willing to pay handsomely."

Oh boy, I thought.

I'd heard the rumors through the ex-SEAL grapevine that Red was into some shady stuff. Ex tier-one operators could get into a lot of trouble and often did. Became mercenaries. And even worse. There was one in probably every prison in Central and South America, they said. Cartels paid amazingly well.

"You're a trusting man," I said. "This how you usually hire people? Closing time in a Key West dive bar?"

"I have decent instincts," he said, staring at me. "Plus, I'm in a pinch, and Red's not here. A friend of Red's is a friend of mine."

"Famous last words," I said.

"So is it a *yes*?"

I looked at him. I needed to get involved in more shady big-money shenanigans like a victim of a shipwreck needs more open water. My life of late had been all about laying low. Though trouble had a funny way of showing up, I thought, staring at the Aussie.

"No. It's a *no*," I said.

"Why?" he said.

"I'm retired."

"I'll make it worth your while," he said. "I just need somebody to watch my back while I do something. Something completely legit."

I stifled a snort of laughter.

"I appreciate the offer, friend," I said, raising my drink. "But look at me. I look like a spring chicken? My swashbuckling years are behind me. Better find someone else."

He peered at me.

"Any recommendations?"

"Besides Red," I said, finishing my drink, "I don't know anyone around here anymore."

I looked at John as he stared down at the table between us.
The ease and calm and confidence had fled. There was real
fear there. A quick flash of it, anyway.

Then he put his charm armor back on with a grin.

"Cheers, mate," he said as he stood.

18

Key West's famous Sloppy Joe's Bar on Duval was a redbrick building with white louvered doors that were open to the street.

Out in front of these louvered doors were people of every variety conceivable. There was a Hispanic guy in a red hoodie on his phone, a rotund white lady, a skinny white lady, a young Black guy in hip-hop nightclub attire, also on his phone.

Just inside the door at a table sat a man with a white Hemingway beard in a dark long-sleeved T-shirt that said *Security* on it. Standing beside him was a small goateed European Spanish man with his hands in his pockets. He had a pensive look on his weathered face, as if he was a restless poet perhaps out looking for inspiration.

What there wasn't, Blackburn thought, watching the video feed of the sidewalk and bar from the truck's zoom-lens camera, was their Australian target, John Hayden.

The bar was on the corner, and they were set up southwest of it on Greene Street about half a block west. All packed into a jacked-up black Ram 3500 pickup, there were four in the team. Lagare in the driver's seat, and Plaskett and Gutierrez in the crew cab, monitoring the cameras and comms back to control.

Blackburn himself was in *the box*, as they called it. The box was a customized shooting platform inside the covered truck bed itself. In it there was just enough room for one man to lie prone behind a rifle.

That's what Blackburn was doing, lying on his belly beside a Remington Model 700 kitted out with an AAC Cyclone suppressor. The feed of the roof-mounted superzoom camera was just to his left, and with a press of a button a small door in the tailgate dropped, allowing for a shot.

But the problem, Blackburn thought as he rolled a kink out his neck, was there was nothing to shoot at.

The first team they had relieved had gotten a lead. They had shown the target's photo to a street kid who swore he saw the target talking to one of the bartenders at Sloppy Joe's.

But so far there was nada, nothing, no sign.

In the warm truck bed, Blackburn pulled the tablet closer as a pretty blonde middle-aged woman came out of the bar laughing as she held hands with some lucky tall red-haired guy.

Blackburn thought of his own wife. What was she doing now, back up in Fort Lauderdale? *Snoring*, he thought. She was pregnant with their third. He thought of the bike that had just come for his oldest. It was a no-pedals bike, a *balance bike* they called it.

He smiled, imagining his daughter tooling around in the driveway. Angelica was petite for a four-year-old, but she was one spunky kid. He still had to put the bike together as a surprise for her birthday next week. Maybe when he went home this morning after this was done.

Whatever, he thought as he squinted back at the video feed, *this* was.

He thought of his wife and two daughters sleeping, thought about how his job was to be the watchman on the wall. But was that really what he was being here tonight? Being the watchman?

Or the hangman? he thought, looking at the bar feed.

Because it was no joke tonight. Something he had only heard about was waiting at dispatch when he arrived, a Title 50 kill-on-sight order.

Kill on sight, take all pocket litter. That was the extent of their instructions.

That this was out of his comfort zone was putting it mildly. He'd seen such orders when he was in Iraq. Find, Fix, and Finish orders, they had called them. But that was Iraq. *What happened in Iraq stayed in Iraq,* as they used to say.

No way were they supposed to be operating on American soil, dropping people. No freaking way.

He'd been prepared to do it. That's what they told him when he was selected for the lobo squad, that he might get such an order. They'd explained to him the necessity of a dirty-tricks squad, one with a license to kill.

But that was training. They said a lot of shit in training.

The rubber was meeting the road here. This was real killing now. And Blackburn found he didn't like it one bit.

Why not get out and quit? came a thought.

Tell Gutierrez and the others he needed to take a piss. Crawl out, walk away, become an Amazon driver. Do anything. Just go home.

Blackburn turned in the tight space as the truck's big diesel growled and they lurched.

"Hey," Gutierrez called back as they began to roll.

"What's up?" Blackburn said.

"Control's got a lead on another bar. It's on Truman. Hold tight because we need to boogie. It's closing right now."

19

Outside the Bartholomew Roberts, a surprisingly strong wind was gusting.

I watched as it blew sand up the gutters of the blue-black street and ruffled the fronds of the palm trees around me with a sound like the snapping of wet beach towels.

I felt it then. How tired I was. It had been more than a one-beer walk. Way more. I took out my phone to see where the nearest hotel might be, so I could rest my barking dogs for a few hours before I caught the ferry, but it was dead.

I turned as the door opened behind me, and John, the Aussie, creaked down the bar steps.

I suddenly remembered the look of dread on his face and felt bad.

"Hey, John," I said as he passed. "Sorry I can't help you. You want me to give a message to Red if I do bump into him?"

He stopped and peered at me again as he reached into the pocket of his khakis.

"Actually, would you give him this?" he said and handed me a card.

It was a business card belonging to a John Hayden. The name and room number of his hotel were handwritten on the back of it.

"Will do," I said, pocketing it. "You wouldn't know where the nearest hotel is, would you?"

"No, but mine's three blocks down this way," he said as he started to walk.

I fell in alongside him.

"So Red used to work for you, huh?" I said as we came past a white picket fence. "What won you over? Was it the sarcasm or the cynicism?"

He laughed.

"I was actually with a client, leaving a bar on the strip on Duval," John said, "when some drunken fool started up with us. All of a sudden, Red had gotten the guy by the scruff of his neck and his belt and proceeded to relocate him to the gutter across the street. I'd never seen a grown human catapulted like that. I had to sign Red up right there."

"Ah, tourist-tossing," I said.

"What's that?"

"That's what Red used to call it when I bounced with him a few times. His signature move. *All in the hips*, he used to say. His favorite was when they got air. Said he wished it could be a real sport, be his chance to shine."

"You've tossed a few tourists yourself, have you?" John said, smiling.

"Me?" I said as we reached an intersection. "Never. You could hurt your back trying something like that," I said, smiling.

"Good point," John said as we arrived on the next corner.

Across the intersection was an all-night gas station with a convenience store.

"Hey, there's a place," John said suddenly, pointing straight in front of us.

In the distance beyond a darkened construction site, about a block up, was a motel Vacancy light.

"Looks like there's room at the inn."

"Must be my lucky day," I said, relieved to be done walking for the night.

"I turn off to the left here. Be well, Mike," John said, giving my hand a shake.

"You, too, man," I said. "Sorry I couldn't help. I hope you find Red."

"Me, too."

20

What a crazy night, I thought as I watched John cross the street toward the convenience store.

That Aussie was a Key West character if there ever was one, I thought as I stepped off the curb.

I wondered what his backstory was. Then I stopped wondering. Some things were better left unknown.

My foot had just hit the street when I heard a sound. It was a sudden loud buzz, and a split second later I halted and reared back like a matador as a moped going too fast through the intersection actually clipped me.

I stood there, hopping up and down like an idiot, wanting to kill somebody, as I waited for my startled heart to stop leaping out of my chest. I looked down the street, but the moped was long gone.

I limped to the opposite corner, had a seat on the shadowed curb, and took off my docksider.

I tried wriggling my right big toe. It hurt like hell. The nail was cracked, but at least the toe didn't look broken.

"This little piggy went to market," I mumbled to myself as I wriggled my toe some more. "And this big piggy got run over by a drunk."

I thought about Colleen then. I wondered what she would

say to me if she saw me like this, sitting in the dark in the gutter. What she would think.

I *knew* what she would say.

She would say *Mike, what on earth are you doing? Don't you think you're a little too old to be out past midnight?* And she'd be right. No argument there.

Had she landed? I suddenly wondered. Of course she had, I thought, looking up at the dark sky. What time was it now? After four. She'd landed hours ago. She was probably at the hospital already, sitting beside her poor father like a responsible human being.

I shook my head. And here I was. Not beside her.

Why hadn't I just gone with her?

Where she was, I realized now staring at my poor toe, was where I belonged.

"Now, you figure it out. Way to go, genius," I mumbled to myself.

I looked up when I heard the muffled diesel grumble.

Up Howe Street from out of the shadows rolled a pickup. I watched it slow as it approached the gas station. It was a brand-new jacked-up Ram that was called a *dually* because it had two wheels on each side in the back. It was all black with dark-tinted windows.

Still sitting on the curb in the shadows, I watched from across the street as the pickup swung in beside the pumps, its glossy black paint shining under the gas station's hard-edged light.

21

When the truck came to a stop by the pumps, Blackburn, now in the passenger seat beside the driver, was already wearing his ski mask.

He was the first one out of the truck. Running past the blurring pumps, his kneepads made a scratching sound against the dirty concrete as he came to a stop by the door of the convenience store.

Kneeling like a soccer star after a goal, he leaned forward and turkey-peeked through the glass. The brightly lit store had several aisles. The counter was on the left, hot dog and fried chicken stations beside it, and drink coolers on the wall opposite the door beyond the brimming aisles.

No sign of the target. No one behind the counter that he could see. Not surprising, considering that it was the graveyard shift. Without turning, he hand-signaled the others behind him.

They set up in the standard stack-and-approach entry, and he felt Gutierrez's tap at his shoulder. A split second later, he was moving, pulling open the door.

His three ski-masked team members before him entered low and fast behind their short-barreled HK UMP .45s. They fanned out from left to right, each to a different quadrant as they had been trained.

When it was his turn, Blackburn pivoted at the door without hesitation and peeled off hard to the right, staying low along the nearest aisle, his UMP's red-dot sight on the bathroom doors directly in front of him.

Midway down the aisle he halted, listening. He wanted to peek left, but the shelves were just too high to see over.

Where was the target? The next aisle over? The bathrooms?

Shit, this place wasn't that big, he thought. Why wasn't anyone saying anything?

"Back room door open," said Lagare in his ear com link.

"I'm going i—" Lagare said, and then there was a deafening gurgle in his ear that made the hair stand up on the back of Blackburn's neck.

The shot came a second later by the counter.

"Lagare! Lagare!" he cried, spinning back to the counter. He was five feet from it when he caught movement at eye level ahead.

Around the end of the aisle, quick as a magic trick, appeared a hand holding a coffee cup. The cup was tipped, and as Blackburn registered this he saw its smoking, liquid contents were already hanging in midair.

A scream tore from Blackburn's throat as burning grease hit his face, his eyes.

Halting immediately, still screaming, he swiped at his skin and then he looked and caught a glimpse of the target, Hayden, lunging at him.

Despite the pain, his training kicked in, and he tried to swing up with the submachine gun.

But he wasn't fast enough.

He lost the grip of it as his nose shattered in an explosion of glass and red liquid from the hard-swung wine bottle that Hayden broke against his face.

Blackburn whited out with the pain and shock for a second as he fell to his knees. He'd just had the UMP stripped from him when he heard firing from the direction of the drink coolers. A shot two-liter orange soda jumped, hissing off the shelf above his head, and then the plate glass window at the front of the store beside him shattered in a deafening blast.

Strong hands seized him, and he was being half carried, half swung back down the aisle toward the bathrooms. A figure appeared at the end of the aisle. He had just enough time to realize that it was Gutierrez before Hayden shot him from point-blank range.

A moment later, Blackburn was body-slammed against the bathroom door, knocking the wind out of him. Hayden knelt on top of him as he tried to scramble up to close the door that was being propped open by Blackburn's legs. Then the bathroom tiles in front of them turned to dust from fire coming straight down the aisle by the counter.

Blackburn felt himself being flipped over and sat up. He saw a white muzzle flash at the end of the aisle.

Plaskett, you stupid jackass, Blackburn wanted to scream as he heard a passing round make a snap by his ear. *No!*

Blackburn himself tried to kick the door closed as Plaskett continued firing.

Hayden got in behind him to use him as a shield. Blackburn heard another snap of a round by his ear before he felt one go in just over his left clavicle.

A gush of hot blood flowed down the back of his vest, and his mouth filled with the taste of metal and he was coughing blood. Another friendly-fire round tore in through his thigh as he turned.

Hayden began returning fire. Down the aisle, Blackburn watched as Plaskett stumbled and fell forward to one knee.

Hayden leaped up and propped himself in the still-open doorjamb. He aimed and opened fire again. Then Hayden turned toward him. Blackburn wanted to put his hands up, but he couldn't move his arms for some reason. Hayden grabbed him by his vest rig and sat him up against the bathroom door.

There was a rip of plastic, and then he felt a wad of paper

towels press against where the round had entered his chest. Hayden took Blackburn's hand and lifted it and placed it over the wad.

"Press hard," he said.

Blackburn pressed hard. Through the blood in his eyes, he looked down the aisle at the shattered glass and orange soda, the fallen glazed doughnuts and the Prestone cans. Then he looked at what was left of Plaskett and started weeping.

"I'm sorry this had to happen, mate," Hayden said.

Blackburn felt himself getting colder, the warmth flowing out. Something was leaking inside of him. He could feel it.

This couldn't be it, he thought. It couldn't.

"If you live, tell them this," Hayden said.

Blackburn looked up at him. He had very blue eyes. He was spotless. Manicured. A man about to play a round of golf.

"You tell them John Hayden is coming, and he's extremely pissed."

22

When I saw the heavily armed men spill out of the truck and head into the convenience store, I sat where I was, in shock.

But when the shooting began, I quickly stood and pulled on my docksider and ran into the dark construction site behind me and hid behind a pallet of concrete blocks to avoid taking a stray round.

Even after the shooting stopped, I crouched there for another minute before I poked my head out. The truck was still there, doors open. Beside it, I could see glass on the sidewalk in front of the store. The plate glass window had been completely obliterated.

I waited to see if anyone would emerge, listening for a siren. I looked around at the darkened houses. No lights were on. Had no one heard this?

I thought about John then, and the sad, haunted look on his face.

Boy, was he right about needing security! I thought, staring at the still-rumbling black truck.

I shook my head, remembering the machine guns the four men were toting. What was that a hit squad for? A drug cartel?

Was John in there bleeding out? And why wasn't there any more movement? I stood there, straining to listen. There was nothing. Even the wind had died down. All you could hear was the idling of the truck's engine. Why weren't the bad guys coming out of the store back to the truck?

No, no, no. Stay where you are, said a voice. *Stay alive.*

But then came another voice: *John was a friend of Red's.*

"Screw it," I said to myself as I stood and crossed the lot and leaped over the orange construction fence.

I bolted across the intersection and then slowed. I approached the convenience store from the side that had no windows, keeping my eyes on the truck. I finally got to the corner of the store and turned and looked through the only plate glass window still intact. And what I saw through it was astonishing. I truly had trouble believing it.

There was a man down on the floor by the candy counter near the front door. He wasn't moving. There was blood everywhere.

It was one of the men from the pickup.

I stared at the aisles, behind the counter. Nothing. Was everyone dead? I stood there and listened, but there was nothing from inside. And still there was no siren.

"Screw it," I said again. I crouched as I approached the front door.

Just in time to hear its bell and see the door open.

I stopped dead still as I looked.

It wasn't John.

It was one of the bad guys. He was grasping the handle, trying to drag himself out onto the sidewalk.

He was in bad shape. His face was covered in blood. His jeans were soaked through with it. And there was a trail of it on the linoleum behind him.

That's when he looked up and our eyes met.

Then I noticed the pistol he had in his other hand.

It went off with a sudden violent bang just as I dove to my left toward the back of the truck.

I knew it! I thought as I quickly scurried around and put the left rear tires between me and him.

The inner dually tire at my feet exploded as another shot came a second later. My heart started hammering then as I crouched there. If I moved from behind the tires, I was dead, I knew.

Why hadn't I stayed where I was?

Another shot rang out. It hit the body of the truck on the other side.

This wasn't good. He'd hit the gas tank next. And where were the cops?

What could I do? I wondered. Run at him? He *was* wounded. Or wait him out?

I was listening for movement when it finally registered that the truck was idling. It had to be unlocked, I thought.

Another shot went off. There was no more time.

I dove toward the crew cab.

The door mercifully opened when I pulled the handle, and I swung myself inside the truck and squeezed through the gap of the front seats.

Then I slipped the truck's transmission into Reverse as I booted the accelerator.

Two more shots went off as I just missed hitting one of the pumps with the edge of the tailgate. The engine bellowed as I stepped down harder on the gas. A third shot starred high in the windshield right above where I was crouching.

The truck jostled violently as the back end finally reached the street.

Staying down, I spun the wheel hard as I put it in Drive, and the diesel engine roared as I floored it.

23

The helicopter was an OH-6 Cayuse.

Called a Loach, or black egg of death, in Vietnam, the exceptionally agile, delicate-looking craft weighed about the same as a Mazda Miata and could do about a hundred and sixty fully opened up.

It was up around a hundred or so as Birch, strapped into its doorless left-hand gunner seat behind the pilot, adjusted the strap on the FN SCAR 20S that he was holding at low ready with the barrel between his feet.

It was an ideal night for flying, light and steady winds with no turbulence. They were over water about three hundred feet off the deck and outside the wind-rushing opening to Birch's right was a line of lights from the Overseas Highway.

Behind them to the north was Naval Air Station Key West, where they had just taken off from. The Loach had been fired up and waiting for him beside the runway where the Criterion Group corporate jet had come to a stop.

Even before they had landed, Birch, with an open line into Control, had been clued in about the search for Hayden. A lobo squad had put eyes on him and had gone to eliminate, but now the team was unresponsive.

That didn't seem possible, Birch thought as he stared out at the lights against the black. They didn't select world-class tactical talent like that from the phone book.

Birch remembered the SASR file on Hayden, the two dead in the German hotel.

This mouse had sharp teeth, didn't he? Birch thought. Or did he already have help?

The latest addition to this mystery of the gone-silent tactical team was that the lobo squad's vehicle was on the move, but no one was answering on the radio.

Birch looked at the computer tablet that hung from the back of the pilot's seat. It showed a map of Key West and two blips. One blip was the helicopter, the other was the transponder on the truck they were looking for.

Whether Hayden was driving the truck or someone else, Birch wasn't completely sure.

Birch pulled the charging handle of the SCAR stripping a 6.5 Creedmoor round into the chamber.

But he intended to find out.

He was searching the spread of lights, trying to orient their position from the map when a strong vibration reverberated through the cabin's floor. He felt a sudden sense of weightlessness, and then gravity was pushing him down into his seat. The pitch of the high buzzing of the rotors seemed to increase as they lost altitude. Birch felt his pulse rise as his stomach dropped.

"What's up?" Birch said to the pilot through his headset as he stared down at the black of the water rushing up.

Then the descent suddenly stopped.

"Just a glitch," the middle-aged Asian American pilot said casually. "Keep your Savile Row shirt on."

Birch turned his attention back to the glowing tablet screen and saw that the transponder beacon in the truck was quite close now.

"You seeing this?" he called to the pilot who had the same screen in front of him.

"Roger."

"What's the range?" Birch said.

"A mile and a half."

Birch looked right and saw headlights moving on the high-way. He tapped the pilot on the shoulder and pointed.

"There, there, there," Birch said.

The nimble aircraft banked, immediately arcing downward. They came level about twenty feet off the water and then swayed and cradle-rocked back and forth as the pilot opened it up.

Birch saw red taillights ahead as they gained on the black pickup truck like a hawk on a squirrel. He adjusted the rifle strap again and tested the seat harness with a tug before he leaned toward the opening.

Coming in a little too hot off the water above the highway, they actually overshot the truck. To compensate, twenty feet above the truck, the pilot rotated the bird slightly left and then spun back. As they came around the right side of the vehicle, pacing it now, Birch raised the rifle to his cheek.

"Come to Papa," he said.

24

I was flooring the big Ram truck north up US-1 when I first heard the faint sound of the chopper. I wasn't sure if there were more hit teams around, so I was headed for the base where I had been stationed. It was the only place I knew that such bad guys would probably avoid.

Down the completely deserted two-lane highway, I blurred past some white storage buildings on my right. A pharmacy, then a gas station. I was flying. I would have gone faster if one of the dually tires hadn't been shot flat.

And why not speed now? I thought, still hyped up with adrenaline. *I should honk my horn at the same time.* I wanted—needed—the cops to pull me over.

Or did I? I thought as I glanced behind me.

What I had found behind me in the truck cab had me worried. There were laptops and kit bags, and inside the bags I found taped-up extra mags, smoke grenades, and a helmet with night vision.

Everything was military grade. It was like a mini rolling war room. Some kind of stealth SWAT truck. I was definitely familiar with such gear from my time in the SEALs and the NYPD's SWAT team, the ESU.

Had I just stepped into the middle of a war between a drug dealer and a rogue SWAT team of corrupt cops or something? I wasn't sure.

To top it off, there was a radio beside me in the passenger seat that kept saying *This is Control. Come in. This is Control. Come in.*

"What have you done to yourself, Mike?" I mumbled as I sped down the highway.

Suddenly all the buildings alongside the road were gone, replaced now with just dark brush on both sides.

What was that stuff called again? I thought as I pinned it past a semi on the shoulder.

Mangroves. That was it. US-1 all the way to Miami would be like this. Just a series of mangrove stands, sandspits, gas stations, and low bridges.

I suddenly snapped to attention when I heard the chopper, now suddenly much louder.

And then the back and front windshields of the truck exploded simultaneously.

That was truly a near heart-stopping shocker, I can tell you.

The truck whipped on and off the shoulder as I yelled wordlessly, shaking glass out of my hair.

When I got the truck straight and looked right, there was a hole in the windshield the size of an eight ball and another in the headrest of the passenger seat. There was smoke coming out of it, and I could smell the burned leather.

I listened to the thunderous eggbeater sound of the chopper directly above me now.

"Shit!" I yelled.

These guys really, really wanted their truck back.

I needed to do something, I thought as I looked up, or the next shot would be going through my head. I guessed that I was probably still about five miles out from the naval base. It was too far. I wasn't going to make it there.

That's when I saw some kind of turnoff up ahead on the

left. It seemed to be a driveway on the other side of the narrow grass median and highway. I slammed on the brakes as I spun the wheel hard for it.

Maybe too hard, I thought as I felt the truck swell up off its rocker panels, threatening to roll, and its back end swung onto the grass median.

But I didn't flip. I *just* made the driveway. And the fast-approaching, unavoidable chain link fence that stood across it.

There was the pop of one of headlights and a metal crunch of the hood as I blasted through it. I listened for the chopper, fainter now, as gravel rattled off the side of the truck. The driveway curved back and forth through some more mangrove trees.

Was it some kind of utility road? I wondered as I slalomed around a dump truck and then a backhoe.

"Shit," I said again as I heard the rotor chop getting louder.

Through a break in the brush on my right, I saw some other construction vehicles in a clearing. And beyond the clearing, there was nothing. Just the water of the gulf.

Whatever the road was, I realized, I was coming to the dead end of it.

I thought about spinning a U-turn and heading back toward the highway when a shot came through the roof and shattered the dashboard screen. When I wiped the plastic dust out of my eyes, I saw more water to my left and thick brush in front of me.

I killed the one headlight and punched at the overhead light until I heard a crunch. Then I headed straight for the brush.

Then I did something I really didn't want to.

As the truck was still going at a pretty good clip, I opened the driver's door and I bailed out.

I was still doing forty or so by that point, so the gravity, velocity, and friction of the gravel against my rolling, skidding skin was not exactly fun.

But I would have to worry about that later, I thought as I finally came to a rag doll stop. I didn't even glance where the truck ended up with a loud crunch in the mangrove trees ahead of me. All that registered was the deafening sound of the helicopter as I launched myself out into the darkness, running for the water to my left.

As I ran, I realized that the water was actually a canal about the width of a football field, and across it I saw the lights of some houses.

I kicked off the one docksider I still had on as I reached the canal's concrete piling and pencil-dived into the water. Not only did I not get impaled on something sharp under the water, it was deep enough to take me all the way under.

I decided to stay down and swim underwater for the other side of the canal. The water was shockingly warm, like bathwater. I stayed under for as long as I could, and when I popped my head up, I was almost to the other side.

The chopper was still loud but a bit less so. I pointed myself at the house lights and went back under. I swam until my hand found some riprap rocks, and I quickly crawled up them and got back up on my feet.

There was a weird sound then. Right beside me I heard a squawk and then a loud, flapping sound. A large, almost prehistoric-looking bird burst from the rocks beside me. I looked at its huge wingspan as it took off across the canal.

I'd startled a pelican!

I was still trying to not die of a heart attack when at the edge of the rocks, I noticed another fence framing a tennis court. I went alongside it, and when I came around its short side I could hear the chopper coming closer.

That's when I saw it.

Beside the tennis court in the driveway of a house was one of those silver Airstream trailers. I was going to just crawl underneath it, but when I arrived, on a whim I tried the door.

"Thank you, God," I said as I felt the door swing open.

In the dark of the trailer with the door closed, I was gasping like a clubbed fish as the sound of the helicopter passed over my head like the angel of death, and I hit the floor.

"Colleen, I knew I should have gone with you," I whispered.

Then I passed out.

25

When I woke up in the trailer after what was probably three or four hours, it took me a few seconds to remember everything and to realize where I was. For a long minute or two, I truly thought that I had dreamed the whole thing.

But then I opened my eyes and looked into the hot dimness of the Airstream. I listened to the world outside for any sign of things like helicopters or gunshots. Nothing. It sounded peaceful enough, at least.

What an idiot I am, I thought as I lay there, motionless, sweating. How was I going to explain this to Colleen? To my son? Here I was, illegally in someone's trailer after driving around not exactly sober in a shot-up truck belonging to . . . a cartel? Some hit squad? That I wasn't dead six times over was proof of the existence of guardian angels.

I let out a long breath, then tried to put together a game plan for what to do next.

First, I needed some water. All the walking, drinking, running, swimming, and avoiding death had made me pretty parched. I looked around the trailer. No luck. It looked like it was only being used for storage.

Next priority was getting out of this person's trailer. And off their private property without getting shot or going to jail for breaking and entering.

That there were extenuating circumstances which had put me here was a fact. But as a retired cop with some familiarity with the legal system, I knew how facts often could get lost in a shuffle as crazy as the one I'd just been in.

Bottom line, I needed out of here and quick.

I listened, wondering what I was liable to encounter once I did surface.

John, the Aussie, was obviously involved in something way more serious than he had let on. There was at least one dead in the convenience store that I saw, if not two. The guy who was shooting at me looked like he was on the way out as well.

Having taken the pickup truck, did the guys in the helicopter think I was John? That wouldn't be good. And if they wanted him dead last night, wouldn't they still be looking for him?

That was a *yes*.

I tapped my still-damp cargo shorts and found my cell phone. It dripped as I pulled it out. A dead battery was one thing. This was completely shot.

No calling an Uber out of here, I thought.

I pocketed my phone again, and I sat up and then stood and took another look around.

I smiled when I saw what was strapped to the wall behind some plastic storage bins.

Hanging on a custom wall rack was a bicycle. It was one of those super high-end twelve-speeds with the small pedals. I stepped over to it and felt its full tires. *Cervelo* it said on the frame.

After I gave its front wheel a good spin, I tossed through a duffel bag beside it. Inside was biking gear, a red helmet, cleated cycling shoes, and some Oakley sunglasses. There was even a spandex cycling shirt and pair of shorts.

I lifted the gear out. The stretchy shirt was white and had the Swiss flag on the front, and the shorts were black and super tight.

"Here goes nothing," I said.

It felt like I was wearing a sausage skin as I crossed the trailer to the door.

But as they say, beggars can't be choosers, I thought as I undid the door latch. Especially beggars marked for death.

I poked my head out the door. The coast seemed clear. I took the bike down and went out of the trailer.

I was happy for the bike's lightness as I carried it alongside the fence to the rocky shore. I clambered along the rocks behind two other houses and then went in through a gap between two of them.

Then I hopped on the bike, rolling out into what looked like a normal suburban street. It was empty.

Did anyone notice? I wondered, looking around. I couldn't tell. I didn't think so. It was still very early.

I pumped at the tiny pedals, doing my best Lance Armstrong impression.

Maybe I'd get out of this yet, I thought.

26

In the hot, early-morning Florida sun, my head began to throb as I biked alongside the small but expensive-looking seaside bungalows. I was definitely dehydrated. First chance I got, I would need to pick up some water.

After another minute, I rolled around the speed bump that fronted the seaside subdivision and came out of a little street into a busier road. As I made the left back toward the Overseas Highway, I saw a gas station at the corner.

"Just what the doctor ordered," I said.

I was approaching it for some much-needed cold liquid when I suddenly saw a cop car stopped at the turnoff for the Overseas Highway. There was a bulked-up male cop sitting in the driver's seat with a tanned muscled arm jutting out the open window. Immediately rattled, I paused my pedaling and considered turning back.

But there was no way, right?

Even if he was looking for me, I was just some cyclist, part of the wallpaper. Plus, from the casual way he was sitting there, he didn't seem to be looking for anyone.

I was still hanging back and considering a retreat when I saw the cop head into the gas station. I quickly pedaled past the station to the corner and got on the Overseas Highway and made a turn to the right back toward Key West proper.

Making a left wasn't an option as there was hardly anything in that direction, and I would certainly stand out. I just needed to get out of the initial area, get lost in the crowd, and regroup.

But first things first, I thought as I spotted a CVS across the highway. When there was a break in the traffic I cut diagonally across, and once inside the blessedly cool store, I immediately picked up some aspirin and some Gatorade. I was taking it to the counter when I stopped by another display.

"That's what I'm talking about," I mumbled as I selected a prepaid smart TracFone.

"Nice day for a ride," the clerk said, giving me a raised eyebrow at the snugness of my attire.

I almost laughed myself. The fit of my clothes was quite, um . . . remarkable.

"Ride, Baby, Ride. That's my motto," I said as I scooped up my purchases and headed outside.

I biked around to the back of the CVS and sat on the curb in the shadow of a palm tree beside a dumpster. I emptied the bag, and after I swallowed three aspirin with half a quart of Gatorade, I set up the TracFone. It came with the Google Chrome app, which I immediately opened to search the local news.

Deadly Shooting at Key West Gas Station was the lead story.

That this was the lead story was not surprising, but what was surprising was what the reporter said about it.

A Hispanic woman in her late twenties stood in front of the crime-scene tape that had been wrapped around the pumps.

"Last night," she said, "a clerk here at the Gas Plus was gunned down in what the police are calling a *robbery gone bad.*"

It had gone bad, all right, I thought. But I doubted anything had been stolen.

That's when it hit me.

A clerk?

The bad guy with the machine gun who was blown across the Pringles and Snickers bars was no clerk.

"The investigation is ongoing," said the reporter, "and the police are looking to KMBH and the public to help with a video they obtained of the alleged getaway driver."

"What?" I said to the phone as the screen changed. "No, no, no."

But the answer was a most definite *yes*.

The next video was of me, driving out of the gas station at the wheel of the pickup truck.

"If you know this vehicle or the driver or spot either of them," the reporter said, "the Key West police are advising you to please call 9-1-1."

27

Beyond the lip of the hangar, some Latino summer pop music was pumping as a busy maintenance crew cleaned the outside of the Criterion Group Airbus jet with a power washer.

Just inside the hangar beside a storage-parts bay, Birch sat at a battered table with the two jet pilots and the chopper pilot. They were playing hearts, and the two pilots of the jet threw down numbered club cards and Birch threw down a five of clubs. The chopper pilot, whose name was Rob, threw down the queen of diamonds.

"You're not going to try to run on us, are you?" Birch said to the chopper pilot with a raised eyebrow.

"You'll just have to see," Rob said, pulling his cards in close to his chest.

They were on standby now as the higher-ups figured out what to do next. They'd missed whoever was in the truck. It had taken them some time to realize that the driver had bailed, and by then, even with the infrared camera on the chopper, it was too late. He'd obviously escaped into the neighborhood on the other side of the canal, but what were they supposed to do? Start kicking in doors? Birch had been told he had latitude but not that much. They had to have some discretion.

Still, it was a failure. Something that Birch, like all professionals, did not take well.

On a positive note, they'd learned that the driver of the truck had not been Hayden.

Birch himself had seen the video of the shooting taken from the gas station, and Hayden, after remarkably taking out all four lobo squad members, left the rear of the establishment on foot.

The mystery man who took the truck was definitely someone else.

Who was he? Birch thought as he looked at his cards. An innocent bystander? A Good Samaritan? An opportunist truck thief? Just a Key West drunk?

No word on that yet, Birch thought as he tossed down a ten of clubs. Perhaps Criterion Group's Merlin, the computer, could figure it out.

He tossed down all his cards a moment later as his satellite phone rang.

"You need to get to the secure phone on the plane," Control said.

Great, Birch thought. One of the powers that be wanted a word.

"Be there in two shakes."

28

Birch waited until there was a break in the whooshing hiss of the power-washing wand above before he ran around the dripping scissor lift and up the gleaming jet's steps.

On-screen when he got to the rear conference room was a bland-looking sixty-something bald man wearing glasses. It was the CEO of Criterion Group, Albert Viviani, Birch realized. He recognized him from news clips. He was wearing a puffy white parka and was standing on an outdoor deck. Behind him in the distance were very high snow-covered mountains.

"Mr. Birch, at last we lay eyes on each other," Viviani said. "How are you this morning?"

"Disappointed, sir," Birch said. "The task you hired me for is still not completed."

"I like that answer, Birch," he said.

Viviani's accent was European but hard to pin down. Was he French? Italian? German?

Birch studied the imperious way he held his head back, as if he was looking at Birch with his nostrils. There was something old in his manner. Something older than America, older than Europe. Birch could have sworn he'd seen his face before, hovering there in the dark background of an old oil painting, a sultan painted by an old master, glaring, sniveling, coveting.

Coveting. That's what it was, Birch thought. Viviani was a coveter of the highest order from a long blue-blooded line of coveters.

"If you would please explain to me what's going on," Viviani said. "I know you've written a report, but on matters this big, I need to hear it from the horse's mouth."

Birch described what had transpired.

"This man who got away, do you think he is involved? A former employee of Hayden's bank, perhaps?"

"I don't know," Birch said.

"Just a bystander?"

"I don't think so," Birch said.

"Why didn't he call the police?"

Birch pursed his lips.

"A dead phone perhaps," he said.

"Why approach such a dangerous situation at all?" Viviani said.

Because some men have courage and concern for human life, Birch felt like explaining.

"The bars had recently closed. Perhaps alcohol was involved?" Birch tried instead.

The clueless CEO nodded, pondering this. He pushed his eyeglasses up the bridge of his nose with his thumb. A gust of icy wind from wherever he was ruffled the hood of his parka.

"I have already spoken to Mr. Landler, the head of our American corporate security," he finally said. "You are familiar with Mr. Landler?"

Landler was the one who had offered him the contract in London a month before.

"I am."

"Mr. Landler is the former assistant director of the FBI. He and his contacts will be of great use to you in catching up to Hayden."

Birch nodded.

The dead lobo team had been a CIA covert-ops hit squad not allowed to operate on American soil. Which was why another CIA cleanup team had to go in to get the bodies. Having an FBI connection would be much more helpful in a manhunt.

"Mr. Birch, I called this meeting to personally express to you the level of importance inherent in the recovery of this item. There is nothing, literally nothing, on this earth more important than its successful recovery."

"I understand, sir."

"Failure is not an option," Viviani said.

"I understand."

"For *you*, Mr. Birch. Failure is not an option for *you* personally."

"Sir?" Birch said.

"I've read your file. You were in the SAS."

"No, 1st Battalion, Parachute Regiment, 1PARA, sir."

"No matter. Stationed in Iraqi Freedom, correct? Where did you operate?"

"We came in first to soften things up all over. Afterward, I was primarily in Mosul," Birch said.

"Where you were a sniper?"

"Yes."

"How many people did you kill?"

"Three hundred and fifteen, three twenty. Somewhere in there. Maybe more. I lost count."

"All illegal, I'm told. Day after day you woke up and shot people. Your case file said that your fellow soldiers in your unit begged you to stop."

Birch laughed.

"Nannies," he said. "They never knew how to have any fun."

"But you killed women and children."

Birch looked at him. His eyes were wide, curious, intensely interested. He looked like an eager schoolboy wanting to get the dirty details of a bolder friend's sexual conquest.

Birch shrugged, yawned. Screw this wanker. He wasn't one to kiss and tell.

"Are we going somewhere with this, sir?" he said.

"How do you like your freedom so far?" Viviani said.

"After eight years in prison, I like it quite a bit."

"May I remind you, Mr. Birch, that we sprang you because we heard you were exceptionally good at getting things done. No matter what."

"I assure you that we're very close to wrapping this up, sir. I've got a scent on the item."

"A scent won't cut it. As you know, your lawyers are my lawyers, which means your freedom is in my hands."

"So if I don't run this item down, it's back to the clink, is it?"

"I'm afraid so."

Birch smiled.

"This amuses you, does it? There is no action without a motive, Mr. Birch," Viviani said. "You have yours. It is sink or swim time for you and for all of us."

"I'll get you the item on one condition," Birch said.

"Are you really in a position to negotiate?"

"I want a nice place in London," Birch said, ignoring him. "Something really nice in Kensington Palace Gardens where I can rub shoulders with international billionaires, high-profile diplomats, and members of the British royal family."

"Are you mad? A flat there is about twenty million pounds."

"How much is the Criterion Group worth, Mr. Viviani?"

Viviani opened his mouth, closed it.

"Do I have your word, sir?" Birch said.

Viviani nodded.

"Excellent," Birch said, standing. "I'll get back to work now."

PART TWO

LIFE IS A HIGHWAY

29

"T-shirts! Get your T-shirts," I yelled at the passing beach crowd. "Come right up and get your genuine *Most Southern Point of the US of A* T-shirts. Twenty dollars only, folks."

"Do you have a large? It's for my grandson," said a nice old lady in a sun hat and floral swimsuit, clutching a couple of sawbucks.

"Sure do, ma'am," I said, pooching through the sidewalk pile at my side. "Here you go. Enjoy."

It was coming on noon, and I was where I figured the cops would look last for a dangerous, convenience store-clerk-killing fugitive: selling T-shirts at one of the busiest and most popular tourist traps, the Southernmost Point Buoy sidewalk.

For easily a hundred bucks more than the lot was worth retail, I had been able to buy out the old-timer I had found selling them. For an extra twenty, he'd even tossed in his cheap beach chair.

The best perk of my new job was that I was able to exchange my spandex look for a T-shirt and a pair of gloriously loose surfing shorts that returned the blood flow to my lower extremities. As I sat watching the milling crowd, another Conch Tour Train tram rolled slowly by. When it had passed, I noticed that my new TracFone was vibrating.

I leaped up and hurried over to the right of the buoy where people were taking selfies and stood facing the open sea.

"Mike?" said a woman's voice.

"Kit, thank goodness," I said. "Thank you so much for getting back."

Kit Hagen was a really good friend who also thankfully happened to be a really good FBI agent.

I needed to figure out what in the hell was going on. And fast. And if anyone might be able to help me to do that at this point, Kit was it.

"Your son said something was up?"

Without my old phone, I'd had to call Declan to get Kit's number out of my contact notebook at my rental back in Fort Myers. I apologized for not being able to make his game, but he didn't even blink when he heard the serious tone in my voice. And didn't ask questions. Declan understood more than anyone what my life—what our crazy life living under the radar—was all about.

"Okay, Kit, here goes," I said. "I'm down in Key West and last night there was a shooting."

I told her the whole story, my chance meeting with the mysterious Aussie, John Hayden, at Red's bar, how he had tried to hire me for security. I told her all about the gas station shootout and how I'd had to steal the truck to not get shot. How I was pursued by a helicopter full of guys trying to kill me.

"Mike," Kit said as I got to the helicopter part, "are you sure all that sunshine hasn't gone to your head?"

"Kit, I know how this sounds. On the news this morning, they showed *me* on a traffic camera in the getaway truck. The cops are searching for me like I'm Key West's Most Wanted. I was just trying to help, and now I'm running for my life."

She was quiet for a moment.

"Oh, wow," she said. "You're right. I'm watching the video right now."

"*Wow* is right," I said. "I'd turn myself in right this minute to clear this up, except that the cops and media are lying through their teeth. They're reporting that only the clerk is dead. Not true. There were four shooters, all with automatic weapons, and I saw at least one of them deceased. And the one who shot at me didn't look like he was going to make it. Plus, I never saw any clerk. This is a cover-up. Of what, I don't know. All I do know is that a cover-up needs a patsy, right? That's me."

"What can I do?" Kit said, her tone dead serious.

"I need a back channel to someone sane in law enforcement to get this off me. I didn't do anything, and I can easily prove it. I don't feel like being the scapegoat here. I'll be wasting away in Margaritaville with two in the back of my head. Can you find out what the hell is going on? I need some help here."

"Let me make some calls," Kit said. "Stay by your phone."

"Thanks, Kit," I said as I watched a speedboat and parasailer float past out on the blue-green water. "You're a lifesaver."

30

Birch was in the plane, feeding the fish, as he drank a glass of freshly squeezed orange juice when he saw the screen flash back on in the conference room to his left. He headed inside and closed the door.

The middle-aged man who appeared on the screen had a strong jawline and a friendly, lined face that reminded him of Ronald Reagan. He had the same wavy hair and, to add to this impression, behind him on the hunter-green wall of the wood-paneled office he was sitting in was a framed American flag folded into a triangle.

Most Americans drove Birch mad, but he actually liked this one.

"Mr. Birch, hello," said Mr. Landler as he gave Birch a disarming smile.

"Hello, Mr. Landler. We meet again."

"I read your report, Mr. Birch, and have spoken with Mr. Viviani. I have already had preliminary conversations with my contacts to assist you. I'm thinking that if we open a counter-terrorism case on Hayden, so many helpful resources in tracking him down could become available to us. We could even create a task force out of the Miami office. The SAC there was a protégé of mine."

"That sounds like an excellent idea to me, Mr. Landler. By all means."

"Well, there is one hurdle to overcome," Landler said, "that I was hoping you could help with."

"Anything," Birch said.

"We would need a cover story that the agents involved would find credible. I know you've been all over Hayden's file. Is there anything in his past that we could possibly link to? Anything that could plausibly make him a threat to the safety, sovereignty, and security of the United States?"

Birch tapped a finger to his pursed lips as he thought about it. On the screen, Landler lifted a coffee mug. *Fordham*, it said on its side.

Birch suddenly snapped his fingers.

"There is a senator. Mark Clifton from Florida. He's still the senator, right?"

"Yes," Landler said. "He's on the Intelligence Committee. He's up for reelection, I believe."

"Hayden's bank, Northdale Standard—when it was in Key West—made a donation to Clifton's campaign. I recall a picture in the file of Hayden and Clifton at a golf tournament together."

"And . . .?" Landler said.

"Northdale Standard is under investigation by regulators in Australia for a deal they did in Thailand. It was even in the paper over there."

"Go on," Landler said.

"How's this for a story? Hayden is desperate. Desperate men sometimes run amok. Hayden is also a former highly trained Australian Special Forces soldier. We can claim that we have top secret evidence that makes us believe that Hayden has lost his bearings and is here in America to assassinate Clifton."

"Assassinate Senator Clifton?" Landler said, giving him a look. "Why?"

"Who knows? A shady deal they did? Clifton pinched Hayden's wife's ass? Does it matter? We already have pictures. Pictures of

Hayden and the Senator. And also pictures of what Hayden has done in Germany and now at that convenience store. Pass a few of them out on the sly to the task force head. Hell, show one to Clifton. Pictures are worth a thousand words, especially blood-splattered ones."

Landler nodded, taking another sip from his Fordham mug.

"He's a foreign terrorist out to kill a senator," Birch said, pacing now before the screen. "He is a highly trained, unhinged former associate of Clifton's here in America on a mission of revenge. That's the story."

"You know what?" Landler finally said. "I like that. I'll buy that for a dollar."

"Not bad, right?" Birch said.

"Yes," Landler said. "The personal-revenge angle is emotionally gripping. That'll do it. Let me make some calls. Sit tight."

31

I was down to about twenty T-shirts two hours later when I saw Kit's number come up on my TracFone.

I leaped up out of my beach chair past a living statue of an alabaster-coated goddess who was setting up beside the Southern-most Point Buoy and headed to my spot facing the water.

"Hey, Kit," I said.

"Mike," she said, "I have a friend in the Miami office and was able to get some news through the grapevine. Brace your-self. It's not good."

"What do you mean?"

"Hayden is a terrorist."

"What?"

"That's what I heard. This guy, John Hayden, they have him on the Terrorist Watch List. It just came over the wire."

"Why? What for?" I said.

"He's a banker from Australia," Kit said. "Not exactly your regular type of bank either. The articles I read seem to indicate that the bank facilitated money-laundering to offshore accounts. And the bank is going down the tubes because of some govern-ment scandal in Thailand or something. The rumor is Hayden killed some clients in Germany, and now they think he's after a US senator who accepted campaign donations from the bank."

I thought about what I was hearing, and then I thought about Hayden. He was some guy on a rampage? No way. He seemed calm, cool, and collected.

"Which senator?"

"Clifton from Florida."

"Clifton?" I said. "He's an intel committee guy, right?"

"Yes."

I thought of the four heavily armed men.

That was a hit squad, I thought. No ifs, ands, or buts.

I remembered the look of fear on Hayden's face. No way was he after any senator. Hayden was on the run. Asking me for help proved that. If anything, the opposite seemed true— that someone was after him.

Behind me, I saw the goddess now standing on her pedestal.

Maybe I'd ask the Oracle of Delphi over there, I thought, shaking my head. I definitely needed some help to figure out something this nuts. Then I realized that I had a more pressing concern.

"Kit, am I on this watch list, too?"

"No word on you at this point, Mike," she said.

"But the Bureau is on this now, right?" I said, looking around.

"Yes. My contact says they're assembling a task force to track down Hayden."

Only a matter of time before they ran me down, I knew.

"This friend of yours, why does he think you're looking into this?"

"I said I knew a curious Key West cop," Kit said.

"That's smart, Kit. Keep covering your tracks. Something this radioactive could escalate quickly."

"You sure you don't want to come in, Mike? Try to work this out?"

I knew I had to clear myself. For Declan's sake. I couldn't have my stupid mistake ruin his life. Not now when things were really starting to click for him.

"How much do you trust your Miami buddy, Kit?"

"He seems like a good guy but . . . trust my life with him? Or yours?"

"That's what I like about you, Kit. You're almost as cynical as I am."

"What are you going to do?"

I took out the card from my wallet that Hayden had given me with his hotel info on it.

"I'm not exactly positive," I said. "I'll have to call you back."

32

When Birch arrived on Stock Island, the other task force vehicles were already parked at the end of the cul-de-sac beside an
open boatyard.

He veered the Cadillac Escalade he had rented next to the
three dark Chevy Suburbans and cut its engine. When he got
out, he could hear the rumble of a generator and the nails-on-
chalkboard screech of an aluminum boat being sandblasted just
beyond the boatyard's chain link fence.

"Special Agent in Charge Dennis Quevedo," said a tall, wiry
guy who popped out of the nearest SUV.

He was wearing a coral polo shirt and biscuit-colored khakis. Miami office casual, Birch thought. He was also wearing
big glasses that were nerdy, but the eyes behind them seemed
cunning. Birch took in the man's deep tan. He wore too much
cologne. Or was it deodorant?

Birch glanced at Quevedo's left hand, at the ring finger. It
had a band of lighter color where a wedding ring would normally be worn. He knew that the ring tan meant that Quevedo
was married but didn't wear his ring at work so as not to reveal
details about his personal life.

Birch smiled. In his line of work, knowing a man's vulner-
abilities was always an advantage.

"Can we talk in your truck?" Quevedo said, leading Birch back toward the Cadillac. "Sweet ride," he said, settling in. "Hey, nice overshirt. What is it? Gucci? No. Balenciaga, right? I love Balenciaga."

Birch wondered how he could politely explain that it was from a bespoke Neapolitan designer above the pay grade of special agents in charge. He failed to come up with anything. He stayed silent as he watched Quevedo place an iced drink in a plastic cup into the drink holder.

"I got you something," Quevedo said. "Some iced tea. Figured with you being English and all."

"How . . . considerate of you," Birch said, glancing at it with savage disdain.

"I didn't catch your name," Quevedo said, putting out his hand.

"Birch."

"No, I meant your first name."

"Birch," Birch said again.

"Alrightee, then," Quevedo said, lowering his hand. "Well, Mr. Birch, I've spoken to Joe Landler and understand what's going on. You need our help tracking down this John Hayden. What am I saying—*our* help? What I mean is, you need *my* help. Because these are my men out there. Ipso facto you need me to help you. There is no *our* without me, comprende?"

"Winston," Birch said.

"What was that?"

Birch lifted the tea and took a sip. It was horrid, but at least there was no sweetener.

"My first name is Winston," Birch said.

"Birch it is," Quevedo said, looking at him with a funny grin.

Birch raised a thick eyebrow.

"Just a joke, Mr. Birch. So before we get rolling here, I'm thinking this thing is off-the-charts important, am I right? I mean, I wasn't born yesterday. Even I know who Landler works for."

"Your point?"

"I help you to bring in this John Hayden or look the other way when you do. Whatever you need to do. I, too, eventually want to work for who Landler works for."

"That's interesting," Birch said.

"How's that?"

"That you would mention this to me," Birch said, looking out to where a boat on the other side of the yard was being loaded with wooden lobster traps. "I'm a contractor, Special Agent in Charge Quevedo. I don't work in HR."

"Whoever you are," Quevedo said, "your lips are near some pretty darn big ears. This comes to a solid conclusion, you put my name in one of them. That's the deal, okay? I'm retiring in three months."

Birch nodded his assent. "As you wish." *But be careful what you wish for,* he thought.

"Awesome. Here," Quevedo said, offering him a leather bill-fold. "Another gift."

Birch opened it. Inside was a nickeled silver badge. *Federal Bureau of Investigation* it said over the top of it. *Department of Justice* in the middle.

"You've just been deputized, Mr. Birch. During this investigation, you are to wear this over your belt here like I do, see? And you are only to speak to me in private. Not to my guys. Just to me. That's how this will work."

Birch hooked the badge over his belt.

"Understood," he said.

"Good. Now, you roll behind us into Key West. We have a lead."

"A lead?"

"We did some data collection," Quevedo said. "We went over all of the Ubers that were in the vicinity of Hayden's flight when he came in. We emailed his picture around. One of the drivers remembered him. We'll head to the hotel where he was dropped off."

33

The rental boat was a fifteen-foot Boston Whaler I'd picked up from Cow Key Marina on the north side of the island.

I let its motor off in the water a quarter mile south of the Golden Bay Villas and dumped the purchases I'd just made out of their plastic bags.

Onto the deck spilled a leather motorcycle vest, a pair of socks, some duct tape and twist ties, a pair of multipurpose stainless-steel scissors, and a fishing tackle box filled with lead sinkers.

I cut two paddle-shaped pieces of leather from the back of the vest and then filled one of the socks with ten of the one-ounce egg sinkers and hefted it. That would do.

I cut the sock away with just enough space to secure it tight with a twist tie and then I laid it down on one of the pieces of leather. After I'd created a sandwich by laying the other piece of leather on top of that, I proceeded to carefully duct-tape all of it together. When I worked as a plainclothes cop in NYC, we always had a sap handy. It hit as hard as a billy club, but you could hide it in your pocket.

Once I was done tape-jobbing up the DIY sap, I looked it over. It certainly wasn't pretty. But when I swung the weighted weapon into my palm, I whistled as it gave out a most satisfying crack. I wasn't sure if John Hayden would be obliging in my request to straighten out my current fugitive status, so I wanted to have a plan B.

I slipped the sap into the pocket of my swim trunks and motored in toward the dock of the resort. There was a concrete seawall just before it, and I left the boat there and dove into the water.

The water was actually quite refreshing. Being busy running around trying not to get shot or thrown in prison for a murder I didn't commit, I hadn't had a shower yet. A saltwater one was better than nothing, I thought, climbing up the ladder.

As I stood on the dock, I could see that the Golden Bay Villas was actually just a large three-story hotel with a courtyard in the middle that had a pool. I walked across the beach and between the rows of Adirondack chairs facing the water. I lifted a towel off one of them and tossed it over my shoulder as I came in under the walkway that separated the pool from the beach.

I stood there scanning the pool. It was packed with laughing children and parents and bronze-skinned old people watching from the lounge chairs. There was no John Hayden. To my right was the doorway for a stairwell. I pulled it open and went up the stairs to the second floor where I opened another door into the hotel corridor.

I had to walk all the way around the square-shaped hall until I found John's room, 267, on the side of the building opposite the bay. I walked past it without slowing and came out of an open-arched doorway into an outdoor area where there was a set of elevators and a railing facing the courtyard pool.

I stood at the railing, searching some more for John at the pool when the elevator dinged and out of it walked a pretty young red-haired woman. She was by herself, pulling a rolling suitcase. Ignoring me, she passed back the way I had come.

Instead of getting into the elevator, I stood there for a moment looking down at the pool. I waited for thirty seconds more and turned back for the corridor that led to John's room. When

I turned the corner, I saw that the redhead was stepping out of his door. She was busy looking at her phone.

I smiled as she glanced at me as I stepped up.

"Hey, are you looking for John? John Hayden?" I said.

She gave me an intense look, a worried one.

"Who are you?" she said with an Australian accent.

Pay dirt, I thought.

34

"My name's Mike," I said, smiling as I scrubbed at my wet hair. "I'm a buddy of John's. Actually, I'm a former employee. I used to do security work for John with Red Callahan. And you are?"

"I'm Natalie. John's personal assistant," she said.

I stared at her. Was that true? I wondered. Was she really his PA? Or was she also lying?

"At Northdale Standard in Australia?"

"Yes," she said.

"Funny, he didn't say anything about you last night when we met at Red's place," I said.

"Red's place?" she said.

"His bar on Howe Street. The Bartholomew Roberts?" I said.

"Oh, yes, of course. John said he was going there."

I still couldn't tell if she was lying. But why would his assistant be here? I thought about what John had said about a legit job. Maybe he had been telling the truth.

"Are you staying at the hotel?" she said.

"Yes, down the hall. I'm in 254," I lied, smiling.

"John doesn't seem to be in his room. Have you seen him today?" Natalie said.

I shook my head.

"No, I haven't, which is strange since he offered me a job.

I've actually been looking for him, too. You wouldn't happen to know what his schedule is for today? Does he have a meeting off-site or something?"

"I'm not sure," she said, looking at me a little suspiciously now. "But I can check for you. You're in which room again?"

"Two fifty-four," I said.

"I'll slip a note under your door and let John know you're looking for him. Mike, was it? And your last name?"

"Just Mike," I said with a wink. "He'll know."

I left Natalie and headed back toward the elevators. I was standing at the railing overlooking the pool when I noticed them. Four men—definitely cops, feds by the look of them—were talking to one of the towel guys.

I immediately turned and headed back down the corridor, half-running.

Natalie was still at Hayden's door.

"Mike? What's wrong?" she said, looking at me as I sped toward her.

"It's the cops," I said. "They're looking for John."

35

Standing behind Quevedo's men at the courtyard pool, Birch, on pure impulse, looked up. And his glance landed on a face by the second-story railing. It was unmistakable.

It was the man in the lobo truck from the surveillance video at the gas station.

The man spotted him at the same time and then backed into the shadow of the hallway above and disappeared.

Birch hurried along the edge of the pool to the walk-through for the beach and pulled open the stairwell door. He slipped out his Wilson Combat 9 mm as he arrived at the second floor. He opened the door. The hall was empty. He thought about the lay-out. The man had been heading in this direction right at him.

There was no other way out which meant that he must be in a room.

Birch listened as he walked slowly down the corridor.

Halfway down the hallway, he heard the distant muffled sound of water running. He stepped past two more doors, then a third. The door on his left was open a crack. The sound of the water, louder now, was coming from behind it.

"John," a woman's voice called out beyond the door, "would you get out of there already?"

Birch's eyes went wide when he heard her Australian accent.

Quietly and slowly, he palmed the door open and slipped inside all in one motion. There was no one in the short corridor leading to the bedroom. The sound of the shower was coming from the half-open bathroom door on the left.

He moved silently from the hall door into the bathroom, his gun pointed level at the shower curtain dead ahead. Steam billowed above the curtain and obscured the mirror. He purposely slowed, his heart keeping pace with each step.

He was reaching for the curtain with his free hand when he heard it.

A creak.

It was the open bathroom door behind him closing, he realized, just as something exploded against the right side of his face and neck.

Black dots dancing in his vision, Birch heard the water louder now as his legs went rubbery. Then he was falling face first into the water's roar and steam and the smothering curtain as the lights went out.

36

"The door! Get the door!" I hissed behind me at Natalie.

I heard her close it.

I looked down at the shooter I'd just knocked out with my flat sap. He was a white guy in his forties with slicked-back blond hair. He wasn't overly tall, but he was built like a rugby player.

I'm talking *thick*. Dragging his heavily muscled body out of the bathroom by the back of his shirt into the room was like moving a gun safe.

As I quickly frisked him, I saw he had no ID on him, just a Department of Justice badge.

And a gun, I thought as I lifted it off the tiles.

Not just any gun either. It was Wilson Combat EDC X9 with a silencer. Wilson Combats were about as far from a joke as possible. They were the kind of gun professional marksmen used in match competitions.

I whistled.

A guy built like a middle linebacker with no wallet, no ID, walking around with an FBI badge and a three-thousand-dollar silenced subcompact?

Didn't take a brainiac to figure out what his occupation was.

I slipped off the guy's billowy shirt. The fabric had a nice silky feel to it, I thought, as I slipped it on.

I stuffed the badge into one of the shirt pockets and pulled the shacket down, covering the guy's expensive target gun that I tucked into the waistband of my pants.

I looked at the now-shirtless man. There was a tattoo of a bulldog on his right shoulder. It was holding up a Union Jack on a pole between its teeth. I noticed there was a number on the dog's tag: *33.*

A British assassin, I thought. *Now, there's something you don't see every day.*

I noticed then that he had a fancy-looking watch. I lifted his thick wrist and read the Patek Philippe above one of its many complications. Even I knew a Patek was as expensive as a Rolex.

This killer sure liked the finer things in life, didn't he? I thought as I took it off his wrist.

I didn't want to steal it. Only an animal would do that. But I did unscrew the crown and toss it over my shoulder back into the bathroom and into the toilet with a loud plop.

Swish! Nothing but net! Americans 1, Brits Zed. And the American crowd goes wild!

I couldn't resist.

"What now?" Natalie said.

I saw that the room had sliders to a balcony. I went over to the doors. The balcony faced the bay, and I could see the dock where I had left the Boston Whaler.

"We need to go out this way. Come on," I said as I pulled the door open.

37

"Wake up, sleepyhead. Earth to Birch. Come in, Birch."

Special Agent in Charge Dennis Quevedo whistled from where he sat on the hotel bed, texting.

"Wake up. C'mon. Yoo-hoo," he said.

Birch, his aching head filled with cotton, sat up against the wall. It took him a full minute to realize he was no longer wearing his shirt. He looked around for it.

"How many fingers am I holding up?" Quevedo said, still texting.

Birch rubbed the right side of his head. He had a massive headache, and it felt like his jaw was broken. He probed his molars with his tongue to see if they were loose.

"Wow, you look like shit. What happened?" Quevedo said.

"You tell me."

"You lost the badge I gave you," Quevedo said.

"To the devil with the badge. Where's my shirt?" Birch yelled. "And my gun is gone, too."

"He rolled you, all right," Quevedo said. "What did he hit you with? A bus?"

"Was it Hayden?" Birch said.

"No, the other one. We looked at the hotel tape. It was the guy from the truck," Quevedo said.

"There was a woman, too," Birch said. "An Australian. I heard a voice."

"Yep," Quevedo said, lifting his phone with her picture on the screen. "Her name is Benning. Natalie Benning. Ring a bell?"

"No," Birch said.

"Well, she just checked in and apparently just checked out with the getaway driver."

"You missed them?" Birch said in disbelief.

Quevedo shrugged.

"They must have cut out from the balcony here and split out the back toward the beach. Why didn't you wait for us?"

"No time. I saw the guy from the video on the second floor and went after him."

"There's no *I* in *team*, Mr. Birch."

"What now?" Birch said. He was losing his patience.

"My guys are scouring the area, but those two had a major head start. There's a dock out there, so I put in a call to the coast guard to search for a boat. Too bad there's no cameras on the beach. When I told them I just had a description of the people, they didn't seem too fired up about it."

"Is this Hayden's room?"

"Yes. We went through the whole thing while you were passed out. It's as clean as your clock."

"No," Birch suddenly said, patting at his wrist. "My watch! Where's my watch?"

"Oh, that's yours? Bad news, Birch. It's in the toilet," Quevedo said, thumbing toward the bathroom.

Birch leaped up and rushed to the bathroom. He snatched it out of the toilet with a moan.

His Patek Philippe Calatrava's once-perfect face was already fogged up, condensation clouding the crystal. He held it to his ear. Nothing.

His mind raced in a panic. The gaskets and the seals, he thought. The movement was surely ruined. Rust was already setting in. The gears were probably completely shot.

"No, no, no," he said as he noticed that the crown had been unscrewed.

The bloody bastard!

He moaned again.

"What's up? You want a doctor?" Quevedo called out.

"No," Birch said, holding the now useless twelve-thousand-dollar watch to his ear. "I just need a gun."

38

It was about four in the afternoon when we pulled into a diner called the Sea Queen just off the Overseas Highway in Marathon.

My new friend Natalie went to the ladies' room, and I sat in a booth in the back, my back to the rear wall, my eyes on the entrance of the parking lot. I stared at the sun-bleached concrete, at the cars going by beyond our rented Nissan Rogue.

It was about two hours since we'd left the hotel on the Boston Whaler. I motored it immediately a few miles south to Higgs Pier where I had already parked the Nissan.

They might have a statewide BOLO on us by now, but without a car description, what would that mean? I'd been an NYPD cop long enough to know that, even with a BOLO, if a bad guy was in the wind, it was advantage bad guy, unless he was dumb enough to run a red light.

I had a bolt-hole in Cape Coral, and I was going to head there to try to think this through. But I was tired, and I still had at least three or four hours of driving to do.

Natalie returned to the booth just as the waitress arrived, and we ordered fried eggs, french fries, and pancakes.

I studied Natalie for the first time as we sat across from each other. She seemed to be in her early thirties. She wore her red hair in a bob. It made her look quite polished and professional for someone her age, but what did I know? I'd never been to Australia or worked at a bank. Or even worked in an office, for that matter. I'd lucked out there.

She hadn't told me much on the ride. Only that she was John Hayden's personal assistant and that she had just arrived from Down Under. Due to the twenty-two-hour flight, she had immediately fallen asleep when we got into the car. I certainly couldn't blame her.

"How long have you worked with John, Natalie?" I said.

"Please call me Nat," she said, stifling a yawn. "Five years."

"What kind of bank is Northdale Standard? An investment bank?"

"It's a regular bank and an investment bank," Nat said. "What's called a *universal bank* in Australia. John is the head of the investment side. He travels all around the world. He has contacts with the who's who pretty much everywhere. The phone calls he gets! That's why I like working just for him. John's brilliant, and the work is very interesting.

"And you worked for John in security with Red in Key West? I remember him talking about Red. Some giant ginger, was he?" she said.

I told her how I had met John, how he was looking for Red and for help. The waitress arrived then with our order. But once she stepped away, I got to the part about the shootout. Nat put her head down and closed her eyes when I was done. I thought she was about to cry. She took a deep breath instead.

"Are you sure he's okay?" she said.

"Without a doubt," I said. "If he was dead, this thing would be over."

"I can't believe this is happening," she said.

"I don't mean to pry, Nat, but you and John are . . . together?"

"No, we're not involved," she said.

There was a flicker in her eyes that made me think she wasn't being completely truthful.

"That's what everyone thinks," she said as she folded her arms. "But John's just a really great boss, and he happens to be a really great person, too. He just has a kind of complicated life."

"Complicated?" I said.

She sighed.

"He was married, but his wife died of cancer many years ago, and he raised his daughter, Josephine, by himself. He and his wife had been super close. And, well . . . I don't think he's really fully over her."

I nodded.

"That's why all of this began, I think."

"All of what?" I said.

"This. His . . . plan."

39

I watched as Nat idly began to twirl her hair with a finger.

"Two years ago at the bank," she said, "we discovered something in one of the safety deposit boxes in a branch we had in Wollongong. A man had rented a box but then suddenly stopped paying. We looked him up from his driver's license to contact him, but it came back that the driver's license was false."

She paused as the waitress arrived to clear our table and we ordered more coffee.

"John did some research," she said. "He hired a private investigator that sometimes worked with the bank and found out that in Brisbane, a top machine-learning engineer named Donald Robinson had died by suicide two weeks before the box had stopped being paid for. John showed me the picture from the news story the detective had found. It was the same man who had rented the box."

"What kind of engineer?" I said.

"Some kind of computer scientist. He worked at Google in the States, but at the time of his death, he was working at a government think tank called the Centre for a New Australian Security."

"What was in the safety deposit box?" I said.

"A glass case with a computer chip inside. Turned out it was no ordinary chip. It was a quantum computer chip."

"Exactly what is that?" I said.

"I didn't know either," Nat said. "John explained it to me. Quantum computers are cutting-edge tech, still in the R and D phase. Who knows how they work, but apparently once they're operational, they'll be a game changer. Potentially many times more powerful than a regular super computer."

"Okay," I said. But I guess I still looked confused because Nat continued.

"Imagine you're trying to find a specific book in a massive library with millions of books. To find that book, you would systematically check each shelf, one by one. This process takes time because you're essentially searching through each possible location in a linear fashion. That's classic computing.

"Now imagine a magical library where, instead of checking each shelf one by one, you could somehow look at all the shelves simultaneously. This dramatically speeds up your search, making it exponentially faster. That's a quantum computer."

"Interesting," I said.

"So they have quantum computers that sort of work, but what they don't have is a way to make them work at full capacity. John said the quantum processor chips create these quantum fields called qubits that make the computer really fast. The most advanced quantum chip today has seventy-two of these qubits. John said his can create seven thousand of them, which will fire up the quantum computers they already have like nitrous oxide in a car engine."

"Sounds pretty valuable," I said.

"That's an understatement," she said. "With this chip, all encryption can be hacked. All the government secrets, Bitcoin, everything. At least, maybe. That's the theory."

"Wow," I said. "So why is John in America?"

"I don't know," Nat said, blinking at me. "He wouldn't tell me."

Whatever the reason John was here didn't really matter, I thought. Being in possession of something like this, especially considering it didn't belong to him, meant he was playing with fire and had put himself in a very dangerous situation.

"Why are you here, Nat?"

"John stopped answering his phone," she said. "And I needed to tell him that his partner, Andrew Paxton—who was at a Bitcoin conference in Thailand—is missing."

"Missing?" I said. "Did he know about the chip?"

"Yes," she said. "John thought Mr. Paxton would try to sell it. He knew how dangerous that would be, so he switched out the real quantum chip in the box with a phony. Now Mr. Paxton has disappeared off the face of the earth. His wife was in hysterics when she phoned me. I'm guessing that John is trying to find him."

"Paxton is dead," I said.

"What?" she said. "That can't be."

I thought of the kill team who had entered the convenience store.

"It's true, Nat," I said. "That gentleman we left sleeping on the floor of the hotel wasn't there to bring room service."

She stared down at the table.

"How did you know where to find John?" I said.

She went into her bag and held up a gray Moleskin notebook.

"I went through his desk and found this," she said. "It's his itinerary. For his . . . plan. He left it behind."

Nat set the Moleskin on the table.

"How much do you know about his plan?" I asked.

"Not much. Just that it is the plan to set it all straight," she said. "That's all John would say. He said it would be dangerous for me if he told me anymore. It all seemed so unreal. I thought he was having a midlife crisis or something."

"He seemed pretty together to me," I said.

"I think he thought that somehow this chip would solve

all his problems. He's not thinking straight. There's no telling what he will do. I had no choice but to come here. I just
wanted to . . ."

She trailed off. She looked out at the highway.

"Save him," I said.

She nodded. I could see her eyes were welling up.

"Because you love him," I said.

She nodded again.

That's when she finally did start to cry.

"I don't want him to get killed."

"Nat, it's okay. It's going to be fine," I lied.

I noticed the waitress by the front door, glancing over sideways at us.

"John's still alive. And you have his agenda," I said, tapping
the notebook on the table. "We can find him and warn him.
Where is he headed?"

Nat flipped a page.

"He has a meeting tomorrow."

40

Wired out of his mind on exhaustion and too much bad American gas station coffee, Hayden, heading north on US-17 in Georgia, almost thought he was seeing things when finally he spotted it about a mile before a bridge.

A tractor trailer in front of him changed lanes, and then there it was under the bright sunlight in the center of a murky pond between two spraying fountains.

Jekyll Island the sign said.

He put on the Ford Mustang's clicker and took the exit.

At its end, the two-lane road was new and cut dead east, and after a few minutes he came to the famous mission-style guardhouses. They were from the 1960s, and beyond them grand palm trees towered along both sides of the entry road like an honor guard.

In the flicker of their shadows, Hayden checked his phone for the time, and then the ETA from the directions. He nodded. Barring any more delays, he would just about make it.

He rolled down the window as he got on the causeway itself and saw the incredible view. In the clear light was a sweeping open plain of sea-green salt-meadow grass so bright it looked like it was plugged in somewhere. It went on mile after mile, and to his left in the northern distance, on the edge of this bright, emerald land, he spotted an oil tanker out on a tidal river.

Live oaks began to zip past, mangroves in the mud flats. There were egrets and terns out there in the marshes, he knew. He smiled after he took a deep breath: you could taste the salt in the breeze.

He arrived over the bridge to the island ten minutes later and parked along one of old hotel's winding paths. As he cut the engine between the Spanish moss, he spotted the Jekyll Island resort's famous Victorian tower. He sat staring at it, the soft evening light glancing off its pinnacle like brushed gold. There was a croquet court to his left that rolled up to the hotel's awning like green carpet, and beyond it in the distance, a woman in sunglasses and a white swimsuit was reading beside a sapphire pool.

He shook his head.

Wasn't that like the cosmic joke of life? he thought. Why was it that life suddenly seemed so extra vivid and enticing and hope-filled right before it was to be likely lost?

His grabbed his newest TracFone from the glove compartment, took it out of the box, and used his reservation number to connect to the hotel's free Wi-Fi. He downloaded Telegram and enabled two-factor authentication for end-to-end encryption for secure messaging and began.

How are we looking? he texted to Molineux.

He waited.

Not well, Molineux messaged back. Traffic outside of Atlanta. Will have to stay over. Shall we try for morning?

Hayden sighed.

That's fine, he typed back.

He looked behind him at the entrance of the parking lot.

He remembered the gas station, the men, the blood.

It was not fine, he thought.

He didn't even have to check the news to know he had the hounds of hell nipping at his heels now. Staying still, even for a few hours, was a bad idea.

The TracFone phone dinged.

Have faith, Molineux said.

41

Hayden laughed as he tossed the phone onto the passenger seat.

Faith, he thought as he lifted a water bottle from the drink holder.

What was that again?

He had had faith long ago, he thought as he cracked the cap. *When he was a kid.*

He'd had faith in his country. Faith in reality. Faith that good men did good things filled with dignity and honor. And that he and all the people he knew were obviously on the side of the good guys.

He had been a true believer, all right.

That's why he had joined the army right after high school like his father had done. Soon after boot camp, he was singled out and taken into Special Assignments, a secret army branch.

There he had been put through a different kind of training with some of the hardest and craziest old bastards he had ever laid eyes on. Being able to take what they kept dishing out, they had accepted him as one of their own.

They named themselves the Face Eaters. They were the maniacs you sent in to prove a point, to end things, to change minds by putting two bullets in them.

Some successful liquidations of supposed terrorists later, he

had been taken out of that group. Groomed by some of the upper chaps, he was told to stow his face eating and exchange it
for a happy corporate face as they handed him his fake credentials and shipped him off to America to an Ivy business school.

That had flung the doors wide. Even before he was out of that
program, he was approached by the Outfit to be a special attaché.

The Outfit was the crème de la crème of all the multinational
strategy and management consulting firms that worked hand in
hand with the three-letter intelligence agencies. They offered
professional services to governments. And he was one slick sales-
man for them, wasn't he? It didn't take him too long to realize
that he had been hired to be a different kind of assassin.

One who destroyed entire countries through economic
means instead of bullets and bombs.

He was a real expert backslapper, wasn't he? And what did the
so-called customer country get?

Destruction: genocide, poverty, debt, and death.

Sent by the Outfit, Hayden would go into underdeveloped
countries to hand out loans ostensibly to develop it. They would
offer new highways, new electricity-generating plants, new air-
ports. The condition of these loans was that engineering and
construction companies that were in cahoots with the Outfit
had to come in to build these projects.

This way the loan money never left the corporate colluding
halls of the West. The money was simply transferred from the
Outfit's international finance offices in DC to Outfit-affiliated
engineering offices in San Francisco.

And the lucky backward-customer country was required to
pay it all back with interest, of course.

If his sales mission was completely successful, the loans would
be so large that the customer country would go belly-up. When
this happened—just like the Mafia—the Outfit would demand
the real vig: control over United Nations votes, the right to install a military base, or mining access to natural resources.

For ten years Hayden did this work until he couldn't stand it anymore.

Which is why he eventually wriggled out of the Outfit and started his own bank back home in Sydney. The international contacts he had made were more than happy to connect with his new firm. One that actually made people some money instead of intentionally destroying them.

And he still would have been busily doing that if it hadn't been for Molineux.

42

Phillip Molineux was—what?

An investor? A writer? A thinker? All three?

Maybe he was the rarest thing of all: a good and smart man who cared about people.

Hayden had first come across him when he read one of his books about the corruption within politics. They'd started a correspondence, and soon after Molineux asked if he could write a book about Hayden's career in the Outfit. Hayden had agreed and became the anonymous source behind *Economic Assassin: How the Intelligence Services Consume the Globe for the Elite*.

He had been so hopeful doing that book. He thought it would actually help initiate change.

It did nothing.

Not long after publication, Molineux confided in him that he was part of a small network of patriots that wanted to change things. These men and women were in various branches of the American government and the intelligence services. Where they were not—but wanted to be—was in a central bank. Molineux was confident that with his credentials Hayden could get hired, and they could finally have a man on the inside. Would he be interested?

Hayden had declined. It seemed too crazy, too radical.

He took a long sip from the water bottle.

But that was ten years ago, and a lot can happen in ten years, can't it? Hayden mused.

Suddenly, what was once radical reveals itself to be the only way forward.

That was why when the full-scale quantum chip fell into his lap, a new plan instantly formed in his head. It was a plan that would do exactly what Molineux and his patriotic team were after.

But he would need some help. Especially with the computer programming angle. He had the new hardware. What he needed was the right software.

Which was why he was here.

"Excuse me, sir."

Hayden spilled water on his shirt as he was jolted from his thoughts. He looked to his left where a young man in a hotel-staff jacket was standing.

"Sorry, sir," the man said. "Didn't mean to startle you. The guest parking is around the back of the hotel. This here is for drop-offs and pickups only."

"Yes, of course," Hayden said, resisting the urge to swipe his brow as he turned the engine over.

43

The private luxury compound in Key West near Fort Zachary Taylor Beach had a main house and three other bungalows with a lap pool.

Described as *stunning* on the rental website, the new structures were all white and bright with Tiffany-blue shutters around the windows.

Birch thought that *stunningly plastic* would have been a better term, as he entered the front door. A cheesy reality TV show called *Beach Circus* had been filmed here, according to the compound's website.

Birch sighed.

Made sense. He was smack-dab in the middle of his own cheesy American circus since the moment he'd set foot in the country.

He tossed the keys onto one of the white leather couches in the main house.

But what were they to do? After the hotel disaster, they needed a staging area. He was getting sick of operating from the back of an SUV, so he'd dipped into the Criterion Group Amex card for himself and his new FBI hunting party.

Or was he just being sniffy? It was a nifty-enough place, really. He walked into the kitchen. He noticed how the granite had striking streaks of blue in it. He rubbed his thumb on its smooth surface. Lapis lazuli.

"Accommodations to your and your men's liking?" Birch said to Quevedo as he took two Italian mineral waters out of the Tiffany-blue fridge and handed one to him.

"They'll do," Quevedo said as he set the bottle on the countertop and cracked the lid with an opener he had on a key chain.

Birch went out onto the deck by the pool and sat down in a padded deck chair. He pressed the cool glass bottle to his jaw. Quevedo followed. Birch watched as he sat and put his feet up on the rim of the fire pit.

"Comfy?" Birch said.

"Comfier than you," Quevedo said. "That jaw is purple. You sure it's not broken?"

Birch touched at it gingerly. His head was still aching, but less so.

"No," Birch said. "No word yet?"

Quevedo checked his phone.

"Nada," he said.

Birch closed his eyes.

When he opened them again, he watched as Quevedo's other FBI team members came out of their bungalows in shorts and T-shirts, sitting down by the other end of the pool. There was one pudgy Hispanic man and a tall Indian guy. They seemed to be partners. The other two were a big white guy in his forties with a neat salt-and-pepper goatee and some young Asian kid in his late twenties. He was quite short and slight, almost like a child.

The tapes Quevedo had gotten from Hayden's hotel didn't show the man and woman leaving by car, which meant the theory about a boat escape was pretty credible. They were still running down leads on that end. Nothing promising so far.

But the clock was ticking, Birch knew.

There were no more carpet calls from Viviani, the CEO of

the Criterion Group, threatening to toss him back in prison, so that was a plus.

Perhaps Viviani was just being dramatic, Birch thought. Or maybe cranky. Maybe he had gotten chewed out by whomever ran the team that had been wiped out.

He took another sip of the cold water. At first he'd been pissed by the sandbagging. The bastard taking his badge and gun and shirt. And ruining his watch. But that didn't really matter because, on the bright side, the idiot had left him alive.

If Birch had one goal, it was making the man regret that decision.

He was still having trouble thinking clearly. He moved the cold bottle to his forehead. Maybe his brain was damaged from the clubbing he'd received. At any rate, they needed some luck.

When Quevedo's phone rang a minute later, Birch crossed his fingers. The special agent in charge stood and walked along the lap pool. He disappeared under the shade of the palm fronds and after a few moments came back.

"So?"

"Nothing. No dice."

44

At around one in the morning, Nat and I were on I-95, just past Daytona near a town called Ormond Beach.

I sipped the last of some Starbucks we'd gotten from a truck stop and yawned. I looked over at her, still sleeping.

I'd never heard of Jekyll Island, but according to Nat's itinerary for Hayden, he was supposed to be meeting someone there about his quantum computer chip tomorrow around noon at a hotel. What particular hotel John's notes did not specify, but I had already looked up online that the island had four of them.

I hadn't decided to be Nat's chauffeur out of the kindness of my heart. My number one priority was still the same: getting myself out of this jam. I needed leverage, and knowing where Hayden was put me in front of the pack.

The way these intel types operated had nothing to do with the rules or with the law. They didn't play patty-cake. They would toss me into prison for something like this, if they didn't hand me over to some scum to torture me to death and then toss my dead body in a hole with a bag of lye.

It was ten minutes later when I felt my phone vibrate and saw Kit's number on the screen.

Kit, old FBI buddy, I prayed, *please, have some good news for me.*

But I couldn't answer in the car. This was most definitely a private conversation. I needed to stop and get out somewhere.

As I got off the next exit and was curving around the off-ramp, Nat woke up.

"Are we there?" she said groggily.

"Not even close," I said. "Just need to make a pit stop."

The all-night McDonald's I found was beyond a fruit stand with a billboard that offered citrus saltwater taffy and pecan candies. Nat stayed in the car, and after I grabbed some snacks, instead of heading back to the car I walked to the other side of the lot and redialed Kit.

As I waited, I stood looking out at the forest of palm trees. There was an eighteen-wheeler parked in the sandy dirt of the Waffle House next door. I listened to the sound of crickets and frogs, the wind in the palm trees. I heard the truck start. Its heavy engine rumbled as it left the parking lot.

"Mike," Kit finally said. She got straight to business. "You're now in this up to your eyeballs."

"Tell me something I don't know," I said.

"They have your picture in a BOLO print with Hayden. You are Unknown Accomplice Number One."

I let out a long breath.

"Do they have the car? What picture are they using?"

"The one from the Florida news story," she said.

That didn't mean that much, I knew. I'd been careful to park the Nissan rental where there were no cameras. But who knew these days what kind of shenanigans they would pull with this dragnet?

I looked up at the night sky.

When I was in Afghanistan, they used to have eyes-in-the-sky drones constantly hovering, watching everything, hoovering up all the data. Why not in the States, especially for an operation like this where some crazy banker was running loose with a chip that threatened the powers that be?

I looked out at the dark, deserted road toward the highway.

We hadn't even gotten out of the state and the cameras on the highway were a real—and real-time—concern.

"If you still want to get a lawyer and come in, I can try everyone I know to help. Because if they catch you first . . ."

I knew what would happen.

"No," I said. "Not yet, at least."

It didn't matter, I realized. I needed Hayden to get out of this, and I had a decent head start.

"If that's the case, stay by your phone, okay?" Kit said. "I have a great contact at AT&T that I use for carrier-data requests on the sly. I already contacted him and asked him to keep an eye out for GPS movement on the phone of my contact in the Miami task force. They're still in Key West, but if they move, I'll know and I'll tell you."

I smiled. It was nice to have good friends. Kit was a great one.

"Thank you. What you're doing is above and beyond."

"Be careful, Mike," she said. "I hope you know what you're doing. Remember, keep the line open."

"Thanks, Kit," I said. "I will."

45

Nat was awake when I came back to the car.

"Hey," she said.

"Hey," I said. "I wasn't sure if you were hungry, so I got you something."

I handed her the Mickey D's bag of two cheeseburgers and fries.

"You're a lifesaver. I'm famished," she said as I pulled out.

"And what's this?" she said as I got back onto the highway. She held up a little bag of cookies.

"Have to have dessert, right?"

"McDonald's has cookies?" she said.

"Of course!" I laughed. "How do you not know this? They're shaped like Ronald and the Hamburglar and Grimace and have a glycemic index off the Richter scale. I'm guessing you don't have kids."

"Not yet," she said. "How many do you have?"

"One. A son. He's grown now. In his early twenties. He even has a steady girlfriend. Nearly successfully launched, thank goodness."

"And your wife?"

"She died of cancer when my son was in high school."

"I'm so sorry," Nat said. "So you raised your son alone? That must have been hard."

"It was," I said. "I felt worse for him. My wife was a really sweet person, and she loved the heck out this kid. It was rough times for a bit for both of us, that was for sure. She was the organized one in the family. I could never get laundry right, and I kept breaking the dishwasher. My son—and me, if I'm being totally honest—wore unmatched socks and clothes that hadn't seen an iron for a solid decade."

I suddenly smiled as I thought of him closing out the game the other night.

"But we made it," I said.

"You're a nice man, Mike," Nat said. "I can see why John wanted to hire you."

I looked at her.

"Well," I said, "if I was a nicer man, I wouldn't have been dumb enough to be in that Key West bar after midnight and we wouldn't have had the chance to cross paths and neither of us would be in this big mess."

"Why were you there in the first place?"

"I live in Fort Myers, and I was dropping off a friend at the airport in Key West, and I missed the ferry back. So I unwisely decided to try to visit Red at his bar."

"Which is where you met John."

"Bingo. And Red wasn't even there. Imagine. What an idiot I am. Whoever said you can never go home again was a genius."

"You're not an idiot," she said. "I think you're sweet."

She suddenly leaned over and kissed me on the cheek.

"Um, what was that for?" I said, my face suddenly going beet-red.

"For saving me back at the hotel," she said. "And for helping me to find John."

She took a bite of one of the cookies.

"And for buying me dinner *and* dessert," she said, smiling.

I didn't know what to say after that, so I just smiled back and kept my eyes on the road.

46

Birch's wake-up call came around seven o'clock.

He came out of his bedroom in his robe and slippers and opened the beach house door. Arben and Bezmir stood smiling at him. His Albanian cavalry had arrived.

Hooray, Birch thought.

"Gentleman, please. Entrez."

He noted the wideness of the smiles. They were excited, he knew. Hounds always wagged their tails before a new hunt.

"Hello, Mr. Birch," Arben said.

"Hello, Arben. How was your flight?" Birch said.

They all turned when they heard a shuffle from the kitchen.

"Arben?" said Quevedo, standing there shirtless in the dark. "What the hell is an Arben?" he said.

"Screw you!" Arben said, his dark eyes flashing. He puffed up his thick chest as he stepped forward.

"You have problem or something?" Bezmir said.

"Take another step, lowlife," Quevedo said, not moving an inch, "and find out."

"These are my men, Mr. Quevedo," Birch said.

"Is that right? Are you a rapper or something, Mr. Birch? Because I don't remember hearing anything in our arrangement about teaming up with an entourage of losers."

"Arben," Birch said, patting the Albanian on his chest with his palm, "please wait outside in the car, if you would."

"Yeah, and take the servants' entrance next time," Quevedo said as a parting shot as the door closed.

"Mr. Quevedo, your unhelpful attitude is entirely unnecessary," Birch said.

"Maybe you've done business differently elsewhere, Birch, but I am a federal law-enforcement officer who is in charge of this task force. You understand? You—and whatever else that was—are nothing. And I mean *nothing*. You're a tourist, Birch. One I will put on a flight back to Limeyland if I have to breathe the same air with the likes of that again. Is that clear?"

Birch looked at the man. *My, my. Now we see some cards being laid out, don't we?* He was about to remind Quevedo of the recommendation he wanted Birch to make about a job, but then thought better of it.

He needed Quevedo.

For now.

"Understood, Mr. Quevedo."

"Good," he said. "Now, get some pants on and call up that jet you said is waiting. Our couple on the run got picked up on a highway camera. They just crossed the state line into Georgia."

47

The hotel's grand dining room on the ground floor was a sea
of glowing crisp white linen. At a table beside its west-facing
picture window, Hayden sat looking out as he waited. Beyond
the hotel's pool along the tidal river, a large blue heron was
standing perfectly still, the filleting knife of its white face and
beak angled down.

It still hadn't moved an inch when he heard the footsteps
behind him.

"Phil, you made it," Hayden said as he stood.

Phillip Molineux was a big man in his early seventies with
a trimmed gray beard and a worn, jolly face. In his linen sport
jacket, tan slacks, and madras shirt, Hayden thought the American looked like a character straight out of *The Great Gatsby*.

"Wouldn't have missed this meeting for the world, John," he
said, shaking Hayden's hand heartily before he sat.

"This place is wonderful, just delightful, isn't it?" Molineux
said after the waitress left with their order. "The Gilded Age
meets Southern charm indeed."

"Have you never been here?" Hayden said.

"No," Molineux said. "Never."

"But your book?" Hayden said.

Molineux smiled and folded his leg over a knee as he gazed out the window.

"Just research, son. But I feel like I have been here, oddly enough. All this Spanish moss, the live oaks, the croquet court, and the perfect grounds. You really can see why they chose this place. So elegant and peaceful, yet secluded. Very, very secluded. There was no causeway back then. They had to come by boat, you know."

"They came from the railhead in Brunswick, right?"

"That's right," Molineux said. "Imagine them, there in a US senator's private train car down from New Jersey, the robber-baron bankers and the assistant secretary of the treasury. All of them under secret names so the press wouldn't find out. There they were, these paragons of society, giants of industry, and pillars of the government together, sneaking around in the dead of night like a band of pickpockets."

"To come down here to plan the picking of the biggest pocket of all time," Hayden said.

"Now it's time to pick the pickpocket's pocket, John." His blue eyes squinted as he looked out the window. "Let's get right to business."

He fished into his pocket and tossed John a key fob.

"What's this for?" Hayden said.

"It's all there on an SSD hard drive in my rental in the trunk. I figure under these circumstances you should just take it out of here. The rental, I mean. I'll just get another one. Drop it off at the nearest Enterprise."

He nodded. They wouldn't be looking for Phil's car right away. Driving it instead of his own would buy him extra time that he could certainly use.

Hayden had been in contact with what he liked to refer to as *Phil's people* over the last year. Despite all the evildoers in the system, there were only a handful of truly good people in the government and private sector who understood the full depth of the corruption. Phil, for some reason, seemed to know all the good people.

And once he had approached Phil with his idea, the man had

ramped up a plan with him without batting an eyelash. He knew exactly who to contact to put the pieces together.

For a moment, Hayden thought about the tremendous risks involved in the actual execution of the plan. But finally sitting next to this kind and good old man felt incredible, like a dawn was breaking through after a rainy night.

"So it's all there, right? All the parameters I explained?" Hayden said.

"Yes, it's all there. It'll monitor everything in real time and adjust on the fly," Phil said.

"Has it been tested?"

"Tested?" Molineux said. "Do you have any idea how large this program is? Some things are too large to be tested."

"How long will it take to upload?"

"In plan A, as you describe it, it will take fourteen minutes."

"And plan B?"

"Seven hours," Phil said.

Hayden leaned his elbows on the table and folded his hands, envisioning himself babysitting the upload while every agency on earth was busy trying to pinpoint the source.

"Seven hours," Hayden repeated.

"We're not playing games here, John," Phil said. "Stop and wrap your mind around the scope of this. You're not uploading a bootleg Disney movie."

"But you're sure the software is legit? The programmer is qualified?" Hayden said.

"Yes," Phil said. "The head of the programming team was an MIT artificial intelligence professor."

"You trust him?" Hayden said, looking around the empty dining room.

"I should. He's my daughter's husband," Phil said, smiling. "Don't worry, John. The software program is ready to go. All you have to do after you install the chip is plug in the software, hit Execute, and sit back. That's all there is to it. But I under-stand if you have cold feet and want to back out."

"It's not about getting caught," Hayden said. "I'm resigned to that. It's getting caught for nothing. Getting caught before we can complete the whole plan. That would be devastating."

Molineux looked at him.

"That's a risk assessment you have to make for yourself. No one else can. And like I said, no one will blame you if you choose not to do this. It's up to you. Though, I will say one thing."

Hayden watched the man as he lifted his coffee cup.

"Everyone who worked on this has been dreaming about this opportunity for their whole lives. Many men have noticed this incredible injustice, but there was nothing they could really do about it. Until now. This is the closest shot to breaking free of their tentacles that has come along in both of our lifetimes."

"It's a go, Phil," Hayden said, jingling the key fob. "I'm doing it. No risk, no reward, right?"

"Absolutely. And look what you will win."

"Fairness," Hayden said.

"And, more importantly, freedom," Molineux said, raising a finger. "Freedom, John. And that is everything."

"You're a good man, Phil Molineux. You've been like a father to me."

Molineux leaned over the table and patted Hayden on the shoulder.

"So are you, John," he said.

Hayden shook his head.

"Not yet. That's why I'm doing this. I want to be one. Maybe this will make up for things."

"Just remember, there's no telling what they will do to you if you actually pull this off. There are no lengths they won't go to to punish you. Are you absolutely positive?"

Hayden thought about his daughter, Josephine.

He smiled.

"Phil," he said, "I've never been more positive about anything in my entire life."

48

"Hi there," I said to the desk clerk.

Nat and I were at the Jekyll Island Club Resort, the hotel on the island closest to the bridge we came in on. We had left the car deep in the bushes on a pathlike road that cut east–west across the island and walked the rest of the way.

The car would stay there: they were onto it. Kit had phoned me twenty minutes before to let me know that the task force was in Brunswick, Georgia, now. They were maybe twenty minutes behind us.

So much for covering my tracks, I thought. We had one shot at this. We needed to find John immediately and somehow get off the island without them catching us.

"How can I help you?" the clerk said, smiling.

He was a nice-looking curly-haired kid fresh out of college. I showed him the stolen fed badge I had on my belt. I saw his eyes pop as I flashed it.

So far so good.

He looked sufficiently starry-eyed, completely snowed.

"FBI," I said. "I'm Agent Daley, and this is Agent Ludlow. We're looking for a guy who might be here. His name's Hayden. John Hayden. Agent Ludlow, the picture, please."

I looked at the clerk's face as Nat showed him the pic of Hayden from the Northdale Standard web page.

I saw it there in the clerk's eyes a second later. Unmistakable. A spark of recognition.

C'mon, I thought. *Tell me he's here.*

"Yes," the kid said excitedly. "I saw him yesterday."

Jackpot, I thought as the clerk clicked at his computer.

"What's the name again?" he said.

"H-a-y-d-e-n," I said.

"No," he said, looking at the screen. "No *Hayden* on the register."

"Where did you see him?" I said.

"I saw him sitting in a car yesterday, a Mustang. Right out here by the front lawn. Dark blue. I told him he had to move it. It might be in the parking lot."

"Where's the lot?" I said, already heading for the door.

49

It was one in the afternoon when they got on the causeway and seven minutes past when they topped the crest of the car bridge over Jekyll Bay and rolled down toward the hazy green island.

They were in three vehicles now, two Honda Pilots and a Chevy Tahoe. The Tahoe was in the lead, with Quevedo driving and Birch sitting in passenger seat.

Quevedo said nothing. The only sound was the tires slapping at the concrete segments with a rhythmic pulse.

He had said nothing on the short flight and nothing on landing. But Birch did see his poker face falter and his eyes go wide when he saw the new vehicles waiting for them beside the tarmac at the airport in Brunswick.

"It's only money, Agent Quevedo," Birch had said as he led him across the tarmac.

Birch looked at his phone, checking for messages from Arben and Bezmir. Their chartered flight had just touched down in Brunswick behind them, he saw.

It was silly to have to take two aircraft when the Airbus was the size of a beach house, but Quevedo, with his righteous lawman act, had to be a noodge, didn't he?

Birch flicked his phone screen over to the photo of the man who had stolen the lobo squad's truck. The photo was from a traffic camera on the I-95 turnoff for the island. The woman was with him now. In the photo, it looked like she was sleeping.

They'd learned that Natalie Benning was John Hayden's personal assistant at Northdale Standard and that she had landed in Key West yesterday. She and the man were driving a rental, a silver Nissan Rogue. They had gotten a description of the car after a witness watched the two come in off a rental boat at a dock near the hotel in Key West. They'd already called all the hotels on the island to see if anyone in a silver Nissan had checked in, but no dice.

Birch rubbed under his ear where the man in the photo had sapped him. He studied the picture, examined the man's features, his calm determination. Birch had never been knocked out before. It was not a sensation he particularly liked.

"Peeling off," said one of Quevedo's men over the radio.

Birch turned and watched as one of the Hondas slowed and turned just where the bridge met the island. There was only one main road that made a loop around the outer edge of the island. This way, they could search from both sides at once.

"That's the one thing I like about this setup," Quevedo said as they went past a stand of crooked live oaks.

"What's that?" said Birch.

"It's an island. There's only one way off."

They pulled into the first hotel and drove through the parking lot. Finding nothing, they pulled back out.

When they reached the main street, it reminded Birch of Key West, only newer, shinier, and high-end. Instead of gritty, everything was clean and unpretentiously elegant.

Like me, Birch thought and smiled. *I could get used to this.*

They cruised past some grandparents and little kids coming out of a frozen-yogurt place. Birch looked at the beach's parking lot beyond them.

"See anything?" Quevedo said.

"No," Birch said.

"They have to be here," Quevedo said. "The car came onto the island. No one comes here by accident. Why here, anyway?"

Birch did not wonder. He knew why. But he kept that to himself.

"Yo, Q."

"What?" Quevedo said over his radio.

"I think we found the car."

50

"Freeze!" I yelled at Hayden.

He was reaching into the back of a silver Tesla Cybertruck. He stood slowly and slipped something into his pocket.

"Show me your hands!" I screamed behind the Wilson Combat pistol I was holding on him.

He listened.

"Knees, now! Hands behind your head!"

I rushed forward, put the pistol in my waistband, and cuffed him.

Only then did I help get him up and turn him around.

"You!" Hayden cried.

"Surprise," I said. I emptied his pockets and sat him down in the open truck bed of the Tesla.

"You're a cop?"

"Technically, I'm retired," I said.

I whistled, and Nat came out from behind the conference center where I had left her.

"Nat! What the hell are you doing here?"

"We're here to help you, John," she said.

"Help me? Then, why am I cuffed?" he cried.

I tossed Nat the key fob I'd just taken off John. The task

force was right on top of us now. We needed to get off the island as fast as possible.

"Not time to explain. Get in," I said, pointing with my chin
to the truck bed.

"Are you crazy?"

"I'm not sure," I said. "But the guys here on the island looking for us right now are definitely unstable."

I didn't have any more time to chat.

I shoved Hayden inside and then crawled in beside him.

"What the hell?" he said as Nat hit the button and the cover
began to close. "Get these damn cuffs off me," Hayden said.

"No way," I said. "You and I have some negotiating to do.
Now, face the other side and keep quiet until we get out of here."

51

The raised plastic ribs of the truck bed dug into my own as we went over a speed bump.

"How are we looking?" I called up to Nat through the crack of the truck cab window.

"It's clear so far," she said.

"Are we at the bridge yet?" I said.

"No. Wait. Now we are," she said as Hayden and I slid to the right as the truck turned.

"What's going on, Mike? What is Nat doing here?" Hayden said as I pushed myself back off him.

We were back-to-back now like a married couple in bed after a fight.

"Your business partner is missing," I said. "He's probably dead. She came here to warn you."

"I knew it," he said.

He shook his head angrily.

"She shouldn't have come. I told her not to get involved. She's got nothing to do with this."

We both slid forward against the cab wall as the truck slowed. Then we slid down toward the tailgate as we sped up again.

"Why are you here?" he said.

"Just trying to avoid getting arrested for murder," I said. "Or, more likely, getting killed for being your accomplice."

"What are you talking about? Why would you be arrested?"

"Don't you watch the news?" I said. "The cops think I killed the clerk at the convenience store at your shootout. I'm all over the news, driving away in the kill team's truck."

"The clerk isn't dead."

"He's not?" I said.

"No," Hayden said. "The second I saw the kill team through the window, I grabbed him and shoved him out the back door. They completely made that up."

"It doesn't matter," I said. "They know the rest of those guys are dead, and mine is the only picture they're waving around."

"How did you wind up in their truck?" he said. "I thought you went to that motel."

"I was headed there, but then I heard the shooting. I knew you were at the store. I figured you needed help."

"Went toward gunfire? For me? I'm touched, mate. I knew you looked like a nice guy," Hayden said.

"So much for being Mr. Nice Guy," I said. "Can't say the same for you, John. You wanted my help while you did 'something completely legit.' Remember saying that, Mr. I Stole a Quantum Computer Chip?"

"You're right," Hayden said. "I kind of fibbed there. My apologies."

"What are you doing here on Jekyll Island, anyway?" I said.

"It's a long story."

"Well, you better make it quick, John, since there's an FBI task force armed to the teeth dedicated to picking you up. They're literally minutes behind us."

Hayden said nothing.

"That doesn't concern you?"

"Not in the slightest," Hayden said. "All part of the plan."

"You really are crazy," I said to his back.

He said nothing. I took his silence as agreement.

"How are we looking?" I called up to Nat.

"We're at the end of the causeway. There's a bridge to the right and to the left a sign pointing us back toward I-95."

"Go the bridge way," I called. "We need to stay off the interstate."

"I get it now," Hayden said. "You wanted to catch me to cut a deal for yourself. Use me as a negotiating chip."

"No," I said. "I wouldn't do that. Though, you obviously do need saving, as these guys are out to kill you."

"But you led these guys to me! They wouldn't know where I was if it wasn't for you."

He had a point there.

"Inadvertently," I said.

"With friends like you, who needs enemies?"

"Whatever, John," I said. "I'm in this, and I figured with you dead, they could make up any story they want while *I* get to sit in a jail cell. I needed to make sure you stayed alive so they didn't wipe out my only alibi."

"What do you want me to do? Type up a confession?"

"That'd be a start," I said. "I need iron-clad proof that I had nothing to do with that shooting."

"The video," Hayden said.

"What?" I said.

"I have it," he said. "I took the security-camera hard drive when I left."

"I don't believe you."

"It's true," he said. "*I* needed it to prove it was self-defense."

"Where is it?"

"I mailed it to my lawyer before I left Key West."

"Oh, sure," I said. "Where did you mail it? Let me guess. Australia?"

"No," he said. "New York. I used to work out of New York. I have a lawyer there."

I didn't say anything.

"I'll get you the video. But you have to let me go."

I still said nothing.

"What other play do you have, Mike? You've got nothing else. Unless you want to turn me in to these losers and cut a deal."

"Fine," I said, turning toward him with the key.

We suddenly started to slow.

"Nat, what's up?" I called.

"Oh no," she said as we went slower and slower.

"What?" I said.

"It's the car or truck or whatever," she said, panic in her voice.

"What?" I called out.

"The battery is dead!" she cried.

52

Birch and Quevedo stood side by side outside the Tahoe, staring at the Nissan.

It was parked deep in a stand of trees a couple of hundred feet off the narrow road they had just turned in on. Its doors were open, and several of Quevedo's agents were rummaging through it now. Birch could see that the front of the vehicle was sunk into the marshy ground.

He looked from the ditched car back down the bucolic path beside them. There was a golf course on the other side of the road. A slight breeze was moving the tall trees, and the afternoon sunlight through their leaves softly dappled the pavement of the road. As he watched, a couple of golfers in an electric cart rolled to a stop nearby across the road. Birch smiled as one of them striped a 3 wood straight down the fairway.

"Mr. Birch, feel free to get in there and help my men toss the vehicle," Quevedo said. "Don't be shy."

Birch listened to the chittering of frogs and other creatures in the swamp forest. He waved at some horrid tiny gnats or whatever they were. Were there gators this far north?

"What a generous offer," Birch said.

"I mean it," Quevedo said. "You're looking for a computer

chip, right? You should roll up your sleeves and get in there and take a look."

Birch patted at his pocket and retrieved a cigar. He lit it with a click of his gold Zippo.

"I have complete confidence in your men, Agent Quevedo. Let's give them a chance to do their work and see what they come up with."

He took a deep puff as he glanced back at the golfers.

No doubt about it. His frantic urgency had been replaced by a calm now. Their fox had gone to ground, Birch thought. He'd seen it before. He could sense it. It was all but a done deal. He smiled as he suddenly saw himself on a balcony overlooking Kensington Palace Gardens, sipping an espresso.

"In that case, what do you say we head over to the nearest hotel?" Quevedo said as he thumbed at his phone. "No doubt the two must have walked there after leaving the car."

Birch slapped at a mosquito near his wrist.

"Splendid idea," Birch said as he turned back for the Tahoe.

A minute later, they pulled alongside the meticulously cut front lawn of the Jekyll Island Club Resort and stopped beneath its grand portico.

Now this, Birch thought as he puffed his cigar, *is more like it.*

There was a young clerk behind the desk inside. He smiled happily at Quevedo's flashed badge.

"So did you get him?" he said.

"Get who?" Quevedo said.

"John Hayden."

"What?" Birch cried, almost dropping the cigar.

"How the hell do you know that name?" Quevedo said. "How do you know about Hayden?"

"From the other FBI agents," the clerk said. "Agent Daley and his lady partner."

Birch and Quevedo looked at each other.

"Did they show you a badge like this?" Quevedo said, showing his shield.

"Yes. Exactly like that."

Quevedo gave Birch another look.

"Go slow now, son," Quevedo said. "What exactly did this Agent Daley say?"

53

The Sidney Lanier Bridge near Jekyll Island was one of those new cable-stayed suspension bridges with two pylon towers and cables running directly to the deck like strings on a harp.

A beautiful piece of modern architecture and engineering, isn't it? I thought as I passed one of the harp strings.

Though, I probably could have admired it even more if I didn't think I might, in a moment, be shot and tossed into the Brunswick River below it.

I turned back to where we had left the truck. It was no longer visible. The bridge arched up, and we were now on the downward slope.

"Note to self," I mumbled. "When escaping in an electric vehicle, check the battery level."

I looked back at Hayden and Nat who were walking about twenty feet behind me, still bickering.

I had definitely been right about their mutual attraction. Only people who had the hots for each other bickered.

Despite the new rom-com vibe, things were not looking too good. We were heading away from the bad guys the only way we could—on foot.

Hoofing it was not a good escape plan. I looked down through the cables at the water. There was an oil tanker about a mile away on the river, and beyond it I could see the dark shape of Jekyll Island.

How far away was it? I wondered, staring at it. Ten miles?

We'd made it ten whole miles. "Ten!" I mumbled, shaking my head. The heat was starting to get to me.

Then I ducked and turned away from the flying road grit as the deep rumbling roar of a passing eighteen-wheeler almost blew me over the railing.

"C'mon," I called out behind me. "Let's go, people!"

54

As they headed down the causeway away from the island, the speedometer of the Tahoe was nearing triple digits.

All the stops had been pulled out now. Only three things existed: the blurring asphalt, the blazing sky, and Birch in the passenger seat with his heart pumping one hundred percent pure adrenaline.

Then through a break in the stand of roadside trees, Birch could see the bridge in the hazy distance.

He lifted his binoculars over the sea grass, but the Tahoe was jostling too much.

Birch lowered the window. As his shirt began to snap in the wind, he quietly thumbed the retention nub of the Safariland holster, holding his backup Wilson Combat pistol.

This hunt was over, he thought.

Birch smiled.

He knew his instincts had been right.

It had all come together almost at the same exact time. They had just seen Hayden and the man and woman he was with get into the vehicle from the hotel video when they got the call about a dead Tesla truck on the bridge from the state police radio band.

It was the stroke of luck they needed.

Birch sat in the passenger seat, suppressing the small grin that kept tugging at the corners of his mouth.

Now, now. Stiff upper lip, old boy, he said to himself.

The thrill of the chase was always an adrenaline rush, but he had to stay sharp and cautious. He couldn't afford to get ahead of himself.

He glanced over at Quevedo. He, too, was keeping it cool, his hands loose on the wheel, though they had to be up near a hundred.

This would be a major victory for both of them, wouldn't it? Once Birch had what he had come all this way for, Quevedo would get his wish, his second career with the trillion-dollar company. Maybe with the salary bump, Quevedo could even pick up the kind of aftershave they didn't sell at Costco.

Birch smiled.

You're welcome, you stupid bloody Yank, he thought.

"Can't this thing go any faster?" he said.

"Let's see," Quevedo said.

The Tahoe's V8 growl shifted to a scream as Quevedo down-shifted. There was a clunk under the scream, followed by a pause, and then the heavy truck surged even faster.

"Apparently, yes," Quevedo said as he went around a Mazda Miata convertible like it was standing still.

Birch wondered if Hayden had the chip on him. He had to, right? Even if he had ditched it, there were ways to get him to talk.

He almost wanted him *not* to have it. It had been a while since he'd had a juicy struggle session with a chained-up suspect. He'd welcome something he could really sink his teeth into.

It wouldn't be his beautiful war, of course. He would never have that again. Never have that summer rooftop again where he had been given the life-and-death power of a god.

Quevedo blasted his horn as the causeway ended, and they swung onto US-17, pinning it.

Birch sighed as he looked at the bridge, looming now.

If tearing apart Hayden was all he had to look forward to, Birch thought, then he guessed it would just have to do.

55

Near the bottom of the span of the bridge, I could see Route 17 rolling on in the distance like a beige ribbon laid across a giant lawn. The land that it cut through had exactly zero houses or other structures on it as far as the eye could see. In 99 percent of America, there would be a strip mall nearby to walk to. But not here, not now. Here, there was just open grassland with nowhere to hide.

I swiped the sweat from my eyes. After only ten minutes of walking, my shirt was stuck to my back. The heat and humidity were off the charts. The sun-bleached concrete made it feel like I was like walking on a cookie sheet, even through my shoes.

As another semi roared by, wafting me with diesel fumes and dust, I remembered hitchhiking to the Jersey Shore once with a buddy when I was in high school. It was a grimy road trip, too, I remembered, but back then my biggest worry had been how I'd get back home.

Not how I was about to be executed by some intel goons.

When we reached the very bottom of the bridge, I saw docks on the river off the left side of the road, and on the right beyond a creek, a white multistory building. The building had cars parked in the lot in front of it.

"We'll head there," I said back to John and Nat, pointing to it. "We need to get off this road."

"Aye aye, Captain," John said.

As if we would make it that far, I thought.

We were going to get caught now. How could we not? Someone would spot the Tesla, would call 9-1-1. A squad car would be sent out.

They were already on their way, no doubt. And as Kit had mentioned, we were on the FBI BOLO list.

In five seconds, it was about to be game over.

"Bingo," I mumbled as I saw the traffic camera up on a stick on the concrete jersey barrier at the bottom of the bridge. I stopped myself from giving it the finger. It didn't matter. We were toast.

All this running around—and for what?

For nothing. I started to laugh to myself as I walked. You couldn't invent a jam-up of this proportion without the help of a room full of Hollywood writers. *Wrong*, I corrected myself. All you needed to do was to be foolish enough to miss the ferry and opt for bar-hopping in Key West till dawn.

That's when I sensed the vehicle slow beside me. I looked over. It was a modified pickup, a service vehicle with a white plastic tank in the truck bed.

I read the tailgate.

Roger's Pest Control
Keeping Your Home Pest-Free, the Roger's Way!

"C'mon," Nat said as she ran past me. "That's our ride! I just flagged him down."

The driver was an overweight middle-aged Hispanic guy. He was wearing a traffic vest over soiled Tyvek coveralls.

"That your electric truck back there?" he said in greeting to the three of us.

"Yes," John said. "I'm the idiot. We're on vacation, and I

insisted we get the bloody thing. Forgot you have to charge it after a bit."

"Shit happens," the guy said, staring at Nat. "I'll get you to a gas station, but I can only take one in the front."

"That's fine," Nat said, hopping in.

I watched as John immediately got into the back beside the white plastic tank of pesticide.

"Give me your hand, mate," he said, reaching out to me. "How do you like that? Another truck bed for the two of us. Just like old times," he said, laughing as he pulled me up.

56

Jesup, Georgia, was a small town with redbrick buildings and pickup trucks in the forty-five-degree parking spots. There was an old movie theater with a marquee among the shops on the main street.

Around three that afternoon, John and I stepped into the town's Amtrak train station. I looked around the inside of the quaint one-story building, the size of a small house, as we sat. It had three benches, two bathrooms, a luggage scale, one ticket window—now closed—and two vending machines.

Grand Central Station this was not.

Nat wasn't with us. She was sleeping in the rental car, a '69 Cadillac convertible, that was parked beside the old depot.

It was the second car we'd rented that afternoon. The first was a Toyota Camry that we rented up the road from the bridge in Brunswick at the Enterprise where the pest control guy, Julio, had dropped us off.

But since we figured the bad guys would be onto that in a heartbeat, we drove it directly to a vintage-car rental place we found online that was at an inland town to the west called Waycross. We'd left the Camry in its lot.

If you must get chased by the cops, I thought as I looked out through the depot window at the beautiful boat of a Cadillac, *why not do it in high-style American luxury?*

John came back from the timetable posted on a board by the closed window.

"Twenty minutes, it says," he said as he sat.

We obviously all had to split up now. I would head to New York to get the video from John's lawyer first thing Monday morning.

Though I would miss at least two of my son's games, I was actually looking forward to the trip. It would give me a chance to see Colleen.

I had texted her in the car, but she hadn't texted back, even though it had been a few hours. This either meant that she was pretty upset that I hadn't had a chance to call her or, worse, that things were going poorly with her father.

I figured the best thing to do when I got to New York was to go straight to the hospital and surprise her. Maybe if I showed up out of the blue, I could cheer her up.

"C'mon," John said a few minutes later when we heard the sound of the train. "Maybe it's early."

We headed outside. It was just a freight train. We stood there watching it. It had black oil cars and empty grain cars and wood boxcars covered in graffiti.

"Never mind the regular train," I said. "How fast you think that's going? Maybe I should just try for one of the boxcars."

Hayden laughed.

"I don't think it's gotten that bad yet, has it?"

Rather than going back inside, we sat down on a bench next to the station. It was a high bench with a raised stand for your feet. It took me a second to realize it was an old shoeshine stand.

"John," I said, "now that we have a minute here, suppose you tell me what's really going on. What are you up to?"

He looked at me.

"You have any kids, Mike?"

"I have a son."

"Well, imagine if you had a daughter," John said, folding his arms.

"Okay," I said.

"Now, what would you do if she went away to New York City for a job at an investment bank? And then went out one night for some drinks with the CEO's son? And ended up dead in the hallway of a crack house in Harlem?"

"Oh, John. I had no idea. I'm so sorry."

Those were details Nat had omitted when she'd mentioned John's *complicated* past.

"The coroner's report said cause of death was multiple drug intoxication. They found cocaine, fentanyl, ketamine, and the date rape drug GHB in her system. Put her heart into cardiac arrest, the doctor said."

I sat there shaking my head. A father's worst nightmare.

"Now, what would you further do," he said calmly, "if the investigation into her death hit a brick wall? If there was no accountability for what happened? No punishment. No nothing. Even after it was discovered by my private investigator that the CEO's son had paid off two other women after drugging and raping them. What would you do?"

We watched as another freight train went by.

"I get it, John. I get it now."

"What do you get?" he said.

"You're going to use that chip to take down the CEO and his son."

He shook his head.

"You left out his company," he said.

"What company?"

"It's called the Criterion Group."

"I'm not sure I've heard of it."

"That's just the way they like it," he said. "It's the largest multinational investment company in the world. They have over eleven trillion dollars under management and make about six billion dollars every year. *A year,* I said. They have controlling stock positions in just about every large corporation on the planet. They might be the largest corporation ever."

"And you're going to take them down?"

"All the way," he said. "I'm going to have it so that the CEO, Albert Viviani, will be out on the corner of Broadway and Wall wearing a barrel and selling pencils."

I looked out at the tracks.

"I won't ask you how you're going to do it."

He smiled.

"I wouldn't tell you anyway," he said.

57

Another horn sounded. We looked down the tracks at the approaching Amtrak.

"What about Nat?" I said, pointing my chin at the rental car.

John looked over and then quickly turned away.

"I'm sending her home after you get on that train," he said.

"Say goodbye to her for me," I said.

"I will."

I looked at him.

"She's in love with you, John. You know that, right?"

He looked at me. Then he nodded.

"Yeah, I know," he said.

"Why not go with her?" I said. "That's what your daughter would want. She would want you to be happy, John. She wouldn't want you to sacrifice yourself for her."

The train was getting larger now, and it started to slow.

"It's not just her. I've done some bad shit, Mike. Really bad. When I was a young man, I helped bankers just like Viviani to destroy entire countries. The good people in those countries took me into their homes and fed me. They trusted me."

He bit at his thumbnail.

"And I screwed them," he said. "Not just them, but their children and grandchildren. I ruined them for generations."

"Not on purpose," I said. "You thought you were doing your job."

"Does that matter, Mike? At the end of the day, if you run someone over, does it matter if it was by accident? I helped these bastards get mining contracts in the Amazon. You know what they did to the Indigenous people? They went in with gunships. Shot them like they were wild hogs. I got promoted that year."

I noticed tears on his cheeks now.

He wiped his face.

"It was my first seven-figure check," he said.

I said nothing, just sat looking at him. What was there to say?

"I have to atone, Mike. At least, I have to try."

The train clanged as it pulled in front of us.

I patted him on the shoulder as I stood.

"Be careful, John," I said.

He nodded.

"Go to my lawyer first thing Monday morning. He'll give you the video."

"You promise?" I said as I extended my hand.

"Trust me," he said, and we shook on it.

The train whooshed as it finally came to a full stop.

58

Hayden and Nat drove north in the Cadillac rental on I-95 all afternoon. They stopped once for coffee and to put up the convertible top. When they got back on the road he tried to strike up a few light conversations about the office back in Sydney, but Nat wasn't in the mood.

He looked over at her.

Nat wasn't just beautiful. She was a purehearted person who had seemed to dedicate herself to him selflessly from the moment he had met her.

Who deserved that? No one, he thought. Least of all him.

There was something special about her. How she carried herself, a certain grace that made you want to pull her closer. And he had wanted to pull her closer, many a time. Yet he had held back mainly because of the age difference.

That she had come all this way to save him truly warmed whatever was left of his heart.

It killed him that he couldn't give her the fairy-tale ending she deserved.

They reached Exit 104 for the Savannah/Hilton Head International Airport around three. They passed a heavy-equipment company and a golf course. Then Hayden hit the clicker and pulled under the sign for Departures. The terminal they stopped at two minutes later was a new redbrick building that looked like a high-end mall.

"I don't want to go, John," Nat said.

"I know," Hayden said as he put the car in Park.

"I really don't want to go," she said, looking at him. "I won't. I mean it."

He looked at her, looked down at his lap. He checked his watch. Then looked down at his lap again.

"I thought—"

"You thought wrong, Nat," Hayden said coldly. "You have to go."

"But you want me. I know you do," she said through tears.

"No, I don't. I never did. It was all in your head."

Nat looked at him, a fury rising through her tears.

"You're lying!" she suddenly yelled. "How could you say that?"

"You were an excellent personal assistant. That's all."

She peered at him, wiped her eyes, peered at him some more. Then she started to smile as she punched him in the shoulder.

"You're a giant jerk, you know that, John? You're just acting mean to get me to go. Men are so stupid. You think I'm an idiot? I know what you're doing, and it won't work."

Hayden looked sternly at her. He caught himself start to smile, then laugh.

"That's your problem right there, Nat. You're too smart. Pretty women should never be smart."

"Is that right?" she said.

He nodded.

"Of course. Intelligence is their downfall. Tragic, really. What would be great is if you had a switch that could turn off how smart you were."

"Like a Dumb Barbie Doll switch, is that it?" Nat said.

"Exactly. A brain-off switch. It would be so much better for you."

"Would the switch be just for you?" she said. "Or could I turn it off and on as well?"

"Just for me, of course," Hayden said. "I'd put it right between your shoulder blades where you could never reach it. Two modes on it. Smart or Happy."

"Like Work and Play," she said.

"Now you're getting it," Hayden said.

"Which one do you want now, John?" she said as she grabbed him by his shirt. "Flip the one you want. I don't care. I just want to stay with you. Whatever comes next, I don't care."

Hayden kissed her then.

Then he leaped from the car and opened her door and pulled her out onto the sidewalk.

She was crying as he got back into the car and clicked the locks shut. The sound of it almost made him stop. Almost.

As he glanced back, he saw that she was on her knees like a little girl who had fallen roller-skating.

He slipped the car into Drive and pulled away from the curb, wiping at his own eyes.

59

I fell asleep almost immediately after paying for my ticket. When I woke up against the window of the train, it was near sunset.

Where were we? I wondered as I looked out. North Carolina?

I didn't know, but beyond the window was nothing but trees for a while. I'm talking lots and lots of trees: evergreens, maples, beeches, white spruce, white pine.

The track seemed to start on an upward slope, and after a while, we began to pass small mountain cabins, listing old barns, '80s vans in gravel drives. We slowed as we came across a wide brown river, and a metallic voice on the overhead speaker said something I could hardly make out.

We slowed even more into a station where I saw a sign for a town called Hawk's Falls. Whichever state Hawk's Falls was in, I wasn't sure, but it looked like it had been airlifted into a hilly valley. There was a dollar store next to a furniture store and a really old-looking bank with a clock over the front door. Besides some houses on the narrow streets behind these structures, that was the extent of it.

I looked at the mist rising from the mountains behind the town and wondered for a moment if I was actually in a *Twilight Zone* episode where the train goes back in time. Then the train started up again, chugging and clanging its bell. The mournful horn of the Amtrak sounded out a couple of blares against the tree-filled hills and we were rolling again.

When we passed the baseball field at the edge of town, I remembered how long it had been since I'd called Declan.

"Hey, son. How's it going?" I said when he picked up.

"Dad! You're alive!"

"Yes. Alive and kicking."

"What in the world happened?"

"I met up with an old friend from the service," I said. "And, as much as it pains me to say, one thing led to another and I lost track of time."

What else could I tell him? I thought. The truth? No way. I wasn't about to tell him what was actually going on. I didn't even want to know.

"For days?" Declan said. "You have to be kidding me, Dad. People lose track of time for a few hours at most. Honestly, I was about to start checking hospitals. What the hell are you thinking? Are you on some kind of bender?"

I almost laughed at his righteous outrage. As if I hadn't stayed up countless times in his teenage years wondering if I should call the morgue. It was pretty funny having grown kids, I thought. How quickly the tables get turned.

"Have you spoken to Colleen?"

"No, not yet."

"Well, I think you better. She's texted me about twenty times. I had to tell her that you lost your phone. I don't think she believed me exactly."

"Don't worry, Dec. I'm actually heading to New York as we speak. I'm going to surprise her."

"Dad, what's really going on? You're in trouble or something. Who's after you? You have to tell me. Give me a code word. Say *Santa Claus* or something. Let me help you."

I laughed.

"I appreciate your concern, son. Honestly, I'm good. But you're right. I didn't just go out on a bender and bail on you. I got caught up in . . . something. But it's not that bad. I'm taking care of it. It's a long story, and I *will* tell you. Just not right now, okay? I need to nail something down up in New York, and then I'll fly back in a day or two with Colleen to catch your next game. Speaking of which, how's it going?"

"You're sure you're all right?" he said, sounding calmer now.

"I'm fine. Now, what about you? How did you do against Clearwater?"

"I got shelled. Gave up a walk-off double. But it wasn't my fault. Bases were loaded when they called me in. And I got the save last night against Lakeland."

"Lakeland! I love it. Three up, three down?"

"No, the first guy got a single, then we got a double play, and I struck out the last guy to end it. The stadium reporter actually interviewed me."

I shook my head, picturing it.

"That's awesome, Dec. I'm so proud of you. I can't tell you how much I'm looking forward to being there for your next game. Daytona, right?"

"Yes. Daytona. At home on Friday. Are you sure you'll make it?"

"Son, I promise I will do my best."

60

Birch, mid-cabin on the Criterion Group Airbus, watched the ground lights tilt and swell outside the dark porthole of the window as they banked on final approach.

"What is the room again?" Birch said to Quevedo as the landing gear whined open beneath them.

Quevedo held up his phone at him.

Defense Department 158 Tactical, it said, along with the passcode.

Birch memorized the code.

"You sure you won't come along?" Birch said.

Quevedo gave him the finger in response as he closed his eyes again.

Three minutes later, he walked down the steps of the just-halted aircraft with his Albanian helpers at his heels. He had smuggled them aboard despite Quevedo's misgivings. They headed across the shadowed tarmac into the main terminal.

Because for this part of the operation, they were most definitely required.

Past the sliding glass doors, it looked like a shopping mall. There were airy corridors and skylights. The middle of it looked like a town square with cobblestone-like paths, the scent of fresh coffee in the air.

They walked around a silver-haired man tucking his ticket away, his rolling golf bag making a playful clicking sound as he dragged it across the bumpy floor.

Genteel Southern charm, Birch thought, looking up at the dark sky through the skylights. How . . . American.

The escalator was past the central information desk by the luggage carousel. Fifty steps just ahead to his left was a steel door with the words *Defense Department 158 Tactical* written above it.

There was a box beside the knob. He typed in the code, and the door clicked. Just inside on the right sat a middle-aged woman behind the security desk.

"I'll buzz you in," she said.

"Do you have her phone?" Birch said.

She took it out of a drawer and handed it to him.

Birch arrived at the door and looked up at the security camera.

"Hang back," he said to his men.

The door buzzed.

"Natalie. Now, that's a pretty name," Birch said as he entered.

She was sitting in the opposite corner, feet up on the bench, hugging herself. It was the red-haired woman from the hotel and highway video. She was prettier in person and smaller.

Good, Birch thought.

All of her stuff from her carry-on was spilled out on the table between her and the door. He lifted a pale pink bra with a finger. He looked at it, then her, nodded thoughtfully, and put it down.

"Where's my lawyer?" she said. "I also haven't gotten my call to the Australian consulate."

He nodded.

"Very sorry for the oversight, Natalie," Birch said, placing her phone down between them.

"Here you are. Go ahead. You can call them now."

She didn't look at the phone. Just at him.

"You think I'm stupid?" she said. "You'll just snatch it from me after I punch in my code."

He sighed.

"Stupid would be better for you."

He snapped his fingers. The door buzzed, and his Albanian crew came in with the bags.

"Get your hands off me!" she screamed as she was lifted off the bench.

When she kicked Bezmir in the crotch, his cousin Arben body-slammed her so hard off the table Birch thought it would break.

Birch jumped on top of her with the towel. He placed it over her face as Bezmir handed him the water bottle.

She slipped her face out from beneath the towel in a frenzy of surprising strength.

"Get her head, Arben! Hold it still," Birch cried.

Arben did as he was told and grabbed her hair.

"Boss, wait. Look," said Bezmir standing by her things.

Birch turned. He was holding a notebook. Birch grabbed it.

"An itinerary?" he said, reading the bookmarked page. "It can't be this easy. Key West, Jekyll Island, and oh, lookee here. Your boyfriend is going to be in New York."

Nat stared up at him in horror.

"Nod *yes* or *no*, Natalie," Birch said.

She kept staring.

He grabbed her by the hair.

"Yes or no?"

"Yes, he's going to New York. Yes."

Then she began to cry.

PART THREE

HOME ALONE

61

"Hey, sleeping beauty. Upsy-daisy!" the voice yelled in my ear.

In one movement, I shot awake and rose and thrust away the large figure hovering above me with a savage straight arm to his chest. Something metal crashed to the floor as I flung myself up and out of the cramped slot of the booth-like seat.

I crouched into a fighting position, muscles coiled.

"What are you? Nuts?" said the Amtrak conductor, red-faced.

I stared at him, my mind quickly assessing where I was.

Right, the train, I realized. I noticed then that it was stopped. Outside the window, I saw a concrete platform.

"Really sorry," I said, immediately relaxing. "You startled me."

"I called you ten times, buddy," the conductor said.

He was a thin balding white guy in his thirties. I saw by his expression that I'd really shaken him up.

"Jeez, you can't put your hands on people, you know that?" he said. "I oughta call a cop."

That's all I needed now, I thought in a panic.

I quickly bent and lifted his ticket punch and gave it back to him.

"You really don't have to do that. Honestly, man, I really didn't mean it. I . . . um . . ."

I tried to think up some excuse. "It's just I was in the service.

You know, combat and everything, and I get startled easily. I was out of my head for a second, but I'm okay now. Honestly, it was nothing personal. I feel terrible."

"It's all right. I get it," he said, shaking his head. "My big brother was in Iraq. No harm done. We're in New York. Penn Station."

"Thanks," I said. "Again, I'm really sorry."

"Don't worry about it," he said. "And, buddy?"

"Yes?" I said.

"You're not down south anymore. It's forty degrees out there, tops. Bundle up."

I got off the train and decided to follow the conductor's advice on the wardrobe change. Though, not shockingly, at five o'clock on a Sunday morning in Penn Station, my choices were limited.

After some brief deliberation with no other choices, I ended up purchasing the warmest looking things I could find, a Knicks sweat shirt and matching sweat pants from a Hudson News kiosk along the grim, windowless concourse of the station.

I could have used a coat, too, I thought once I was outside. Florida, this was not. I picked up my pace and hooked a left onto the shadowed sidewalk, my tired eyes scanning early-morning Seventh Avenue's streetlights, steel-shuttered stores, and dark buildings for a Starbucks as I made my way north.

The brightest lights came from the glowing sea-green orbs for the Thirty-Fourth Street subway station two blocks dead ahead. As I passed by them, I thought for a moment about taking the subway to the Bronx where Colleen was at the hospital, then decided against it.

I wanted to get some coffee first, and besides, I could just get a taxi. I needed to stretch my legs and to clear my head.

New York, New York, it's a helluva town, I thought as I looked out at the city.

I'd grown up in the Bronx and had run Manhattan's streets from one end to the other with my friends before we'd even gotten out of grammar school. As I walked, I started thinking about those times. I remembered being down here one summer night and sneaking into some bars during the anniversary celebration for the Statue of Liberty. They were packed with cops and yuppies and firemen like it was a summer version of St. Paddy's Day. I laughed as I remembered how drunk and happy the whole city was.

Those were the days, all right.

Colleen came immediately to mind then. Our time down in Florida. Those long tan legs of hers as she dove off our boat into the sun-splashed water. With the exception of the last few days, I was happier now than I'd been in a really long time. I couldn't believe how much I missed her.

I finally stepped out into the street and waved for a taxi.

"Happy thoughts," I said to myself as I dug my hands into my pockets. "Think *warm* happy thoughts."

62

Just inside the entrance of Montefiore Medical Center on East 210th Street in the Bronx, two EMTs, a doctor, and a couple of nurses were hovering over some poor soul on a stretcher.

"Sir, can you wiggle your toes?" one of them said as I skirted the semiorganized chaos toward the reception desk.

Colleen's dad was on the third floor. I passed a nurse in blue scrubs and a face shield before I found the room. The door was open a crack. I knocked softly as I peeked in.

Mr. Doherty was asleep in his hospital bed, and on the other side of him Colleen was sleeping in a chair beside the window.

Standing there, I felt something soar in my heart as I watched her. Wow, was I happy to see her! I should have been with her the whole time, I knew. I walked over to her. Even tired, she was so beautiful. When I touched her wrist softly, her eyes fluttered, then opened.

Then they went wide.

"Mike?"

We went out into the hallway. An approaching young doctor in a white coat with a stethoscope around his neck did a double take when he spotted us hugging like we'd just won lotto.

"Take a picture, Doc. It lasts longer," I whispered in Colleen's ear, making her laugh as he passed.

"Mike, I've missed you so much," she said. "You don't understand."

"I think I do, dummy," I said, hugging her some more. "Why
do you think I'm here?"

"What about Declan? His games? He needs you."

"He's a big boy, Colleen," I said. "You need me more. How's
your dad?"

"Better than they first thought. He's lost a little memory, but
he seems mostly back. They think he can go home tomorrow."

"Thank God. What a relief," I said. "I'll help you guys get
him settled. What time does he get released?"

"Noon, I think they said."

An old lady with a walker shuffled out of a room down the
hall.

"Can I get you out of here for an hour? Can you eat something?" I said.

"Definitely. My aunt is actually on her way to relieve me,"
she said.

As I offered her my arm, I suddenly heard something. It was
church bells coming from outside. I remembered it was Sunday.

I checked my watch. It was five to eleven.

"Hey, I need to go to Mass. Have you gone already?"

"Last night. But let's do it. My dad can use the extra prayers."

"Wow," I said, grabbing her hand and pulling her down the
hall.

"What?" she said.

"A man who has a woman who will go to Mass twice for
him," I said, giving her hand a squeeze, "is one lucky man."

63

"So what happened to your hand?" Colleen said over the Irish music.

We were in the back booth of an Irish pub across from the hospital. I placed my cheeseburger down and looked at the back of my hand that I had scraped when I bailed from the pickup truck. Then I looked at Colleen's beautiful Irish eyes.

They weren't smiling. She didn't miss a trick, did she? I thought I could keep her out of this, but apparently I had thought wrong.

Though I had been planning to tell her all morning about all the insanity, the thought of breaking the news still made my stomach churn. More than just the words themselves, I was afraid of what they would mean for us.

I really did have a knack for getting into massive amounts of trouble. Did she really need that level of chaos in her life? Maybe not.

Then again, she did know about my past. She'd known me since childhood, after all. She must know what to expect. Right?

I looked at her, smiling across the table, and tried to keep my nerves in check. The soft clink of silverware and quiet chatter around us seemed to increase in volume as the seconds ticked.

"Well, it's a long story," I said.

"Do tell," Colleen said, still looking at me sternly. "Now, please."

I told her. Everything. How I missed the ferry. My poor decision to go see Red. Meeting John Hayden. The shooting at the convenience store.

I watched her closely as I said these things.

Her expression seemed to shift with every other word.

At first, I could see the incredulity in her eyes. She literally couldn't believe what I was telling her.

This was not a surprise, I reassured myself. I could hardly believe it.

Then I noticed her hands clenched on the table as she leaned forward. She was definitely ticked.

But the anger quickly left her expression, and I could see the worry spread across her face. I had expected her to be upset, but I didn't anticipate the level of fear that began to show in her eyes.

I wasn't sure which reaction I disliked more.

Disbelief, anger, and fear, I thought. *Not exactly the way to a woman's heart.*

Then, when I was completely done, Colleen just stared at me in wide wonder.

"I leave for five seconds and this is what happens?"

"It gets worse," I said.

"How?" she cried.

"I'm a fugitive. I'm wanted in Florida," I said.

Before she could open her mouth, I reached across the table and took her hands in mine.

"Please, take a breath, Col. Luckily, I have a way out of this. Hayden took the security footage from the store. It proves that I had nothing to do with any of it."

"Did he give it to you?" she said.

"Not exactly," I said. "He mailed it to his lawyer here in New York. So first thing tomorrow morning, I have to go to his office down in Manhattan to get it. Then I'm going to get my own lawyer and call my FBI friend, Kit, and we're going to hash this thing out and get my name cleared."

She seemed speechless.

"I know. I'm sorry. I should have come with you."

"Damn straight," she said, crossing her arms.

"Colleen, I'll never make that mistake again."

She let out a breath and placed her hands flat on the table. She looked me in the eye.

"*I'll* get you a lawyer."

"Thank you," I said, smiling with relief.

"You're welcome. And once you get your name cleared, then I'll go back to being mad at you," she said, trying not smile but failing miserably.

64

At 840,000 square feet, the Javits Center on Eleventh Avenue between West Thirty-Fourth and West Fortieth Streets on New York City's Far West Side is the largest convention center in the eastern United States. Its main feature is its cubist Crystal Palace–like dome above its main entrance near Thirty-Fourth Street, and underneath it lies a sprawling exhibition hall eight football fields wide.

It was five in the morning when Birch and Quevedo rolled past in the Chevy Impala undercover car that had been waiting for them at the airport. Hayden's itinerary that they had snagged off his assistant was coming in very handy indeed.

Birch looked out from the passenger seat.

With its overhead grid lighting system and see-through glass curtain wall, in the still-dark sky Birch thought it looked like a fireworks display going off inside of a giant greenhouse.

"Seriously?" said Quevedo, behind the wheel as he and Birch made the right off Eleventh Avenue onto Thirty-Fourth Street. "You're not serious, right?"

"What's that?" said Birch after a yawn.

"He's going to be here?" Quevedo said. "Here? This place is as big as Yankee Stadium. What am I saying? This place could swallow Yankee Stadium with a glass of water. We're going to have to look for him here?"

"If these things were easy, Mr. Quevedo," Birch said, "they wouldn't refer to men like you and me as *heroes*."

It truly was a behemoth, Birch thought. The truck entrance they came in off Twelfth Avenue near Fortieth had to be twenty feet high.

The security personnel at the booth directed them to a parking area beside a freight elevator. As they got out of the car in front of it, the elevator rattled open. The three young women who disembarked were wearing rhinestone tiaras and were dressed in silver sequin gowns that had sashes across the front of the low-cut dresses. The sashes of the two dark-haired ones said Miss BMW and Miss Audi, and the blonde was Miss Cadillac.

A lanky Hispanic man with a goatee and a lanyard over his well-pressed dark suit came out behind the women.

"Frank Rodriguez, Head of Security here at the center," he said, shaking their hands.

They all watched the backs of the three beauties as they headed in through a door to the convention hall.

"Must be tough working here, Frank," Quevedo said.

"Oh yeah," Rodriguez said. "It's hard work, but someone has to do it."

They stepped into the sleek, modern lobby beside the freight elevator. It must have been just remodeled, Birch thought, because the walls looked freshly painted and you could still smell the Sheetrock and joint compound.

"I'll take you to the elevator for the Security Operations Center," he said. "It's our eye in the sky. We run everything from cameras to crowd control up there."

"What's your setup?" Quevedo said as they got on.

"We've got all the latest bells and whistles," he said. "A completely comprehensive integrated system. It's less than a year old. We've got everything from CCTV monitoring to intelligent lighting systems. You'll see."

Off the elevator and down another shorter hall, they reached a set of steel doors.

On its other side, the Security Operations Center was a sleek, dimly lit room filled with rows of computer monitors. Beyond them up on the wall, two huge screen displays showed a grid of smaller screens, each one showing different parts of the convention center in real time. Between the monitors was an illuminated map of the enormous facility with markings of the locations of all the cameras.

Even this early in the morning, a team of security personnel wearing headsets sat at desks, scanning the screens.

Birch looked to his left down through the window of the skybox-like elevated perch. Down on the floor forty feet below was a display of cars, rows and rows of them, their mirror finishes flashing under the spotlights.

"You guys get in early, huh?" Quevedo said.

"For the car show, we do," Rodriguez said. "The New York International Auto Show is our largest event in terms of attendance. We usually get about a million people."

Quevedo gave Birch a wide-eyed look as he shook his head.

"Over how long?" Birch said.

"Ten days."

"A hundred thousand a day?" Quevedo cried.

"A little more on weekends," Rodriguez said. "I know it sounds like a lot, but managing it is doable. Here, let me show you."

He led them to a desk in the back where a giant touch screen displayed the entire floor plan of the center. It looked like something out of a sci-fi movie. An intricate map of exhibit halls, service areas, emergency exits, and cameras.

"This is the nerve center," he said. "We've got real-time surveillance of every inch of this building, from the main hall to the freight areas. If there's an issue with an entry point or something's going wrong with a load-in, we know about it instantly."

He tapped the screen, and the front entrance was blown up on the big screen.

"See?" he said. "We've also got security officers stationed at key locations. Entry points, high-traffic areas, and restricted zones. They're all equipped with two-way radios, so if anything comes up, were on it in seconds."

"This is impressive," Quevedo said. "I've seen operations centers before, but this is next-level."

"Precisely," Rodriguez said. "All of the cameras are equipped with facial-recognition tech, and you've already given me your target's picture. Watch."

He tapped the screen, and Hayden's face appeared on the big wall screen like a billboard in Times Square.

"If your guy Hayden comes in here," he said, "we'll spot him right away."

65

The bakery door jingled shut behind Hayden as he stepped out onto Fifth Avenue in Bay Ridge, Brooklyn, with the white box in hand.

He crossed to the black Mercedes G-Wagon parked at the curb, a rental he'd picked up when he'd finally arrived at Newark Airport. He slid in behind the wheel and carefully placed the box in the passenger seat.

He pulled out onto Fifth heading east. He looked out at the shops and cafés, the brownstone stoops lined with plants. Fifteen minutes later, at Twenty-Fifth Street, he took a right onto a curving drive in through the iron gates of Green-Wood Cemetery.

He maneuvered his way to its center until he thought he was near. He parked and opened the passenger-side door and carefully lifted out the white box. He was off by quite a bit, he realized after a few fruitless minutes of searching through the rows. The gravesite was actually beyond where he had parked, a steep walk up a hill.

When he reached the top, he turned and took in a stunning view of the glass-and-steel skyline of Manhattan to the west. He stood staring for a moment, the wind blowing. It took him another twenty minutes to find the headstone. He took a deep breath as looked down at the slab.

JOSEPHINE HAYDEN, it said across the white marble. *"Jewel of My Heart."*

"Hey, sweetheart," Hayden said as he knelt down on the grass before it. "Surprise," he said as he opened the box.

He took out the two banana cream cupcakes inside. They were the same kind his daughter had picked out to celebrate her birthday with him back in her tiny studio in Brooklyn Heights two months before she'd been murdered.

He placed one on the headstone, then took out the pink candle he had bought, stuck it in, and lit it with a Bic lighter.

He closed his eyes.

"Happy Birthday to you," Hayden sang. *"Happy birthday to you. Happy birthday, dear Josephine. Happy birthday to you."*

He thought he would break down and was surprised that he had held it together. He finished his cupcake and licked vanilla cream off his thumb and blew out the candle.

He stood staring at the Manhattan skyline as the cold wind blew.

Even though it was all planned out and there really was no going back now, doubt began to creep in.

Had he really thought of everything? he wondered. Was it really this simple?

Was it even the right decision?

He looked up the gray sky.

Or was he actually crazy, as everyone would soon say?

He thought about it. All of it. Weighed it. The pros. The cons. Even now he could stop it, he knew.

He stared down at his daughter's headstone.

He nodded his head.

It was happening. He was going through with it. All of it.

He turned and began to walk down the hill.

And there wasn't anything anyone could do to stop him.

66

There was a short and clear overhead ding, and the elevator opened directly into the apartment on the eightieth floor. It was still under construction, but Hayden hardly even noticed as his eyes were immediately drawn to the wall of floor-to-ceiling windows.

At eight hundred and twenty feet off the deck of Park Avenue and East Fifty-Seventh Street, facing west, in the clear, spring morning sunlight, you could see damn well near everything.

Times Square, Central Park, the bright white stone facade of the Empire State Building, New Jersey.

Hell, Pennsylvania probably, Hayden thought.

Far below were not just ant-sized people but the roofs of office buildings. At this elevation, even the cars were indistinct. Flowing along the grid of streets, they looked like drops of liquid in a chemist's tubing.

Or, Hayden thought looking down at them, *drops of blood in a vein*.

"So it's the tallest building in the Western Hemisphere?" he said.

"No," the broker said, smiling from where she stood beside him, staring out at the airplane view. "It's the second-tallest building in the Western Hemisphere."

Her name was Samantha. She was about thirty and had a smile that could light up a room.

"But it's the tallest *residential* building in the entire world," said the slick, super cocky broker with her.

"What's your name again?" Hayden said, turning to him.

"Alex," he said, handing him his card.

Hayden looked at it. He rubbed his thumb over the embossed letters that spelled Viviani.

He wasn't the one who had raped and killed his daughter. He was the younger brother.

"How much is it? Twenty million?"

"Twenty-two million," Samantha said.

"Twenty million?" Hayden said again, looking at Alex.

"Why, yes, it is," said Alex, no dummy. "To a serious buyer, at least."

"Do I not look serious, Alex?" Hayden said, smiling at him.

The kid peered at him.

"Actually, you do," he said with a laugh. "So what are we doing here?"

Hayden pressed the barrel of the gun he produced from his pocket to the center of Alex's forehead.

"What we're doing here," Hayden said, "is getting your attention."

Samantha, suddenly taking a step toward the door, yelped like a lapdog in the pistol report. The bullet Hayden fired had trimmed the edge from the fresh Sheetrock beside her left temple.

"This isn't about you," Hayden said to her calmly, the gun already pointing back at Alex's head. "Just sit down, Samantha. And you'll be fine."

She sat down.

"Now, do I have your attention, Alex? I do, right?" Hayden said.

He swallowed, nodded.

"Take out your phone and call your father," Hayden said.

"My . . . father?"

"Is there an echo in here?" Hayden said, cocking his head. "Call your father right now, and make sure you put it on Speakerphone."

He pressed the buttons.

"Dad?"

"Alex? What is it? I'm busy on the other line."

"Hi, Albert," Hayden said. "Let them wait. You'll want to take this call."

"Who is this?"

"Josephine's father."

There was a pause.

Viviani's silence spoke volumes.

Cat got his tongue, I guess, Hayden thought.

"Leave my son alone," he said finally. "What do you want?"

Hayden listened to Viviani's voice crackling with uncertainty. He could almost see the sweat on his brow, the panic rising with every passing second. Viviani had nowhere to turn now.

"What I want couldn't be simpler," Hayden said. "I want you to answer a question, Albert. Do you want me to put a bullet in Alex's head, or do you want me to throw him out of this eighty-story window?"

Samantha screamed then. Alex started to shake. Hayden took the phone from him as he fell to the floor whimpering.

"Please, no. Please," said the CEO.

"*No* what, Albert? *No*, don't put a bullet in his head? Or *no*, don't toss him out the window?"

"Please."

"See, because if I had the choice," Hayden said, "I would have chosen a bullet in my daughter's head instead of what your other son did to her. But I didn't get a choice, did I? But I am giving you one. So which is it?"

"Please."

"You have three seconds. Three."

"Stop!" Viviani said.

"Two," Hayden said, raising the pistol at Alex's head.

"No!"

"One," Hayden said and pulled the trigger.

Hayden disconnected the call, cutting off the howl that had erupted from Viviani's throat.

He looked down at Alex and then at the bullet hole in the wall next to him. Then he looked at his watch.

When he glanced back at the two hostages, they were staring at him, their eyes filled with fear.

He had prepared for this moment in his mind countless times, but the reality of holding the gun on innocent people wasn't something he was accustomed to.

He turned his gaze to the phone in front of him, letting the silence stretch, more than eager to let Viviani stew.

Even so, the pressure was suffocating. No matter how many times he had imagined this part of the plan, nothing could prepare him for the cold sweat dripping down his neck, the sound of his own breath so loud in the heavy silence.

His heart pounded as he let the seconds tick glacially by. It didn't matter. He had to hold his nerve, not just for his survival but for the plan to work.

He looked at his watch again.

It was time.

"When I redial, you say hello first. Got it?" Hayden said.

Alex nodded.

Hayden hit Redial.

"Dad! Dad! It's okay. I'm okay," Alex said.

"Isn't that glorious, Albert?" Hayden said. "Your child lives. Mine does not. But the good news is that I'm not here in New York for your kids, Albert. You're not getting off that easy."

"What do you want? Anything. Please."

"No," Hayden said. "Not *anything*, Albert. *Everything.* I'm here to take everything you truly love, you son of a bitch. So sit back and be patient. Because I'm not just coming for you, Albert. I'm already here."

67

The view from the thirty-third-floor Midtown window looked south. The Empire State Building was huge, directly ahead, followed by a long, low concrete carpet of smaller buildings. Far in the hazy distance like the Emerald City in *The Wizard of Oz* were the skyscrapers down on Wall Street, glittering in the morning sun.

"Can I help you?" said the voice of the female receptionist behind me.

I was at Vasbinder and Lowen, Hayden's lawyer's office on Lexington Avenue across from Grand Central in the Chrysler Building.

Whatever else Hayden was, I thought as I looked at the marble walls and the impressive view of Manhattan, the man didn't seem to be pretending to be a player.

At C-suite level, I thought, this was living about as large as humanly possible.

"I hope so. I need to see Nicholas Renton."

Boy, did I. He had the evidence to clear me of all of this nonsense, and I wanted my life back. That video would give it to me.

"Mr. Renton is in court all day today," she said without looking at her computer.

I stared at her for a beat. She was a middle-aged, light-skinned

Black woman with green eyes that were as cold and hard as cash. Her beige pantsuit was designer.

One tough cookie, I thought.

"Could you please contact him for me?"

"I can try," she said. "What did you say your name is?"

"Mike. I'm a friend of John Hayden. He'll know who I am."

I looked for some kind of reaction in those money-green eyes at the mention of Hayden's name, but there was nothing.

"Please have a seat," she said.

I went back to the window. It was coming on twenty minutes later when the receptionist finally addressed me.

"Excuse me," she said.

I walked to her desk.

"Mr. Renton is not answering his phone, sir. I tried several times. This is not unusual as he is currently on a very important court case that requires all of his attention."

I couldn't believe this garbage. I was going to be in court myself if I didn't speak with him. Man, I needed that tape, I thought.

"But you must have a way to contact him, say, if a 9-1-1 situation is happening here at the office."

"Yes, of course," she said.

"Could you use that?" I tried.

"No," she said without a blink.

"I'm really in a bind here, Miss—"

"Ms. Flanders," she said.

"Ms. Flanders, truly, I— Is there nothing you can do?"

"I'm sorry, sir," she said. "I'm sure your situation is important to you. But we have protocols here I must adhere to."

She lifted a pen that was on her desk and clicked it.

"Here's what I can do. If you will leave me your name and contact information, I assure you I will give it to him when he does call."

I looked at the packages behind her. Was it there? The impulse to leap over the desk and start rifling through them was strong.

No dummy, Ms. Flanders detected my demeanor and the direction of my interest.

She glanced at the packages, then back at me, her eyebrow raised in a fierce FAAFO glance.

"Thank you so much, Ms. Flanders," I said as I took out my burner phone to determine its number. "A call back from Mr. Renton would be fine."

68

There was a huge crowd out on Eleventh Avenue even before the auto show opened, and now at midmorning the Javits Center was packed.

Birch looked over the shining hoods of the concept cars at the crowds edged at the shin-high barriers. Behind most of the cars were huge screens showing car commercials in HD. Jeeps slaloming in deserts, sports cars racing through forests or across wintry tundra.

He remembered what Quevedo had said about the center swallowing Yankee Stadium. With all the massive, flashing 4K screens of the cheesy American car ads, it looked like it had swallowed Times Square as well.

Birch weaved his way through a cluster of slack-jawed Americans listening to a young woman in a push-up bra rattling off an Audi supercar's engine specs. Then he tapped the PTT button on the Kenwood TK radio hidden in his coat pocket.

"Tac 3, this is Tac 1, radio check, over," he said into a Bluetooth lapel mic clipped under his shirt collar.

"Tac 1, this is Tac 3, loud and clear," he heard in his earpiece. "Anything?"

"You'll be the second to know," Quevedo said.

As Birch continued to search the crowd, he still could hardly believe what that bastard Hayden had done. He had abducted Viviani's youngest kid and then pretended to shoot him while Viviani was listening on the phone. Only to leave him alive and let him go. He hadn't made any demands.

This guy wasn't playing games, he thought. He shook his head. When they had said that Hayden was a terrorist, they actually weren't far off, were they?

Because he was terrorizing Viviani, that was for sure.

What would Hayden do when he showed up here at the auto show? Birch wondered. He checked his watch and then took out his phone.

The one with his even more important contacts on it.

"Bezmir, friend, how are we looking?" Birch called out.

His Albanian cavalry, of course, were waiting outside the convention center.

Once Hayden was spotted, no matter what Quevedo said or wanted, there was not going to be any arrest.

Viviani was out for blood now. Birch was told that whoever laid hands on Hayden and brought him before the CEO would be getting a bonus.

Five million dollars if he was dead.

Ten million dollars if he was alive.

The second Birch saw him, he'd snatch him, take him to a warehouse in the Bronx, and torture him. At the end of which, the chip would be in Birch's possession.

Then he would bring Hayden to Viviani one way or another and cash in.

"Bezmir, hello? Are you there?" Birch said, struggling to hear him.

The murmur of the thousands of people mingling around the convention center was almost deafening. The volume toned down considerably when he arrived at a space between the EVs and commercial vehicles.

"What did you say?" Birch said.

"All of my cousins are in place," he said.

Bezmir's cousins were New York Albanian mafia. Even the Italian mob in New York City were said to be afraid of them.

Perfect, Birch thought.

"We have four cars, one on each corner, all in position," Bezmir said.

"Excellent. I will keep you posted."

Birch looked out at the crowd.

The trap was set.

Now all they needed was the mouse to show.

69

At a little past eleven, Birch was up in the conference room, beside the eye-in-the-sky control.

He was switching out the new radios that a contingent of FBI agents from the New York office had brought when he heard the bells and whistles going off next door.

Quevedo had just beaten him into the control fishbowl when they saw Director Rodriguez beside one of the techs by the front.

Looking over the director's shoulder at the tech's screen, Birch watched the red computer square that was following a figure wearing a gray hoodie.

It was a man. He was down on the exhibition floor, standing beside the display for a new electric pickup, with his hands in his pockets.

"Talk to me," Rodriguez said.

"It's him. The guy, Hayden," said the tech.

Birch peered at the face on the screen, but the gray hoodie, pulled almost across the face like a monk's cowl, was in the way.

"How the hell can you tell it's him with the hoodie like that?"

"I didn't see him. The computer did," the tech said. "The facial-recognition program picked him up and made the match. He must have slipped the hoodie off and looked up at the camera and put it back on again."

Quevedo and Birch looked at each other.

"Don't lose him. Guide us to him," Birch yelled as he blew past Quevedo, beating him to the elevator.

The elevator dinged open onto the showroom floor.

Birch looked to his left over the heads of the crowd where it said EVs.

"Where is he?" he cried as he bolted.

"Left of the elevator," said Rodriguez in his ear. "About a hundred, a hundred and fifty yards. He's toward the back by a yellow dump truck now. He's just standing there."

"Hey, watch it, jackass," someone said as Birch, threading his way through the crowd, shouldered a civilian.

He swiveled around and saw the yellow truck.

"Hold up! He just bolted," Birch heard Rodriguez exclaim. "He's on the move! He's walking fast away from you. Now he's running!"

Birch started running himself now.

"Where! Where is he?"

Far ahead, he saw a gray blur dart into a doorway on the left.

"I see him. He entered a doorway to the west," Birch cried.

"Shit," said Rodriguez. "That's the vendors' access. Where is Lopez? Lopez? Gray hoodie running. Gray hoodie. Stop that son of a bitch."

Birch, flying now, dodged around a huge display of tires, and then he was in through the same doorway in a back corridor. It dumped out onto an access road beside an indoor parking lot. There was a scrum of people ahead on the asphalt by the lot's entrance.

"I got him! Suspect down!" Birch heard in his ear.

Birch raced up. A security guard was lying on top of the gray-hooded guy.

Finally, Birch thought as he pulled the hoodie back.

Then Birch stood there, stunned.

What on earth?

"Get your hands off me," the guy said.

It wasn't Hayden. It was some short skinny kid no more than twenty, a college kid.

"What the hell are you guys doing? I didn't do anything. Leave me alone, man," he said.

Not only wasn't it Hayden, in fact it didn't look anything like him.

"It's not him, you idiots," Birch said to the skybox.

That's when Birch saw it. Some rolled-up paper sticking out of the kangaroo pocket of the young man's hoodie. He pulled it free.

It was some kind of paper mask with a rubber band around it. He unrolled it.

And looked into the eyes of a color photo printout of Hayden's face.

"No!" he said.

He looked at the college kid, his heart suddenly pounding. What was this?

It was a head fake, Birch thought. He had tricked them!

He sneered down at the college kid.

"Where's Hayden?"

"Who?" the kid said.

The kid cried out as Birch gave him a whistling kick to his ribs.

"You know who, you cheeky little bastard. Where is he?"

"Hey," the security guard said as he shoved Birch back. "What are you, crazy? He's already cuffed."

Birch's hand twitched at his back where his pistol was. He looked down the access road that led to Twelfth Avenue.

Shoot the guard, lift the kid, call the Albanians to meet him, he thought.

But he was too late.

"Birch," Quevedo said, finally arriving and pushing him away, "get a grip. I'll handle this now."

70

Hayden, sitting in the Mercedes G-Wagon on Thirty-First Street three blocks away down Eleventh Avenue, watched as the young man approached.

He unclicked the lock on the door as the guy stepped off the curb.

He was a tall, wide-shouldered young man who looked like he played football. He was wearing a tracksuit jacket that said *Fordham* across its back.

"Piece of cake," the college kid said, handing over a black plastic box with two magnets on it.

Hayden looked at the key holder that the kid had just retrieved from the wheel well of the new Ford Focus on display. It had been placed there by Hayden's contact in what was known in intelligence services as a *dead drop*. His contact wanted nothing to do with meeting Hayden in person, so they agreed to do one at the New York auto show.

Hayden popped open the box. Inside was a blank blue electronic security badge, and on it on a piece of green painter's tape was a passcode written in black marker.

The last piece of the puzzle, Hayden thought with a smile.

"You did great, son," he said to Kenny Molineux.

He was Phil's grandson. He went to school here in the city,

and Molineux had told him to give him a call if he needed some help.

Hayden handed him an envelope with two thousand dollars in cash.

"Make sure you split this with your buddy. Nick, right?"

Kenny nodded. "Yep. Will do."

"And he has the lawyer's number?

"Yes."

"He'll stick to the script, right?"

"Nick? Of course he will. *That he got paid to do it by some Spanish drug-dealer-looking guy.* He won't crack. And even if he did, he doesn't know why I told him to do it. Kid's a loon. That's why I love him. Everyone does. That crazy little daredevil would have done it for free. He was the one who told me to wear the Fordham hoodie in case they ever trace it back to me. Get the cops going over to the Rose Hill campus to roust those snobby Jesuit Fordham Rams. Rams eat shit, after all."

"You're at Manhattan College, right?"

He nodded.

"Technically, Manhattan University now," he said. "Fordham's rival and greatest Bronx school ever, where Giuliani went, and billionaire writer James Patterson, too. Home of the Jolly Jaspers."

Hayden laughed as he suddenly noticed the beer on his breath.

"You haven't been drinking this morning, have you, Kenny?" he said.

"Hell yes. Kegs and eggs. You think Nick and I would do this sober?"

Hayden laughed again as he turned the electronic badge in his hand.

He was so close now, he thought, looking at it.

So close.

He checked his watch.

Twenty-four hours to go, he thought.

71

It was coming on eleven when I got out of a taxi in front of the Javits Center.

"John Hayden, where are you?" I said.

I must say I was pretty pissed now. Not only had Hayden's lawyer's office not called me back, they had stopped taking my calls. And Hayden wasn't answering his burner phone.

Burner, I thought as I crossed in under the glass dome of the convention center. It looked like I was the one getting burned.

"We'll see about that, John," I mumbled as I paid the twenty-five dollars at the little box office just inside the door.

I went inside under the big dome entrance and stood in the middle of the swirling crowd, gaping at the forty-foot ceiling.

Living and working in New York, I'd driven past the Javits Center plenty of times, but I'd never actually been inside. The place was gigantic. I slowly moved my way in deeper. Off to my right, maybe a hundred people were crowded around some kind of futuristic-looking Porsche.

And ten feet directly in front of me, another fifty or so people were in line beside a vintage Rolls Royce to take selfies with a super tall, tattooed Black guy in a white leather Knicks jacket.

I should have worn my Knicks sweat shirt, I thought. *I could have gotten it autographed.*

I walked past him and saw nothing but more cars and hordes of people.

Oh boy, I thought. This was no joke, was it? I had about as much of a chance of bumping into Hayden as finding a cab in hurricane.

"What now?" I mumbled to myself when I sensed some movement from the corner of my eye.

When I turned, along the wall about a hundred feet in front of me I saw that an elevator door had opened. It was what was inside the elevator that really caught my eye.

It was the guy from Key West. The tidy-looking English guy who'd tried to kill me and Nat at the hotel. The one I had sap-slugged back in the hotel room before I stole his gun.

Uh-oh, I thought, just as he saw me, too.

Then I saw him speak into his lapel.

Not good. I looked around.

Through the milling crowd surrounding the entrance, I suddenly saw uniforms everywhere. About a dozen or more white-shirted security guards. And if I didn't know any better, it seemed like they were coming directly at me through the crowd from all sides at once.

I looked left and saw a big white security guard with a beard staring dead at me from ten feet away. He was close enough for me to hear the radio he was holding in his hand crackle and spit.

That's when I figured out what I had to do next.

It was simple.

Completely and utterly insane.

But simple, nonetheless.

Behind my back, I took out the assassin's pistol I had stolen and quickly unscrewed its silencer.

"Gun!" I screamed and then proceeded to pop, pop, pop rounds into the carpeted floor at my feet.

The violent pops of a 9 mm are unbelievably loud next to those not wearing any ear protection, I knew. We're talking a party-balloon-pressed-onto-a-pin-next-to-your-ear kind of loud.

That did it. I didn't have to scream it twice.

In fact, a second later, I wasn't the only one screaming.

Like a firecracker tossed into a herd of cattle, the milling crowds of people scattered this way and that. Most of them were headed in the direction I started running, back out toward the Eleventh Avenue main door I had come in.

I looked back quick for the assassin. But where he had been was now a sea of surging people.

Good, I thought, only to turn back and see one guard—the same huge white guy—eyes on mine, lunging at me from my left about five feet away.

Then the big Black guy in the Knicks jacket, running for his life for the door, blasted the guard into next week.

Next week? Next month, I thought as the guy went spinning down to the floor.

It was as if the Knicks guy was my defensive end. And he had thrown the world's most crushing block.

Then I was outside, running south down Eleventh Avenue like there was no tomorrow.

72

I thought I had gotten out of the convention center pretty clean until I saw the black Mercedes Sprinter van double-parked near the corner of Thirty-Fourth.

As I watched, four large, formidable guys got out of the van and looked directly at me. As an NYPD cop, I'd seen mafia street-soldier types before. These ones looked to be Albanian or maybe Russian.

As they started to run at me, I decided I didn't care to find out which ethnicity they were. That's why I made the only move I could under the circumstances.

I walked out into the street and into the open side door of the UPS truck that was waiting on the light.

And I put another round into the ceiling of it.

"Out of the truck now!" I screamed at the driver.

The driver didn't need to be told twice. She leaped out the open passenger door as I got behind the wheel and roared the truck up onto the sidewalk, forcing the four thugs to dive for cover as I blasted past them, cutting the corner onto Thirty-Fourth.

I floored the UPS truck down Thirty-Fourth at the Hudson River, its engine protesting as I pinned it. I gripped the wheel tightly, heart racing, as I suddenly looked into the side-view mirror and saw the flashing blue and red lights of a police car.

"Great," I said as I ran the red light and careened right onto Twelfth Avenue.

I spotted some more police lights ahead in the distance, so I made a right onto Fortieth back toward Eleventh. There was dead-stopped traffic ahead and some kind of construction site on the right with an open gate.

I didn't even hesitate.

I cut the van sharply and headed diagonally across the inter-section into the construction site.

Through the opening, there was a recently poured concrete foundation on the left where a front loader was swinging. But to the right was an open dirt field with a gravel path.

I tried to keep the truck straight on what passed for a road, but it wasn't easy. Especially when I followed it between a large bulldozer and a porta-potty with about a centimeter to spare.

"Think, think, think!" I yelled to myself as I squeezed the van through a corridor made by a stack of lumber and a pile of rebar.

I saw a construction trailer at the other end of the worksite to my right back up near Tenth Avenue, which, to my mind, meant there was a way out.

It wasn't much of a plan, but it was all I had.

Without hesitation, I pinned the accelerator and headed straight for it.

That's when the gravel path suddenly ended and I was driv-ing on dirt. The steering wheel felt like it was slipping from my hands as the truck bucked violently against the bumps and dips. After a second, the back of the truck suddenly sounded like a Jamaican steel drum as all the packages in it began flying around, rattling off the metal walls.

As the tires struggled for traction in the dirt, I glanced in the side-view mirror and saw that the police car had stopped at the construction site's edge.

I pressed the accelerator harder as I stared at the trailer, dar-ing to hope that I might actually make it out of this mess. Then

I heard a boom at the bottom of the truck and felt a jolt so hard it made my teeth click.

The truck bounced off the ground and landed with a sickening crunching sound beneath my feet.

Even with my foot pinned on the gas, the engine was almost silent and the truck was at a dead stop. The engine sputtered and stalled, and the dashboard lights flickered and finally went dark.

"No," I cried as the rough hands of two burly construction guys pulled me out of the truck a second later.

"What are you, frickin' nuts?" one of the hard hats said to me.

That's when I saw what was behind them, and my eyes popped.

I couldn't believe it.

It was three of the mafia guys. They had come from the Tenth Avenue end of the site, and one of them was holding a shotgun with a pistol grip.

"Whoa, whoa," said one of the construction workers as two of the thugs grabbed me.

"Who are you guys?" I said to the one with the shotgun as I was bum-rushed out of the gate. The van was there, its back doors wide open.

As if in response to this, he punched me in the mouth.

And then I was being lifted up and chucked into the van like a sack of potatoes.

73

"Hey," I said as I was shoved deeper into the work van. "You guys aren't cops. Who the hell are you?"

"Shut up," one said, and I got clocked again, this time right in the teeth.

Definitely Albanian, I thought, fingering the blood on my lip as we started to roll.

My hands were pulled behind my back then, and my wrists and ankles were zip-tied. Whoever tied me up must have worked on a cattle ranch, because he knew what he was doing.

"Come on," I cried as they popped a bag over my head.

We roared up the cross street of Thirty-Fifth for a while and made a right.

Onto where? I wondered.

It felt like Broadway. Broadway meanders its way down the island of Manhattan, and it didn't feel like we were driving dead straight like on other avenues.

We were heading downtown now.

Why? I thought in shock-laced wonder.

When I was a kid in high school, we used to go downtown on the subway from the Bronx to Astor Place to get New Wave shaved haircuts.

Maybe that was where we were headed, I suddenly hoped.

Maybe me and the Euro crew would go get ourselves cool hair-cuts, buy some beers, and then try to get some Park Avenue prin-cess's phone number. Sounded like an afternoon to me.

My unhinged mind started to actually believe this could be true. I even smiled as I imagined these happy things, my mind busy at work trying to patch together memories and hopes to come up with something—anything—so I wouldn't just start screaming at the terror that was pounding at the door of my brain like the Big Bad Wolf.

No doubt about it. I was pretty mentally out of it by that point.

Take it from me, letting off guns in public, running for your life, getting into car crashes, and getting abducted and beaten isn't the best for maintaining your rational mental health and stability.

I was still using my imagination to float away somewhere safe in my terrified head when it started.

It turned out, I hadn't seen anything yet in the crazy de-partment.

A minute later, the loud roar of an engine filled the van. It was coming from outside on my left. There was another vehicle chasing alongside us, pacing us on the driver's side.

I could hear the Albanians going bananas when the roaring sound got even louder.

Tires screamed then, a sharp, high-pitched screech, and before I could even brace myself, the van was hit. The metal-on-metal bang on my left was deafening, like a sledgehammer slamming into a steel door beside my head. The van lurched to the side, throwing me off-balance and knocking the back of my head into the cold metal wall to my right.

A moment later, there was the violent screeching of the truck's tires losing traction as we started to swing sideways.

No! Please, no, I thought as the wall beside me started to tilt. We were going to roll over. I could feel it.

It happened a split second later. The thud of the van crashing onto its side was so hard, it actually bumped me up into the air. When I landed, I got the wind knocked out of me. Then there was the sound of glass shattering and metal tearing as the van, on its side now, scraped against the pavement.

That's when we hit something hard and stopped moving.

Well, just the van stopped moving. Everything inside—including me—kept moving. Quite rapidly, in fact.

The last thing I remembered as I had liftoff toward the cab of the vehicle was that it didn't feel scary at all.

I remember it felt gentle and happy, like Mommy was putting me to bed.

74

"Mike, wake up. Open your eyes," someone said.

I tried to. It wasn't easy. My eyelids felt heavy, as if someone had put little lead X-ray blankets on them. After a bit, I was able to crack them open slightly. I did some weak blinking. The light hurt, stung as if I'd just been given eye drops.

I could feel myself breathing, but there was a weird sense of detachment from my body.

As a kid, I'd had anesthesia once, when I broke my right leg badly playing sandlot football, and that's what it most felt like. It was a cotton-headed, dizzy, free-falling feeling that was both exhilarating and vaguely scary at the same time.

"Mike, come on. Wake up," the voice said.

I heard a snap.

"Try this," the voice said. "Take a breath."

I did. There was a sharp smell, acrid ammonia.

My eyes snapped open. I was sitting upright in the passenger seat of a car. A really nice car, with a Mercedes symbol on the dash.

When I turned, I saw John Hayden sitting behind its wheel. He tossed the smelling-salt vial out the open window beside him.

"How are you feeling, mate?" he said.

I wiped at my watery eyes. I still felt woozy.

"Okay, I guess. Tired."

"You had a concussion, but there's no blood in your ears so there's no brain bleed, thank goodness. How many fingers am I holding up?" he said, making a peace sign.

"Two?" I said.

"How about now?" he said, giving me the finger.

I laughed.

"That's better," he said, smiling. "Do you remember what happened?"

I thought about it. Law firm, the unhelpful receptionist, getting out of the taxi at the Javits Center, then . . . flying through the air.

I nodded slowly.

"So you do remember," John said.

"That was you who hit the van?" I said.

He nodded.

"As you came running out of the convention center, I was on Eleventh, and I followed you. That escape attempt with the truck, Mike? Wow, that was creative. When those thugs grabbed you up on Tenth and started taking you down Broadway, I knew I had to do something before I lost contact. It was the only thing I could think to do to bust you out."

He lifted his phone off the dash and showed me the screen where a CNN feed was brought up.

Mafia War Comes to Manhattan said the chyron, and the broadcast showed the thugs' van up on a sidewalk. It was on its side, and the front of it looked like it was embedded in the face of the Flatiron Building.

"We hit the Flatiron?" I said.

"The Albanian version of Mario Andretti must have zigged when he should have zagged, I guess," John said with a laugh.

"I'll say. Look at it."

"You must have some guardian angel, Mike, because when I came to get you out of the wreckage, I thought you were definitely toast. But you were just knocked out. I tossed you over my shoulder and got us out of there."

I shook my head.

"I would have been a goner if you hadn't saved me, John. Thank you. And to think I thought you had suckered me."

"Suckered you? How?"

"I went to your lawyer like you said, but I got the run-around. They said he was in court. Then they stopped taking my calls. Then I tried to call you, and you weren't answering."

"Had to lose that burner phone," he said, taking out another. "I'll clear this up right now."

He put it on Speaker.

"Hello?" said a groggy voice.

"Nicholas, it's Hayden, and I'm pissed at you."

"Pissed? Why?"

"I told you to prioritize that video I mailed you. To make copies of it and to hand it off to my friend, Mike, when he showed up. He tells me you're giving him the runaround."

"So, sorry, John," he said. "I've been stuck in—"

"I don't care where you've been," Hayden said. "I don't pay you that retainer for excuses. If that tape isn't in my email in twenty minutes, you're fired."

He hung up the phone.

"This won't take long."

"How long have I been out for?" I said.

He checked his watch.

"Eighteen hours."

His phone buzzed.

"Ah, see? What did I tell you?"

He thumbed open the video from his email as he handed me his phone.

I watched John inside the convenience store as he took out the first guy with his own gun and then burned the second one with the contents of a coffee cup.

"That's some set of skills," I said. "Did you pick that up in the service?"

He smiled.

"The Australian version of the SAS. The SASR."

"Oh, I remember you guys. Redbacks, right?" I said, recalling a group of them I had met in Iraq.

"Yep."

"Were you in Mosul?" I said.

He shook his head.

"I was already out by then."

He started the car.

"Where are we going?" I said.

"I'll tell you when we get there," John said. "You can send that lawyer of mine your address, and he'll mail you a hard copy of the video if you want."

I emailed the video to myself.

"Thanks," I said as I handed back the phone. "This will do for now. I really appreciate it."

"Anytime, soldier," he said, pocketing his phone and putting the car into Drive.

75

We pulled into a small parking lot in a lightly wooded area. I looked out through the windshield. There was a beat-up soccer field in front of us with a small sign that read *Yorktown Youth Soccer Club*.

"Where are we?" I said.

"Beside the belly of the beast," John said.

"Say again?"

"Down there right across the road," he said, pointing to our right, "is IBM's Watson Research Center. Inside of it is the world's most powerful quantum computer, and—" he checked his watch "—in about twenty minutes or so, I'm heading in there to meet with a friend who's going to help me wire up my chip."

He smiled.

"And that's when the fun is really going to begin," he said. "Because that's when I drop the ring into the volcano."

"What are you talking about?"

"You know," Hayden said. "Like in *The Lord of the Rings*? Frodo has to destroy the way in which evil can take over the world. You've read *The Lord of the Rings*, right?"

"Yes."

He clapped me on the shoulder.

"Well, I am Frodo, at your service, sir. We are now here at the walls of Mordor, and I'm about to melt the magic ring."

I stared at him, his bright eyes wide.

"What have you been smoking this morning?"

He laughed.

"I don't need drugs. This is better than drugs. See, I haven't been *completely* honest with you. My intention is to take down the Criterion Group—and I will, don't you worry about that. But there's actually a bit more to it."

"Like what?"

"Do you know what money is? Paper money, I mean."

"The green paper you use to buy stuff, last I checked," I said.

"Do you know where this custom came from, using paper to buy stuff?"

"No."

He suddenly rubbed his palms together.

"Brace yourself, Mike," he said, checking his watch again. "I'm about to deliver a history lesson that's going to blow your mind."

76

"Before the seventeenth century," John said, "all the money in Europe was gold and silver coins instead of paper. There were these merchants called *goldsmiths* in London who had vaults where you could keep your gold safe. When you parked it there, the goldsmiths issued paper receipts as proof of your deposit."

John took out a dollar bill from his wallet and handed it to me.

"These paper gold receipts is where paper money started," he said. "They could be exchanged for the gold or silver at a later time. But as these receipts became more widely used, goldsmiths noticed the paper itself was being passed around and used as gold. They also noticed that people rarely came to ask for the actual gold. That's when they decided to issue *more* paper receipts than they had *actual* gold on deposit, and voilà!—banking with paper money was born."

"What?" I said, looking at the dollar. "They were handing out receipts that had nothing backing them? But that's fraud."

"Yep," he said. "That's exactly what money is. A fake gold receipt. A piece of paper that seems to be backed by some value that does not exist. It used to be backed by gold. But in 1971 in America, they took the dollar off the gold standard, so now it's just paper. No different than Monopoly money."

"But that's cheating," I said. "It's counterfeiting. That's illegal."

"Precisely!" John cried. "Printed paper money invites counterfeiting, which was why gold and silver were historically used in the first place. You can't counterfeit gold, and unlike paper, you can't print it from thin air. But when the central banks got started, they shifted everything from gold and silver to printing paper funny money.

"It's digital now, of course, in the electronic age. But it's no less fake and much simpler to counterfeit. It's just numbers on a computer spreadsheet invented from nothing. Digital air. But what this digital air does is make that dollar in your pocket worth less and less and less. The central bank picks your pocket without lifting a finger. The value of your money goes down and is transferred to them."

"So you're saying these bankers loan out fake Monopoly money that they print from thin air?" I said.

"Yes. It's called fractional reserve banking," John said. "In a nutshell, if you deposit a thousand dollars, then the local bank gets to lend out nine hundred dollars of it."

"So they have a little printing press in the back of every bank?" I said.

"No, they just have one gigantic press at the Federal Reserve. If you come back and ask for your thousand, the local bank quickly calls the Fed and says, 'Mike wants his money back. Print us nine hundred bucks quick so he doesn't find out we stole his money and gave it away to someone else so we could earn interest on it.'"

"But I thought the Federal Reserve was the bank of the government," I said. "The US Treasury."

John laughed.

"That's what they want everyone to think."

He pointed at the top of the dollar in my hand.

"See what it says there, Mike? *Federal Reserve Note.* Not *US*

Treasury. The Federal Reserve is a private bank that is not federal and has no reserves."

"That scheme is no different than if you parked your car in a lot and you found out the lot was renting out your car when you weren't there," I said. "That can't be true."

"It's true, Mike. That's exactly what bankers do with your money when you park it at a bank."

"That's just criminal," I said.

"You're right," John said. "Money is supposed to represent real work, real goods and services. That's the purpose of it. It's a work voucher that we can all use to easily and fairly exchange our work for goods. But that's only in a fair system.

"Our fractional reserve system, in essence, gets to print fake work vouchers. Printing money causes inflation, and when prices go up, your money is less valuable. Banks do no productive work in a society, yet they profit. While you get poorer, bankers get richer by both using and devaluing your money at the same time."

"So the purpose of banks is to drain the working lifeblood of society by forcing workers to work harder to pay the banks for borrowing money that the bankers themselves invented out of thin air."

"Exactly," John said.

"This is a giant scam," I said.

"A giant multi-century counterfeiting scam run by criminals."

"How can that be?" I said. "No one in their right mind would agree to such a system."

"You're right," John said. "That's why the Federal Reserve was started under cover of night back in 1913 at Jekyll Island."

That got my attention.

"A US senator and the heads of all the biggest US banks sat down with J. P. Morgan and a German-born banker named Warburg whose family had been running the same central banking paper money scam in Europe for hundreds of years. Warburg hashed out what they had to do, and then the bill bringing the Federal Reserve into law was passed on Christmas Eve when no one was looking."

"So that's why you went there," I said.

"Yes," John said. "I needed to go there and see with my own eyes the place where these crooks had pulled off the crime of the century."

He looked at me.

"Especially now that I'm about to bring their racket to an end," he said.

77

"What do you mean, John?" I said. "I thought your problem was with Viviani."

"Oh, no, Mike. I'm not just taking out Viviani," John said. "I'm about to fry all the fish at once."

He smiled out at the soccer field.

"I'm going to take down the Federal Reserve."

"That sounds nuts."

"And I want you to help me."

"What?" I said.

"Watch my back when I go in there," John said, pointing his chin toward the IBM facility. "Wait outside with the car running. With this quantum chip and that super computer in there, I'll be out in a jiffy. You're a good man, I know you are, Mike. What's going to happen in there will undo all this evil."

"You're crazy," I said.

"Was Andrew Jackson crazy?"

"The president?" I said.

"Are you really American?" John said. "Yes. The seventh president of the United States. The Fed back then was called the Second Bank of the United States, and in 1832 Jackson vetoed its charter, declaring it unconstitutional and corrupt. He then withdrew all federal deposits and placed them in smaller, state-chartered banks. This effectively crippled the bank, and by the end of Jackson's presidency, it had ceased to exist. He had 'beaten the bank,' as he proudly said at the time. It was his greatest achievement."

John smiled.

"Now it's my turn to beat the bank," he said.

"I don't think that sounds like a good idea," I said.

"It's the only way, Mike. Democracy is supposed to be the rule of the people. But with this hidden money power, a handful of insiders rule it all. The Fed allows the corrupt politicians to print money whenever they need it, creating a limitless slush fund to finance wars, to conduct military coups and—my personal pet peeve—to issue global loans to destroy entire countries," John said, shaking his head.

"I used to help them. Now I'm going to stop them. Once the Federal Reserve is shut down, this entire corrupt system is going belly-up."

I looked at him.

"Wait, didn't they try to kill Andrew Jackson?" I said.

"So you do know some history," John said. "Will you help me?"

"Can't do it," I said.

"Why not?"

"I can't even balance my checkbook, John. I wish I could help you, but I can't."

He let out a breath and reached over, opening my door.

"Then, this is where we part ways, mate," he said. "Glad to have met you."

I got out of the car.

"Mike," he called at my back.

I turned.

"You have any money in the stock market?"

"Not really."

"Good," he said. "You have any money in a bank?"

"Yes," I said.

"Withdraw it and buy gold."

"Yeah?"

"This is the best insider tip you'll ever get in your life," he said as he pulled out, leaving dust in his wake.

78

When Birch opened his eyes in the security break room of the Javits Center, he felt suddenly nervous.

Why did he feel so troubled?

The Albanian fiasco had just been chalked up to a mafia problem. He was completely insulated there. What was it, then?

He would fail.

He could feel it. Sometimes, he would get premonitions. In Iraq, for instance. Once, right before a very routine mission, something told him not to get on the convoy they were about to roll out on.

This feeling of doom was so strong that, coming out of the muster room, he had stuck a finger down his throat and puked up his breakfast to fake being sick. The convoy had been hit, all the men killed. ISIS had tortured two of his comrades to death, and their blackened and burned bodies had been hung from a highway bridge.

With Arben and Bezmir both killed in that car crash, it was déjà vu all over again, wasn't it?

And he knew full well it was Hayden who had done it. He was obviously on a kamikaze mission to see Viviani put in a pine box.

And it wasn't hard to guess who was standing directly in the way of this maniac's intended target.

"I'm not taking a bullet for this piece of shit," he mumbled.

Viviani would be quite useful come payday. But Birch could only cash his check if he was alive.

He should just go, he thought. Disappear into America. He was on his own. He could fake reports and drain the expense account. Viviani himself said he was going to see him back in prison if it didn't work out. And he wasn't going back there.

They would track him down, though, wouldn't they? If he bailed on them now, they would only send someone like himself to square the account.

When he looked up, Quevedo was there.

"They think they got something," he said.

Birch followed him into the control center.

"What is it?" he said to Rodriguez.

"Okay," the security director said, pointing at the screen, "just to recap. As the prank went down, the kid here in the Fordham hoodie goes under this car here, and he clearly gets something."

"We know that already," Birch said, rubbing his eyes.

Rodriguez ignored him as he rewound the video.

"Here's the car being placed in its spot on the floor in preparation for the auto show. As you can see, there's nothing on the floor under it."

Before Birch could say anything, Rodriguez continued.

"But check this out."

He clicked a button, and the screen changed to the outside of the Javits Center.

"On Saturday, as they were bringing in the car, this happens."

They watched as a man put something under the wheel well.

"We got him from a camera here," he said, pointing to the map of the facility.

"Do we know who he is?" Birch said.

Rodriguez smiled.

"He popped. He has a security clearance."

"What?"

"Guess where he works. You ready?"

"Where?"

"The IBM quantum computer center in Yorktown Heights."

79

The IBM Thomas J. Watson Research Center was a large, ominous-looking black glass building that was the shape of a half circle.

Plonked down among the suburban Yorktown Heights tennis courts and four-bedroom colonials, it looked like a malevolent alien ship that had touched down in the middle of a 1950s TV sitcom.

Hayden locked the Mercedes and looked at the sleepy people heading toward the building across its parking lot.

Most of them were actual geniuses, Hayden knew. Year after year, this building churned out more patents than anywhere on earth. Not just in quantum research but in cloud computing, block chain, AI. More brain power was collected in this building than probably anywhere on the planet.

Yet how many of their brilliant inventions, he thought, were being used for the good of humanity today?

AI-powered drones and robots were already ramping up more war and turning the world into a soulless, detached, techno-cratic nightmare, where algorithms rather than people made life-and-death decisions.

Too bad these smart people weren't smart enough to see the dystopian-nightmare future they were building for themselves, Hayden thought.

Too bad they didn't understand that every new, world-changing innovation they came up with would just give the powers that be more power to imprison or even wipe out their children and grandchildren.

As he followed the sleepwalking geniuses toward its curved black facade, Hayden suddenly thought that the building looked like a modern version of the Colosseum.

He smiled.

Only today, he thought, patting his briefcase with the microchip and the software program inside of it, the Christians were going to chow down on the lions, for a change.

He was just coming under its spacey front awning when he received a text. It was from his contact inside. One word.

RUN

He looked at the message, looked at the front door.

Right here at the finish line? he thought.

He closed his eyes. There was no time to be disappointed.

Move, idiot. Now. You planned for this.

Hayden turned and headed back toward the Merc, walking as quickly as he could.

"Plan B it is," he said, eyeing the exit of the lot.

PART FOUR

CLOSING BELL

80

From the Croton-Harmon Metro-North station steps, the view was incredible. Beyond the parking lot, the Hudson River widened out, and on the other side of the water in Rockland County, there were several rolling green hills.

Two hours after John's early-morning history lesson about the financial system, I was sitting on the steps waiting for a train into the city. I was sipping a coffee and eating a Starbucks egg-white sandwich, enjoying the morning sun as I looked out at the view.

I felt more at ease than I had in a long time.

No doubt about it, I thought, I was a happy man. Finally, I had my evidence that proved I was innocent. I had Colleen waiting for me back at her dad's house. I had a hot breakfast and no broken bones. What else was there?

I had gotten myself into one strange jam, but now, I thought as I looked at the slate-gray roll of the Hudson, I was home free.

Colleen, who worked at a law firm, would help me to get a really good lawyer to smooth things over with the authorities, and we'd be back in Florida to follow Declan's season in no time.

I thought about everything John had told me about money and the Fed. It definitely sounded just about right to my ears. The rich really did always seem to get richer and the poor poorer.

That this was no coincidence, but rather a sneaky calculated move built into the system itself, made a truckload of sense.

But since I was just a cop and all economics tended to hurt my head, I was happy to leave John to his own high-finance fun and games.

As a wise man once said about ambitious friends, "To the edge of the fire I will gladly walk you. But into the fire with you, I cannot go."

I did, however, decide to hedge my bets and took his advice. Using my burner phone, I had converted a chunk of my cash into gold American eagles that were now sitting in a vault in North Dakota.

"Good luck, John," I said, lifting my coffee to the sunny sky.

I heard the whistle for the train.

"I think," I said.

A minute later, I took a seat on the non-river side of the car that faced backward to the movement of the train. I was still enjoying my coffee when I saw two police cars outside the window. They were gray NY State trooper cruisers. As I watched, they drove down the hill toward the station and into the parking lot.

That we weren't moving as this happened made my spidey sense tingle.

But I dismissed it because it didn't seem possible that they could have caught up with me.

And besides, even if they were here for me, I was good now. They had nothing on me anymore.

"You," I heard from behind me. "Let me see your hands."

81

An hour later, I was in White Plains, the largest city in West-chester.

I was sitting by a metal table in a folding chair with my right wrist handcuffed to a bolt in the concrete floor.

Not home free, after all.

I thought the troopers who picked me up would have driven me down to the FBI headquarters in New York City, but instead they had taken me here to what I guessed was the closest office.

"Michael Gannon," bellowed a tall, tan Hispanic man wearing glasses as he burst into the windowless room.

"And you are?" I said.

"Special Agent Quevedo," he said. "You're a hard guy to get an ID on, you know that, Mike? I put your picture into the database, and it came up flagged as *Top Secret*. Never saw that before. Under normal circumstances, if I asked for more info on something like that, the spooks would have said to piss up a rope. But these aren't normal circumstances, are they, Mike?"

He pulled up a chair close so that our knees were almost touching. The agent liked his cologne, I noticed.

"So they sent me your jacket," he continued. "You're a strange one, aren't you? Your Navy SEAL and NYPD records are im-peccable. But ever since you retired, you've managed to piss off a lot of really powerful people. What's wrong, Mike? You've never heard of this thing called golf?"

I stared at him. He seemed out of place. He must be the head of the task force, I realized. He was from the Miami FBI who had been chasing us all the way up from Key West.

I stifled a laugh.

"And?" I said.

"And? Let's see. You shot up the New York auto show. Then you stole a UPS truck," he said, folding his arms. "That wasn't very nice. We've got aiding and abetting a terrorist, attempted murder with an unlicensed firearm, grand larceny. How many felonies so far? Four?"

I yawned.

"Where's my phone call?" I said.

"We just want to know one thing, Mike. Where is he?"

"Where's who?" I said.

"Hayden," he said, banging on the table with a fist.

Agent Quevedo looked angry. In fact, he looked very angry. And his anger didn't seem like the good cop–bad cop kind. It seemed real.

I held myself back from smiling some more.

Because I thought they had actually caught John. But considering this guy's mood, I guess they hadn't. I thought of the old Buster Keaton movies with the Keystone cops running after Keaton, who always just manages to slip away.

John must have slipped the dragnet again.

"I have no idea where John is," I said truthfully.

"No idea?"

"No. And why is a British guy working with the FBI? Is he here? How is his jaw feeling?"

"Where's Hayden?"

"Where's your coat?" I said.

"My what?"

"Your coat. Your *red* coat."

"What is that supposed to mean?" the agent said.

"You're working for the Brits, right? The Redcoats? You're the Benedict Arnold of the twenty-first century."

"Where is Hayden?" he said again.

"I have no clue," I said. "And apparently neither do you."

"Really?" he said. "We know you're working with him. We know he has a stolen quantum computer chip and is in cahoots with a guy at the IBM in Yorktown Heights. We know he went there this morning, but now there's no sign of either of them at the facility. Then we look around and see who? You. The guy who has been seen aiding and abetting this known terrorist since Key West, just strolling around near the facility. But you don't know anything, is that right?"

"Wait a second. I do know something."

"What?"

"I have the right to remain silent," I said.

"I'm not sure you want to go down that road," he said.

"Au contraire," I said, putting my free hand behind my head. "As it says in my file, I was a cop. It's you who doesn't want me to go down that road. I know all about that. As for me, I'm taking up full residence on that road starting now."

"You want to play hardball, Mike?" he said. "Let's. You have a son, right? Pitching in the minors?"

I stared at him.

"I will say this once," I said. "You may bring my kid into this, Quevedo, if you wish. But if you do, I hereby do solemnly swear that making you regret that decision will become the focus of my every penny and thought and breath and action from this day forward till the last second of your life on this planet."

"Is that a threat?" he said.

"It's a promise," I said.

"We can put you in prison. Right now. You know that, right?"

I mimicked turning a lock on my lips and swallowing the key. Then I shrugged and looked at the wall.

82

Birch and Quevedo sat in an empty office in complete silence for a full minute after Quevedo came back from the interview room.

"Gannon doesn't know where Hayden is," Quevedo said.

"Why do you think that?" Birch said.

"Why isn't he with him?"

"They had a falling-out?"

"Then, why isn't he ratting him out?" Quevedo said.

"I don't know," Birch said. "But at least now we know *why* Hayden is in America. He's got the software, but now he needs the hardware. He's here to physically put the stolen chip into one of the big US quantum computers."

"To screw Viviani," Quevedo said.

"Yes. Hayden blames him for the death of his daughter and, almost as important, for screwing him out of the justice she deserves."

"Yeah, but now that he's been locked out of the IBM one, which quantum computer will he use?" said Quevedo.

Birch shrugged.

"You tell me. How many are there?" he said.

"Oh, between fifty and seventy operational ones. And they're scattered throughout the entire country. You have them at IBM, Google, Honeywell. At national labs like Oak Ridge in Tennessee. Then you have your universities: Stanford, Harvard, University of Chicago. And that doesn't include all the new start-ups which probably have a hundred prototypes they're working on."

Birch clasped his head in his hands.

"I thought there was a handful. This is a bloody needle in a haystack."

Quevedo had his phone out. He put it on Speaker.

"Alice. Get me up on the secure FBI Command Line. I need Assistant Director Price."

"Now?" she said.

"Yesterday," Quevedo said.

"What's our move?" Birch said.

"I don't know what you call it in England, but here in America, we call it kicking it upstairs," Quevedo said.

"Agent Quevedo, what's the status?" a man's voice said thirty seconds later.

"We've got a situation, Jack," Quevedo said. "The suspect, Hayden, is still on the loose. We closed in on him near the IBM facility in Yorktown Heights here in New York. We believe he was trying to gain access to a major quantum computer. We think that's why he is here in the US. He's trying to plug in his stolen chip. If he succeeds, if that chip actually works, Jack, there's literally no telling the amount of havoc he could wreak."

"You've got to be shitting me," Price said.

"No, sir. This guy could potentially crack all encryption codes, destabilize all secure communications, and undermine the nation's most critical data. He could unravel our entire security apparatus, the financial system infrastructure, the power grid. All of it. This could be the big one."

Birch and Quevedo looked at each other.

"What do you need from me?" said Price.

"I need the green light to issue a nationwide lockdown order for all quantum computing facilities," Quevedo said. "We need to cut all external access to the hardware of these systems immediately. No exceptions. National laboratories, top universities, private companies—all quantum systems spread across the country need to be shuttered tight. I'm talking federal authorization, and this needs to happen now."

"Are we sure this is the only option?" Price said. "Do you know how complicated this request is?"

"I understand the size of the ask here, sir," Quevedo said. "But you have been looped in with intel, right? This guy isn't playing around. He killed four CIA operatives in Key West. He's basically the Unabomber on steroids. He's on a do-or-die mission of destruction. We blocked him here at IBM, but this guy is smart. He has to have a plan B."

"Which is?"

"Accessing another large-capacity quantum computer. We need to catch him before he gets the chance."

"Okay," Price said. "Understood. I'll loop in Homeland Security and CISA and the Department of Energy. Shit, you'll probably need clearance from the White House for this type of federal order. I'll call you back."

Quevedo hung up.

"What's CISA?" Birch said.

"Cybersecurity and Infrastructure Security Agency," Quevedo said.

"Alphabet soup," Birch mumbled.

The two men sat silently until the phone rang on the desk seven minutes later.

"Okay, Agent Quevedo, the order is being drafted," Price said. "Homeland Security is on board. We've got full support from the White House. The lockdown is approved. I already have staff on the phone with CISA, the Department of Energy, and the private sector. We're shutting it all down. Now, run this son of a bitch down, Quevedo, you hear me? Or we'll both be posted in Alaska."

"Thank you, sir. I'll keep you primed."

"Now what?" Birch said.

"Now that we shut the mouseholes," Quevedo said, "we just need to catch the mouse."

83

Hayden, pulling his rolling suitcase, texted the car service as he walked through the sparse predawn crowd at O'Hare.

The driver, when he found him, was a roly-poly bald middle-aged Black guy with a friendly smile. As he approached him, the man tipped an imaginary cap.

"Welcome to Chicago, Mr. Teagle," he said. "Please call me Ben. Let me get that," he said, reaching for the handle of the carry-on. "This way, sir."

Hayden smiled as he followed the driver. The airport was almost deserted this early. Outside the automatic door, he shivered in the ice-cold breeze, staring at the snow. It was coming down hard. He looked at his phone. It said it was twenty-three degrees.

The driver didn't seem to mind as he opened the rear passenger door of the Escalade at the curb.

"You seem used to the cold, Ben," Hayden said, attempting to rub warmth back into his arms after he fell into the plush captain's chair. "Are you from the area?"

"Born and bred, Mr. Teagle. And I'm guessing you're Australian?"

Hayden nodded. "It's summertime there now."

"In that case, perhaps you'd like to adjust your personal heat and massage settings," Ben said, directing Hayden to the controls

of the center console. "Any stops you'd like to make before heading to the hospital?"

"No stops, thank you, Ben."

Hayden was headed to St. Philip Neri Children's Hospital.
It was just north of the Loop downtown, and it specialized in
cancer cases.

Over the last year Hayden, posing as a retired Australian
mining executive turned philanthropist named Mr. Teagle, had
been donating embezzled funds siphoned from his bank to ramp
up the construction of a quantum computer to aid in cancer research.

His original plan when he came into possession of the full-
scale quantum chip was to have a quantum computer of his own
built to utilize it. But there was a problem. Building quantum
computers was eye-poppingly expensive and complicated. It had
to have a cryogenic cooling system. The cleanroom lab itself
that it all had to be placed in cost at least ten million.

Too expensive, it had turned out, even with him dipping
into his clients' offshore funds.

That's why he had come up with a different solution: to become the largest donor to the quantum computer-building
project that was already underway here in Chicago at the hospital. The project was near completion now. That's why he had
asked if he could come to take a look at it before the grand un-
veiling that was set for the following week.

He took out his phone.

Hi, Pierre. Just got in. Should be there in half an hour, he
typed. I hope I haven't woken you.

Pierre Garnier, a former Caltech professor, was the head of
the computer-building team. He had already agreed to come
in early to meet Hayden at the hospital.

I'm already here, Pierre texted back a moment later. Please
let me know when you arrive. I'll meet you at entrance.

Looking forward to meeting you, Hayden messaged back.

84

The cleanroom on the top floor of the hospital hummed and whirred with the sound of the cooling pumps.

"Voilà," Pierre said as he led Hayden inside.

On the right-hand side as they entered was a table with a desktop computer on it, and behind it was a massive stainless-steel cabinet that was six feet high.

This was the supercooling dilution refrigerator that contained the vacuum pumps and gauges, Hayden knew. Attached to the back of this unit were what looked like several huge stainless-steel wheeled kegs on a large rack along the rear wall. These metal kegs were filled with the supercooling helium gases.

From this industrial array came spaghetti strands of steel hoses that snaked up the wall, across the ceiling, and then down into the computer itself that filled the center of the room.

It didn't look like a regular computer. With its multiple tiers, it looked almost like a massive chandelier, or an upside-down stainless-steel wedding cake. This was the quantum computer's cryostat where, with each descending layer of the cake, the temperature dropped until reaching the smallest layer at the bottom where the quantum chip was stored.

Hayden stared at the bottom layer.

Only there at the bottom of the cryostat could the state of

near-complete zero be achieved, allowing for the supercon-
ductivity and superposition of the qubits inside the chip to operate. It was this near-zero temperature state that allowed the
computer to execute calculations at a speed never before imagined, let alone achieved.

"As you can see, the cleanroom itself is still pretty raw. We
have some major aesthetic work to complete," Pierre said.

He was a tall, thin, black-haired man of twenty-seven. His
round glasses and his boyish face gave him the look of an aging
Harry Potter.

"But you have fired it up like you said in the email," Hayden
said. "All systems are go?"

"Yes," Pierre said. "We haven't opened it up fully yet, but
the first test parameters all came up green. The temperature di-
agnostics are near perfect. We were also able to link up online
in the initial testing. That private fiber optics network you insisted we install was such a great idea, Mr. Teagle. The band-
width is off the charts."

"It's the least I could do," Hayden said, resisting the urge to
pump his fist.

The network he'd had installed was actually referred to as
dark fiber.

With the high frequency trades he now needed to execute,
so much of their success or failure would come down to the
data lines. That's why instead of relying on the snail-slow regular phone company lines, he had hired a dark fiber company
to string a direct, dedicated fiber line from the hospital's quantum computer six blocks to the north into the colocation service
company located in the same building as the Chicago Mercan-
tile Exchange. Through this CME colocation was a fiber link
into the CME, which had a direct access fiber line into the New
York Stock Exchange.

Though all of these fiber links were lightning fast, it was
the distance in the fiber line between the CME and the NYSE
that was going to make the execution of Hayden's plan the nail-

biter. The direct link between the quantum computer in York-town Heights and the New York Stock Exchange only had to go through thirty miles of glass fiber.

From Chicago, these trades would have to travel through about a thousand miles of glass. It was this thirty-times-larger distance in fiber length that was going to make the entire up-load take thirty times longer. Seven hours instead of fourteen minutes.

But at least it was operational, Hayden thought as he stood staring at the cryostat.

This was going to be the most stressful workday of his life, he thought as he waited for the upload to complete.

But he was all in now.

85

"You've done an amazing job, Pierre," Hayden said, gazing at the cryostat. "And you're ahead of schedule. I can't thank you enough."

"It is I who should thank you, Mr. Teagle. To put me in charge of such a large project is such an honor. I know you were the one who was the deciding factor in my being hired despite my youth."

This was true, Hayden thought.

He had insisted to the hospital board on hiring a new, much younger project manager.

Not only because the summa cum laude graduate of Europe's version of MIT, ETH Zurich, was obviously brilliant, but Hayden wanted as impressionable a young person as possible who he could control.

All for this very moment.

"Pierre, hiring you was a no-brainer," Hayden said, smiling warmly. "Now that I'm finally meeting you in person, I'd like to share with you a surprise that I am hoping you of all people will most be able to appreciate."

"A surprise?" Pierre said.

Hayden placed his briefcase on the desk and popped the clasps.

"Voilà, Pierre," Hayden said as he removed the shockproof case and handed it over.

"Oh, my goodness. What's this? A processor?"

"Yes," Hayden said. "That's exactly what it is. A *new* processor. A brand-new kind."

Pierre stared at it, his eyes lighting up like a jeweler who had just been handed the Hope Diamond.

"I've never seen anything like this. Where did you get it, Mr. Teagle?"

"Not important," Hayden said with a wink. "I asked around Australia for the best processor possible, and I believe I received it. And I want you—us—to be the first to bring it online. I think with this new chip, this hospital will possess the best quantum computer in the medical space not just in America, but in all the world. We could change things with this, Pierre. I really think we could."

"I . . . I hardly know what to say. I'm amazed," Pierre said.

"Can you install it?"

Pierre stared at it.

"Now?" he said with hope.

Hayden smiled widely. He had him.

"There is no time like the present. Let's fire it up."

Pierre immediately hurried to a worktable on the other side of the helium tanks. There was a hiss like a balloon losing air as he began to snap at an electrical box on the wall.

"How long do you think it will take you to install the chip?" Hayden said, checking his watch as Pierre, now with a ratchet in hand, stepped to the cryostat.

"An hour. Probably less."

An hour would make it 6:20 a.m. EST.

Three hours before the market opened.

Hayden smiled.

"Perfect, Pierre," he said, taking off his coat. "Tell me how I can help."

86

Birch, sipping an espresso, was in a hangar at the Westchester County Airport watching the mechanics switch out the left taxi light on the Criterion Group jet when his phone rang.

Oh boy. Here we go, he thought.

It was Viviani.

"Birch, listen to me very closely," he said. "What is the status? Where is John Hayden?"

"We still don't know," Birch said, putting down the cup. "We traced his car to the Westchester County Airport. I'm here right now. The FBI team I'm working with is in the air traffic controllers' office right now, running down his possible locations."

"We're too late," he said.

"Sir?" Birch said.

"He must have already found another quantum computer. I can't believe this is happening."

"What's happening?" Birch said.

"We have an issue," Viviani said. "Something is wrong with our trading platform. We can't access any accounts. We've been locked out of everything, trading logs, client data, everything."

Birch's jaw dropped. The Criterion Group was responsible for trillions of dollars.

"IT and Cybersecurity are scratching their heads," Viviani

continued. "We have probably the most advanced anti-hacking software in the world, and they have no clue what's happening. If our ETFs are still frozen at 9:00 a.m. EST when the market opens, nine hundred billion dollars will be stalled at the station. By 9:05 the board will call me. By 9:10 I . . . I don't know what will happen. The sun explodes? It's beyond my capability of reckoning. You need to find that son of a bitch."

"Can you wait a moment, sir? It's my other phone. Hold the line."

"Here's the latest," Quevedo said on Birch's other line. "Hayden wasn't on any of the commercial flights, but a private charter left an hour after the car was left in the long-term lot. We're pretty sure he was on it."

"Where to?"

"Chicago. It landed about an hour ago."

"How many quantum computers are in Chicago?" Birch said.

"We are still tallying, but there are at least three major ones that we know about. You've got the University of Chicago, Northwestern University, Fermilab. More probably, but they're the major ones."

"He's already at one of them," Birch said. "I have Viviani on the other line. The Criterion Group's computers are off-line."

"You have got to be shitting me," Quevedo said. "Hayden is not messing around."

"Hey," Birch called up to the pilot yawning by the steps. "It's Chicago. How long?"

"Hour and a half," he said.

"I can be there in an hour and a half," Birch said to Quevedo. "Which one do I search first?"

"Get to the University of Chicago," Quevedo said. "That's the main one. I'm already in contact with agents at the Chicago office. And my boss, Price, said I have Hostage Rescue from DC at our disposal. I will call now and have them meet you there."

"On it," Birch said.

Birch put down one phone and raised the other.

"Mr. Viviani," he said.

"What?"

"We just got a lead. Looks like Hayden is in Chicago. There are only a handful of quantum computers there. The FBI is on it, and I'm on my way."

"Tell the pilot to drop the hammer," Viviani said. "You need to get him before the opening bell rings or we're cooked. Get him, Birch. Go get him *now*!"

87

I was sleeping on the cold, hard floor when the door opened and Quevedo came in followed by two more agents. One was Hispanic and the other one was a thin Indian guy. They both looked pretty young.

They were probably from Quevedo's task force, I thought. Like myself, they looked like they could use a shave and a cup of coffee. Though, I doubted they had spent the last twenty-four hours chained to a bolt in a concrete floor here at the FBI office in White Plains.

As Quevedo watched, they unlocked me and then cuffed my hands behind my back.

"Where are you taking me?" I said when I was brought out of the room.

We got on an elevator. As the door rattled shut, Quevedo turned and popped a pair of noise-canceling headphones over my ears.

Down in the underground parking lot, we piled into a gray Chevy SUV. I looked out the window as we drove through the predawn to the Saw Mill River Parkway.

We were heading toward the city now for some reason. To process me, probably. Colleen had to be worried sick.

There was a ton of traffic, so it took us about an hour before we crossed the Henry Hudson Bridge into Manhattan and got onto the West Side Highway. We exited way down in southern Manhattan. I thought we would go to the FBI headquarters at 26 Federal Plaza, so I was surprised when we passed by it on Broadway and kept going.

I looked out the window as we entered the Financial District.

When I was an NYPD cop, I had never worked all the way down here, but I always found it fascinating. It was the oldest part of the city, home to the stock exchange and the first fancy stone skyscrapers.

We made some turns, and I looked out as we slowed alongside an old building that was more imposing than the ones around it. It was about fifteen stories high and took up the whole block. Its sturdy limestone blocks and black wrought iron bars along its lower windows gave it a medieval vibe not unlike an Italian castle.

We stopped before the entrance of it on Liberty Street. I saw that a gold number 33 was painted on the glass above the doors.

"What is this place?" I said.

Quevedo took off my headphones.

"You'll see," he said.

I suddenly remembered the bulldog tattoo on the British assassin.

"Thirty-three, huh?" I said.

Quevedo looked at me.

"That's an interesting number," I said.

"It sure is," Quevedo said. "It matches the thirty-three reasons we have to throw you in jail for the rest of your life."

88

"You wanted to see me, sir?" Quevedo said as the assistant left the wood-paneled office.

William Harper, the president of the Federal Reserve Bank of New York, put a finger to his lips in a shushing motion from where he stood behind his desk. Then he snapped his fingers as one would to a trained dog and pointed to the chair in front of the desk.

Why Quevedo had been summoned down here with Gannon in tow he wasn't sure, but he had the funny feeling it had to do with what Birch had told him about the Criterion Group's frozen computers.

Quevedo wasn't the only one in the know. It was ten o'clock now. The market had been open for an hour, and already it was in the financial news that something very odd was up at the trillion-dollar investment firm. The rumors were flying that people couldn't get into their accounts.

In just a regular community bank, that would be troubling. In the largest investment firm in the world, it sent ominous ripples across the financial system of the entire globe.

That's why Quevedo's orders from his boss had been simple.

He was to do anything and everything Reserve President Harper told him to do.

"I'm sorry to keep you waiting, President Harper," came a Middle-Eastern-accented voice out of the phone on Harper's desk a moment later. "The sultan has been unavoidably detained. He will call you back in five minutes."

The Sultan? Quevedo thought.

"Perfectly fine, Amir," Harper said pleasantly. "I'm here waiting."

The speed with which Harper's soft blue eyes flashed to anger after the click of the line would have made a traffic light jealous. He seemed to leap as he stood and came out from behind his desk.

"Okay, Agent. Listen to me very carefully. I need to know what you know, and I need to know it now. Tell me everything up-to-date you have about this nutjob, Hayden, and his quantum chip."

"We think he's in Chicago," Quevedo said. "He landed there a few hours ago. We're running down all of the quantum computer labs there. That's the latest we have."

"How many can there be?" Harper cried. "Why haven't you found him yet?"

"There are five computers, sir, that we know of so far. But there may be more."

The president stared at him. He opened his mouth. No words came out. He closed it.

"Why is he doing this?" Harper said. "Why the hell has he frozen up our computers?"

"Wait, what did you say?" Quevedo said.

"You need a hearing aid?" Harper said.

"Your computers? But I thought it was just the Criterion Group. The Fed's computers are down, too?"

"*Yes!*" he cried. "At the opening bell, all of them went off-line! Why the hell do you think you're here, you idiot? We've been locked out of all our accounts! Not just our accounts, but the GSA is now inaccessible! Come Thursday, you and every employee of the federal government won't get a check, Quevedo. As of nine this morning you can hang a Closed sign on the White House, and Congress, and the Pentagon, too! This is an act of war! Now, what in the name of the universe is this maniac doing?"

"We're not exactly sure, sir," Quevedo said. He wasn't sure if he had the go-ahead to continue, but the situation seemed to call for it.

"We think a lot of it has to do with him seeking revenge for his daughter."

"His daughter?"

"Yes. Hayden's daughter. Her name was Josephine. She was an intern at the Criterion Group. She was found dead two years ago from an OD in a Harlem crack house. The CEO Viviani's son was one of the last people to see her. No one was ever prosecuted. So Hayden, we believe, is settling accounts his own way."

"You've got to be joking! How come I haven't heard about this?"

"It was kept out of the papers, sir."

"That son of a bitch," Harper said. "I knew it had something to do with Albert."

"If I may, sir, what is it that you know about Mr. Viviani?"

"Do you know where Hayden got that chip from?" Harper said.

"No, sir."

"From the Criterion Group itself. Viviani has dumped billions into creating the first full-spectrum quantum chip in a secret lab in Australia. Then the idiot lets it walk out the door, and now look! I'm going to fry that slimy bastard before this is over."

"This guy who was with Hayden, you have him in custody, right?"

Quevedo nodded.

"Who is he?" Harper said. "How the hell is he involved?"

"The suspected associate is named Gannon. He's a retired NYPD detective. He claims he was in the wrong place at the wrong time, but we have a jacket on him of engaging in sub-versive activity going back several years. He also let off a gun at the New York auto show yesterday where we suspected Hayden was going to be. But like I told my boss, he's not talking, sir."

"Get him in here!" Harper said, his eyes flashing rage again. "He'll talk to me!"

89

We were still sitting in the SUV in front of 33 Liberty Street when one of the feds babysitting me answered his phone.

"Yep, you got it, boss. Be right in," said the Indian guy.

The inside of the building was even more impressive than the exterior. The huge entrance hall looked like a cathedral minus the stained-glass windows. Its vaulted stone ceiling had to be thirty feet high.

No, I thought as I stared at it, remembering its address. It was probably thirty-*three* feet high.

I was guided down a stone corridor to the right and through a wrought iron doorway.

"Where are we?" I said. "Is this a museum?"

"Shut up," the agent said, texting something on his phone.

"Hey, wait," I said to his back. "I saw this movie. This is where Nicholas Cage found all the Templar gold, right?"

"If you had an inkling of the shit you're in," he said as we stopped in front of a large closed door, "you wouldn't be joking, bud. You'd be crying."

Just then, Quevedo stepped out of the door. I was shocked when he took off my cuffs.

"You're going to have a sit-down in the office here like a normal person," he said. "We're going to be right out here. If you cause trouble in there or try to leave, I'll gladly come in and shoot you, got me? Blowing your brains out would make my year."

I looked past him as a tall, thin woman in a tailored navy pantsuit appeared in the open doorway.

"I'm Alexandra, President Harper's assistant," the gentle-eyed young woman said as she led me inside.

President of what? I wanted to ask but didn't.

"I'm Mike," I said instead.

She brought me into a little ante room and then through a door into a huge wood-paneled office with a beautiful walnut desk and wood louvers on the high windows.

"Excuse me, Alexandra," I said as I was offered the seat in front of the desk.

"Yes?" she said.

"Where are we?" I said.

She looked at me patiently.

"The Federal Reserve Bank of New York," she said.

Wow, I thought. Hayden hadn't been kidding. Things were getting more serious by the minute.

"Coffee?" she said, smiling warmly.

"I'd love some. Milk, no sugar, please."

As Alexandra left through another door, I looked at the huge canvas on the wall to the left of the desk. The painting featured a Greek temple, and lying on the steps of the temple was the head of a Greek statue next to what looked like a rubber kitchen glove.

It was nothing if not evocative, I thought.

If I'd had any doubts before, I was sure now that I had to get out of this place immediately.

90

A man came into the room from the door Alexandra had used. He was tall and handsome in his early sixties with perfectly cut silver hair and sparkling blue eyes.

"Good morning, Mr. Gannon," he said as he crossed behind the desk.

His blue suit was made of silk, and his tie had the tiniest periwinkle dots on it. It was the most amazing tie I had ever seen.

He was model-thin and radiated health. He must run marathons or something, I thought, because he appeared to have almost no body fat. As I watched him walk toward me, he looked like a movie star at the Academy Awards about to accept an Oscar.

"Morning," I said, smiling at him.

"I'm Bill Harper. I'm the president here. How are you today?"

"Actually, Bill, not that great. I'm not sure if you've ever been illegally detained, but it's not very pleasant."

He nodded and pursed his lips.

"Mike, I'm not going to beat around the bush. I need your help."

Alexandra came in then with my coffee in a paper cup.

"Thanks, Alexandra," I said as she left.

I took a sip. I thought it, too, would be impressive, but frankly Bronx bodegas had better coffee. You'd think with all the funny money, they'd at least spring for some Starbucks.

"Mike, I need to know what's going on with John Hayden. What is he doing?"

Harper seemed to be losing his cool now.

"Here's the thing, Bill," I said, peering at him.

I took my time as I placed the paper cup on his desk.

"If I start talking, then you implicate me in this thing. You'll say I'm his partner. Whatever Hayden does, if there's blowback, I'm going to be the scapegoat. But I'm not his partner. I'm just some guy who was in the wrong place at the wrong time. And I can prove it now.

"You seem like a nice guy, but in the interest of my personal legal situation, I'm basically unable to say a thing. So feel free to indict me or whatever."

"Listen, Mike. If we indict you, the judge can deny bail before your trial."

I sat up.

"And then just keep delaying the trial," he said. "With no end in sight. You want to go to Rikers, Mike? You were in the NYPD. I don't have to tell you what happens to cops out on Rikers Island."

"You're threatening me now?" I said. "Look in my eyes, Bill. Do I look scared? Try it. I'll do Rikers standing on my head."

This was pure bluster. You better believe I was scared. Because I did know what would happen if I was tossed in Rikers. A shank in my kidney or worse. Much worse.

"You don't think I can fight you," I continued bluffing, "but I can, *Bill*. I know what a lawyer is, too. And I didn't get mine by reading an ad off the side of a Megabus, so my advice, back off."

Harper let out a breath.

"We've gotten off on the wrong foot, Mike. My apologies. Let's keep it simple here. What does he want?"

"What does who want?"

Harper suddenly leaped up behind the desk.

"Enough with the horseshit! Hayden wins. He's in the driver's seat. He can have whatever he wants, okay? We just need to know *what* he wants. He can name his price. Sky's the limit! Does he want Viviani to step down? Done! Does he want justice for his daughter's death? Done!"

I said nothing.

"Let's just make a deal!"

"You seem worked up, Bill. Maybe you need a vacation."

That's when it happened.

All the lights went out. The room was lit now with only the dim light coming through the louvered blinds.

Not good, I thought as I sat up. *Not good at all.*

I heard the cough of a generator, and the lights flickered back on.

John, you crazy nut, I thought, *what have you done?*

91

I watched Harper storm out of the room, slamming the door behind him.

"All of our computers are down," Alexandra said as she came in and took my coffee cup. "That's why President Harper is so upset."

I couldn't help smiling then. I mean, an ear-to-ear grin.

Alexandra just stared at me and left the room.

John had done it, I thought. He'd actually hacked the Federal Reserve.

The door flew open. Harper was back. He didn't seem any happier.

"You think this is funny?" he cried.

He stepped over to me. He raised his hand. I thought he was going to slap me across the face, but the look I gave him convinced him otherwise.

I found it pretty stunning that he'd actually considered resorting to violence. That's the thing about being an American. We grow up thinking everyone is just like us, a regular joe with goodwill toward men. So it makes it hard to believe in human evil. That anyone—let alone a fellow American—would actually harbor true ill will toward another just boggles the mind.

But evil is a slippery little eel that finds its way, doesn't it? I thought as I looked into Harper's beady eyes.

I started to laugh then. It was all I could do.

"Stop it! Stop laughing!" Harper cried. "What did Hayden do? Why can we not get into our computers? What is he doing?"

"I don't know," I said, "but I have a feeling it isn't going to be good for you guys."

"Not just for me, you idiot!" he cried. "Your friend's stunt is going to cause a global financial meltdown. The repo market is already in free fall. We're talking a complete credit freeze, an upending of the supply chain! All of it is going to grind to a halt. This is going to be the worst financial disaster in the history of the world. In a matter of days, there won't be food at the supermarket. There'll be riots. It'll make the Great Depression look like a Sunday picnic."

I looked at the banker with his thousand-dollar silk tie. He was suddenly worried about the downtrodden, was he?

"Let's get real, Bill," I said. "I can't stop John. You can't stop John. No one can. John's in control, and he is really, really angry. His daughter was murdered. Drugged and raped and murdered. His only child. And you people thought you could just sweep it under the rug. You thought regular rules don't apply to billionaires. Well, guess what? You thought wrong.

"John has the chip, and now he's the one in control. And he's had it. We've *all* had it with you sanctimonious criminals pissing on all the world's regular working folks for too long. We do the real work and make real things. You print fake dollars and steal the real stuff we make.

"Now the shoe is on the other foot, and you can't handle it. Time for you guys to face the music. Denial, anger, bargaining, depression all in just a matter of hours, Bill. And all of that is over now. All you've got left is acceptance."

"Acceptance?"

"Of you and your fellow banksters' total, complete, and utter destruction."

He stared at me silently.

I looked at his creepy painting on the wall.

"Tell me, Bill. How much is that eyesore worth? If you want, I'll help you get it down so you can sneak it out of here."

"What?"

"You're going to need something to sell. Something tangible. Your passport up-to-date? By the closing bell, the stock market is no longer going to exist, and they're all going to blame you. You know that. What you need is an exit strategy now. While you still have time."

I saw him swallow as he stared me.

"It's closing time, Bill. You don't have to go home . . ." I said, looking around his office. "But I'm pretty sure you can't stay here."

92

The conference room on the ground floor of the Federal Reserve was a vast, opulent, windowless, wood-paneled space, and through the center of it ran a boardroom table of dark varnished mahogany that gleamed under the light of an elaborate chandelier.

When Quevedo came into the room on the heels of President Harper at three that afternoon, he counted a dozen men seated down the length of the polished wood runway. All of them were wearing crisp banker suits with their somber expressions.

As they arrived at the side of the table opposite them, the only sound was the ticking of a grandfather clock standing by a portrait of Woodrow Wilson to the right of the arched door. Harper just stood there for a moment, gazing down at the bankers like they were dog shit he had just discovered on his Italian shoe.

"Ladies and gentlemen," he said, "may I remind you of 2008. Your predecessors, or in some cases, you yourselves, sat right here with the very same mission. To save the financial system of not just the United States, but of the world."

"What the hell is this?" cried one of the suits. "What is happening?"

"Agent Quevedo, please explain."

Quevedo blinked as the men in charge of most of the planet's wealth stared a hole through his forehead.

"This morning, around 8:58, a man named John Hayden, a banker from Australia, gained unauthorized access to the computers of the Criterion Group and . . ." he cleared his throat ". . . the Federal Reserve System."

"What in hell?" someone yelled.

"How?" cried another of the bankers.

"Silence, silence," the president said.

"Well," Quevedo said, "we believe Hayden is in possession of game-changing computer technology, a new quantum chip."

He paused, letting the silence stretch for a moment.

"We have been in pursuit of this man for the last week. This same man killed two government agents in Germany and another four intelligence operatives in Key West, Florida. And this morning, he initiated the hacking of the Criterion Group and the Fed."

"Hacked? You mean with a new virus? Another data breach?"

Quevedo shook his head.

"No. This is something far worse. This quantum chip is a new piece of technology that can break through any security system we have today. Your data, your transactions, your entire financial infrastructure—all of it—is now compromised. He could potentially get into any system, any database, passwords, personal data, financial transactions, government secrets, you name it. He could drain all the accounts. Or delete them. He owns the cloud. He can do anything he wants."

"And there's no way it can be stopped?" said a suit.

"No," Quevedo said.

"What is he actually trying to do?" said another of the bankers.

Harper cleared his throat.

"We are not positive," he said, "but at 9:01, Hayden sent out a forged emergency memo that appeared to come from the Federal Open Market Committee."

Harper stared at them.

"This memo instructed the Fed to immediately announce an emergency interest-rate cut."

"Holy hell! Some son of a bitch just up and cut the interest rate?"

"Yes," Harper said. "This fabricated report spread quickly through global financial networks, triggering immediate panic. You saw it. With that and the rumor that the Criterion Group wasn't accessible, the market reacted with sheer terror. By ten o'clock, the US dollar began to plummet, and investors started fleeing to other assets, causing widespread global market turmoil."

"You don't have to tell me," said one of the bankers. "We're down eighteen percent."

"Eighteen? We're down twenty-five," cried another.

"Please," Harper said. "That's why I have brought you all in here. Now, we still don't know how bad it will be as the situation is still ongoing."

"You haven't caught this guy yet?"

"No," Harper said. "That's why we need to hit the ground running. In order to prevent the total collapse of the financial system, just as in '08, I have initiated another emergency rescue plan. The moment this is over, I'm announcing a massive liquidity injection into the financial system. We're going to flood the market with fresh cash to stabilize the currency. We've activated currency swap lines to prevent a total collapse of global trade, and you, ladies and gentlemen . . ."

He flung a folder across the table at them followed by a pen.

" . . . will be the first to sign up for it on the dotted line."

There was a moment of silence as the full impact of his words began to sink in.

"What's to stop this from happening again tomorrow?" one of the bankers wanted to know.

"You don't have to worry about tomorrow," Harper said, folding his arms. "If we survive today, it will be an actual miracle."

93

Hayden, sitting at the computer terminal, checked his watch. He looked at the steel door of the lab. He had already posted the Closed sign on its door. Then he looked at the screen again where the download bar was past the halfway mark.

Two more hours, he thought.

Two more hours to go until the closing bell.

He had already checked the financial channels to see that the first part of the plan had gone off without a hitch. The market was in a free-fall panic to tell the grandkids about.

But it was the second part of the plan that was the most important part.

Without that, none of it would matter, he thought.

He looked at the snail's pace of the download progress.

"Come on," he urged it. "Come on."

He focused intently on the computer screen and was all but oblivious when he heard a quiet shuffle two minutes later.

The hairs on the back of his neck stood up as he turned.

Pierre was standing there unbound, a pair of needle-nose pliers in hand.

Hayden leaped up, immediately blocking the path between Pierre and the door.

"Let me out of here," Pierre demanded.

"I can explain," Hayden said, keeping his voice calm and steady. "It's not what you think."

But Pierre was already moving forward, menacing with the pliers.

Hayden's eyes flicked to the desk, where his gun lay, just out of reach.

They both noticed it at the same moment.

Everything seemed to slow then. Hayden moved first. His heart thudded in his chest, his training kicking in, as he dove for the gun.

As he grabbed it, he heard Pierre sprint past him for the door.

When he turned, he saw Pierre at the door, one hand on the lock, his back turned.

Hayden raised the gun and aimed at his back, his finger hovering over the trigger.

Instead of pulling it, he closed his eyes.

He couldn't do it.

The lock clicked open with a soft metallic sound, and Pierre pushed the door open and bolted out into the hallway.

Hayden hurried to the door and locked it. He looked around and then moved the desk in front of the door. He went over and looked at the laptop where it said one hour and fifty-eight minutes to go.

How long before the cops arrived? he thought. Twenty minutes? Then, SWAT, another twenty or thirty. How long till Homeland Security figured out what was going on and cut the power? An hour probably.

It would be close. It would be damn close.

94

The quantum computer lab at the University of Chicago was in a research center building on Ellis Avenue in Hyde Park behind the library.

"First there was Jekyll," Birch mumbled as he burst out of the SWAT truck into the snow, watching the flow of students for any sign of Hayden. "Now we've got Hyde."

He was rushing through the center's front doors behind SWAT when his phone rang.

"Drop everything," Quevedo said. "We have Hayden. He took over the quantum lab at the St. Philip Neri Children's Hospital downtown. Get there now."

Birch whistled at the FBI SWAT team.

"Back on the pig. St. Philip Neri kids' hospital."

"Where is that?" yelled the driver as he climbed back in.

"Google it!" Birch cried. *"Go!"*

"Is anyone else on scene?" Birch called back into the phone at Quevedo.

"The local cops so far. Hayden's barricaded himself in the lab. He had one hostage who just managed to escape."

"Cut the bloody power!" Birch said.

"We can't," Quevedo said. "Three surgeries are underway, and the mayor's office said no."

"But this bastard is liquidating the global economy! Any more of this and there won't be a Chicago to be mayor of!"

"It doesn't matter. You need to get there, Birch. Kick in the freaking door! Shut this shit down now!"

"On my way," Birch said as the driver let the air horn rip.

He was met by Chicago PD SWAT Team Leader Captain DeRosa at the ER entrance twenty minutes later.

The sound of their boots echoed in the stairwell as he and Birch ascended the stairs two at a time. They hit the fourth-floor landing and were met by six Chicago SWAT cops already there behind their ballistic shields.

"He's in the lab across the corridor to the left," DeRosa said.

One of the SWAT guys opened the stairwell door. Birch looked out. There was a sterile scent of antiseptic and the faint hum of hospital machinery. The door looked too solid to kick in.

Shit, he thought as he ducked back into the stairwell.

"The door's locked, I take it?" Birch said.

The SWAT cop, a short, hard-eyed little Black guy, nodded.

"We need a breaching charge. You guys have any C-4?" he asked.

The SWAT guys looked at him as if he was crazy.

Birch glanced at his watch: 3:45 p.m. Since Hayden was still in there, it meant whatever he was doing wasn't finished. He peeked his head back in the corridor.

"Where is the hostage?"

"The French guy?" the Black commando said.

"Yeah. Whoever he is, we need him. Get him some paper, a pen, and a clipboard."

They brought the scared-looking man up the stairs two minutes later. He was holding a dry-erase board and a marker.

Close enough, Birch thought.

"What does the inside of the lab look like?" Birch said, grabbing the board and the marker.

"Look like?"

Birch drew a rectangle and the door and held up the board.

"This is the door on the corridor. Draw me the rest of the inside. Like we're in kindergarten."

The French guy drew away.

"Here is the refrigerator and desk, and the cryostat is here in the middle."

"Cryo-what?" Birch said. "Kindergarten, remember?"

"That's where all of the computing is coming from. The cryostat," Pierre said.

"That's where the chip is?" Birch said.

"Yes."

"And where is it in the room?"

"Precisely five feet to the right from the door. It comes down from the ceiling of the room."

"Where is it hanging? Around chest height?" Birch said.

He nodded.

"You're positive?"

He nodded again.

"Okay. You can go now."

"What are you going to do?" the SWAT leader DeRosa said.

"Hand me that rifle, Captain, and close the door to the hall behind me," Birch said. "Get down."

95

The upload had five minutes remaining when the firing began.

The wall to the right suddenly blew open where Hayden sat at the desk with the laptop, and bullets began flying through the lab like a swarm of angry wasps. Several of them clanged as they peppered the side of the cryostat.

"No!" Hayden cried.

He leaped up and tried to push the refrigerator toward the hole in the wall. It wouldn't budge. He groaned as he felt something go in his lower back. Finally, there was a terrible screech as the fridge began to move and Hayden pushed it into place, covering the hole to protect the cryostat.

A moment later another blast of fire cut through the wall next to the refrigerator where Hayden was standing. Something stung at his wrist, and as he turned he felt another sting in his upper left back.

He dropped to the floor and crawled over to the desk and grabbed the laptop. He headed toward the helium kegs. Once he was safely behind them, he looked down at the keyboard. His blood began to drip through the spaces in the keys. He stared at the screen where the download continued.

Four minutes, it said.

When he looked back around the kegs, the hole in the wall

was so big he could see into the corridor. There was a guy in a flak jacket out in the hall.

"Hayden, shut it down!" a British voice yelled through the hole. "Shut it down and you live. That's the deal."

Hayden fired his gun through the hole, and the man disappeared.

He got up and flipped the desk up and over, covering the hole. Then he stumbled back and checked the download bar.

Three minutes.

He looked down at his feet. The amount of blood on the floor was amazing. His pants were pretty well covered with it.

Two minutes, said the screen.

He heard a rattle at the door.

Two minutes, it still said.

He lifted the gun and fired a warning shot into the wall beside the door. The door rattled again. It seemed to almost open as there was a thud.

They were kicking it in now. He wasn't going to make it. He was bleeding out. They would come in and stop it.

There was another louder thud at the door.

He would lose at the last second, at the very last second, he thought.

Then his eyes fluttered over to where the helium tanks sat all around him.

And he smiled.

He raised the gun and aimed and pulled the trigger and shot the tank closest to him. He heard the hissing. He shot again at the one behind. More hissing. He fired again and again and again until all ten of the spare helium tanks were hissing wildly.

Thirty seconds later, a loud alarm began to sound from overhead. He crawled over and hunched over the laptop.

One minute to go now.

He hugged it to his chest as the alarm and the hissing continued.

After another minute, he suddenly felt sleepy.

The glorious hissing in his ears sounded like a crowd at a parade, he thought. He began to imagine them as he lay on the floor with the laptop. He smiled, seeing himself walking down Broadway, the crowds behind the police sawhorses. Ticker tape was falling like snow as they cheered. He looked to his left as he felt a warm little hand grip his.

"Oh, Josephine," he said to his daughter. "Isn't this incredible?"

"Yes, Daddy," she said. "It's amazing."

Hayden could still hear all the cheering as he bent down to pick her up, and then he slid under and everything went black.

96

"Birch! Birch! What's going on? Talk to me," Quevedo cried.

"I don't know," Birch said into his phone as he came out in front of the hospital into the snow. It was quite deep now. "I tried to shoot the bloody thing through the wall to shut it off, but now there's all kinds of alarms ringing all over the place, and they're calling an evacuation. They pulled me off the floor."

"What happened?"

"They're saying one of the helium tanks was hit. In an enclosed space, the gas sucks up all of the oxygen."

"Did you shut the computer down?" Quevedo said.

"I don't know. Maybe. Who knows? I can't get in there."

"What about Hayden?"

"If he's in there, he's dead," said Birch. "I can't get back in there until the helium gets vented. They're sending over the fire department hazmat team. I'll go in with them when they get here, but they said this snow is going to slow things down. I'll let you know when we're going in."

Quevedo returned to the conference room and found President Harper at the now-empty table.

"What's the situation?" Harper said.

"They found Hayden," Quevedo said. "He's at the children's

hospital. He took a hostage, but it seems to be over. He's dead in all likelihood."

"And the computer? The chip?"

"We can't get into the lab yet. There was shooting that apparently resulted in the release of some hazardous material. The hazmat team is on its way, but there's a major snowstorm right now in Chicago that could delay things."

"But it's him? You're sure?" Harper said.

Quevedo nodded.

"It's Hayden. It's over."

"It's not over," Harper said.

"Sir?"

"You have to get the chip, Quevedo."

"The chip?"

"Yes. Now that you've stopped Hayden, what's to stop someone else from trying this again? Get that chip and bring it to me. It won't ever be over until we have that chip."

"Okay, sir," Quevedo said.

"Head out to Teterboro now. I'll have a jet waiting for you. You need to go now."

"To Chicago?"

"No, to the moon," Harper cried. "Yes, Chicago. Go get the chip and personally bring it back to me so we can finally put this damned thing to bed."

97

Birch hit Speed Dial on his other phone.

"Mr. Viviani, good news," he said. "We got the bastard. It's over. He was holed up in a children's hospital in Chicago, but the situation is under control now. I'm right outside."

"It doesn't matter. It's too late. It's gone."

"Gone?"

"They restored partial access to our data," Viviani said. "It's all gone. The accounts. He drained them all."

Birch looked up at the fourth floor where the lab was.

"What do you mean *drained*?"

"Trillions of dollars of assets, Mr. Birch, have disappeared. Every last cent. All the government pensions. All of it is gone."

Birch felt dizzy.

"How is that even possible?" he said.

"We don't know," Viviani said. "Our Forensic team is saying he moved the funds through layers of anonymized block-chain accounts through the dark web. Our stock is down twenty percent. It'll be down the other eighty tomorrow once this gets out."

"He stole trillions of dollars? With a *T*?" Birch said.

"The SEC is on the way to the New York office to shutter the doors, Birch. They're saying we are responsible. The tidal wave of consequences hasn't even begun. The lawsuits, the criminal trials." His voice trailed off.

"Sir?"

"Get the chip."

"Get the chip?" Birch said.

"You're there where it is, right?"

"Yes."

"I don't know who you have to kill to get it, but get your hands on that chip and get on the jet and meet me in Geneva. That bastard, Harper, at the Fed thinks he's got me by the balls. We'll see about that."

"I don't understand," Birch said.

"Hayden just showed us that the chip actually works. Hell, even those Bitcoin idiots are about to have to get a job if they don't bow at my feet. We'll be the new Bitcoin. The unhackable quantum Bitcoin."

"I see," Birch said.

"Do you, Birch? You wanted a flat in Kensington, right? You get that chip, and you'll own Kensington itself. Now, go."

98

The place that they hid me away on the second story of the Federal Reserve building with two of the FBI agents looked like a common room inside an Ivy League dorm. There were leather couches and a huge flat-screen and an elliptical machine. There was even a little kitchenette with a cabinet and a sink.

Best of all, there was a regulation-size pool table that we spent several hours taking turns playing each other. But after two hours, the agents had to leave for some reason they wouldn't tell me, and I was locked in alone.

When they left, I tried to turn on the TV to see what the hell was going on, but there was no on button, and I couldn't find a remote. After playing some more pool by myself, I got hungry and went to the pantry and found a couple of cans of Campbell's chicken noodle soup. I poured them out with some tap water into a pot that I found in an upper cabinet.

When I opened a drawer to look for a spoon, I found the TV remote and went over and turned it on. It was already tuned to the financial channel, and on the screen, a red banner was streaming across the bottom.

MARKETS IN FREE FALL—DOW DOWN 60%

"John, you crazy nut," I mumbled.

Above this declaration of doom, the normally composed anchor, some willowy man-child with an expensive haircut, looked sick, panicked as if he could barely hold it together.

Behind him on several screens were stock prices in a sea of red, plummeting with each passing second.

"We are in unprecedented territory here," he said. "Let's not sugarcoat this. The markets are in free fall. This is not a correction. This is systemic failure."

Beside him, an older female financial analyst shuffled through papers, her face tight, strained.

"We are now receiving reports that the Federal Reserve's systems have gone off-line. No official confirmation yet, but banking insiders are telling us that interbank transfers are failing across multiple institutions. People are talking cyberattack. We still have yet to hear from the president. Ken, what is the latest?"

The camera cut to another figure, an older professor type wearing glasses standing in front of the White House.

"Alicia, we're still waiting for a statement from the president. But if what you're saying is true—if the liquidity operations are frozen and payment systems are down—we are looking at something that goes far beyond a market crash. We are talking about a full-scale financial paralysis."

The screen split, showing another commentator, a short loud animated man who was usually mocked for his perpetually bullish stance no matter the circumstances.

"I—I—listen. I've seen crashes, I've seen recessions, but I have never seen this. It's like someone just switched off the economy! If these corporations can't access their funds, if the banks can't process transactions, then we're looking at an instant liquidity crisis. We're watching the wheels come off in real time!"

Coverage cut back to Ken in front of the White House, holding his earpiece.

"The White House remains silent, but we are told emergency meetings are underway at the Treasury and the Fed. We have no confirmation that this is a coordinated attack, but with major firms like Amazon, Microsoft, and J. P. Morgan reporting outages, the question must be asked: Are we witnessing the largest cyber event in financial history?"

"That's exactly what you're seeing, buddy," I said to the television.

I continued to follow the mayhem for another hour or so before I fell asleep on the couch.

It was around six o'clock in the evening when one of the agents woke me up. It was the Indian guy.

"Put your hands behind your back," he said, lifting his cuffs.

"What now?" I said. "Rikers, is it?"

"Just come on," he said, taking me outside into the hall.

I was led to the lobby through the vaulted entryway and back outside. The cops had cleared out the entire street, and there were sawhorses all around the building. We arrived in front of the SUV when we suddenly halted and the agent undid my cuffs.

I looked at him.

"You're free to go," he said. "You'll be contacted if we need you."

"What's going on?" I said. "Where's Quevedo? Are the computers back up?"

He didn't answer. He just turned and went back inside the building, and I was standing there alone on Liberty Street.

I walked out from behind the sawhorses and headed west. The entire street seemed empty. In fact, all of downtown seemed pretty deserted. It reminded me of 9/11, working down here at the pit. How they'd put a fence across Broadway.

That's what it felt like now. Like a bomb had gone off.

Was Hayden alive?

I had a feeling he wasn't. It seemed to me that if he was still on the loose, they would want to keep me around.

I thought about Nat. How she had come all this way to help John and to try to bring him home. She was going to be crushed if he hadn't made it.

I walked up onto Broadway. I didn't catch the name on the neon sign of the bar I walked into a block to the north, but it was a Western-themed joint with cowboy hats and snakeskin boots hammered up on the black-painted walls.

"What can I get you?" the bartender said in a Northern Irish accent.

"A shot of Jameson and a Heineken," I said absently, taking out my phone to call Colleen.

"Cheers to you, John," I said, lifting my whiskey after the bartender left. "I hope you got what you wanted."

99

It was still snowing as Birch, now driving a borrowed Chicago PD unmarked Ford, weaved through the I-90 traffic and got off at the West Loop exit where the industrial areas and cargo areas for O'Hare were. He wasn't used to driving in the snow, so he was glad when he saw the sign for General Aviation.

There it was just beyond the chain link on the tarmac. The Airbus. His ride out of here.

What did the Yanks call it? he thought. *The end zone.*

He patted at the retrieved chip in his pocket.

Touchdown, he mumbled.

His heart pounded with glee as he got out of the car. He had done it yet again. He had won.

"Kensington Palace Gardens, here I come," he sang to himself as he lit up a victory cigar.

"Hey," said a voice.

Birch lowered the Zippo lighter and moved the stogie to the edge of his mouth as he turned.

"Leaving without saying goodbye?" Special Agent Quevedo said suddenly from beside him now. "How could you, Birch?"

His piece came up. It was a Glock.

"After all we've been through?"

"Whoa there, Quevedo. What gives?"

"You give," he said. "You give me that chip or you're going to learn the definition of the words *bloody hell* the hard way."

"Quevedo, how dumb are you?" Birch said. "You're doing this for what? America? America is over. Did it ever even really exist? Do you really think that any countries still exist? They don't. Don't you get it? It's never changed."

"What are you talking about?"

"The king still sits on his throne, you fool. He's never stopped owning it, all of it."

"Hate to burst your bubble, Birch, but he's just a figurehead."

"Oh, you are an idiot. You think he's what? Mickey Mouse? Ronald McDonald? Do prime ministers have to dress in tails to be in the presence of Ronald McDonald? The king and his family and friends are the lords and everyone else on this earth is a filthy peasant. As it was and so it ever shall be. There are just winners and losers. Now, put down that gun and come with me on that plane and be a winner for once in your life."

"You've got it backward, Birch," Quevedo said. "I win, you lose."

The screech of the jet firing up drew Quevedo's gaze left. It was all Birch needed.

To pull a trigger for an untrained person takes the better part of a second on a single-action pistol. For a double-action pistol like the one Quevedo was holding that had to cock back a hammer before the pin hit the primer, the time was twice that, Birch knew.

With the muscle memory of a world-class pistol shooter like himself who could draw and fire in two-tenths of a second, it was no contest at all. Birch hip-shot the Wilson Combat, and in a flash, Quevedo went flying back toward the ground, his eyeglasses sailing in the other direction.

Birch smiled when both Quevedo and his glasses hit the asphalt simultaneously.

But only for a moment.

As the agent's hand hit the pavement, the Glock went off. And Birch felt a hard tap at his chest.

He dropped his Wilson Combat as the asphalt of the parking lot suddenly smashed into his knees. He opened his jacket and looked down to see blood above his heart.

He dipped in two fingers and lifted out the chip.

He stared at it.

It had been shot clean through.

The greatest shot of the idiot's life and he wasn't even alive, Birch thought.

Birch stared at the chip. It was dust now. Gray dust. Metallic ashes, he thought as he watched them flutter to the wet pavement. He thumbed at them in his hand.

Birch started laughing then.

All for nothing, he thought as he tossed the shattered chip.

His shirt was filling with blood. It felt sticky. He felt dirty.

He remembered the apron he had worn at The Grill. The filthy apron. He started to cry as he lay down on the pavement on his side. When a snowflake fell on his lip, he licked at it.

So cold, he thought, and his eyes fluttered and then closed for the last time.

EPILOGUE

100

John Hayden's funeral took place at Rockwood Cemetery in Sydney, Australia, three months after what was called the greatest "flash crash" of all time.

It had been delayed because the authorities wouldn't immediately release John's body to his family, claiming it was part of a crime scene. As if. The powers that be would have put his head on a pike if they could have gotten away with it after what he had done.

There was a lunch afterward in Sydney at a very nice restaurant back on the water called The Quay. Colleen and I were sitting at a table by the window looking out at the breathtaking views of the Sydney Opera House and Sydney Harbour Bridge.

"Hey, look, an opera house, your favorite," I said, teasing her as I squeezed her hand.

"Don't think we're getting out of here without a visit," Colleen said, squeezing it back.

The waitress took our order, and after she left, I found myself looking out at the water, reflecting on everything.

Hayden had been basically a good guy—maybe even a great one—but there was something about our time together that left me with more questions than answers. I had to admit, the way things had unfolded, a lot of pretty bad people had been called to the carpet, which definitely felt like a win. Yet despite this, the chaos that had been unleashed was still reverberating.

Had what John done been worth it? Was it really for the best? I definitely felt conflicted. I couldn't shake the feeling that, somehow, we were still stuck in the middle of something unresolved.

I looked over at Colleen, smiling at me.

Well, at least I was sure about something.

My sweet and beautiful girlfriend had forgiven me for everything. And shockingly enough, the Feds seemed to have forgiven me as well. I thought they would come after me with an army of prosecutors, but so far, so good. Besides, I had a really great lawyer thanks to Colleen's connections. If they charged me, I would start blabbing, so I guess they just wanted the whole thing to simply and quietly go away.

The media had spun the whole incident with the story that the culprit was just a lucky hacker with mental issues, which seemed to satisfy the public, and everyone moved on.

Though, there had been no mention of the quantum chip in the press, I noticed. Where was it? Did the Feds have it? They probably did.

What was a real puzzler, though, was all of the Criterion Group's missing money. The twelve-trillion-dollar firm had had to file for bankruptcy. The CEO, Viviani, was in Switzerland fighting extradition.

Where the trillions had ended up was anybody's guess. Hayden hadn't been working alone, so did his group get it? There was still no word on that.

I turned away from the view to see Nat, who had arranged the whole memorial service, approaching our table.

"Mike," she said, pecking me on the cheek. "Thanks so much for coming."

"Of course," I said. "This is Colleen."

"Nice to meet you, Colleen. I love your dress. So how's Key West these days?"

I laughed as Colleen raised an eyebrow at me.

"I wouldn't know," I said, smiling. "No more midnight margaritas in the garden of Key West for me. I learned my lesson there."

"Have you seen this?" she said, showing me a news story on her phone.

GOLD REACHES 20K!

"I did see that," I said.

I left out the word *happily*.

"John did that, right?" I said.

She nodded.

"How?" I said. "How did he actually do it? What did he actually do?"

"Come with me," Nat said.

101

Nat led Colleen and me outside to the terrace beside the bar.

"When I came home, there was a letter from John for me," she said. "He had a lawyer send it in the event of his death. It explained exactly what he had done."

"Which was what?" I said.

"He bought it," Nat said.

"Bought what?"

"All of the gold," she said.

"All of what gold?"

"All of the gold available on the market," she said. "He drained the Fed and the Criterion Group accounts and used them to buy all the available gold for sale in the world."

"In the world?"

"Yep. Both physical and futures contracts. In a matter of hours, John had cornered the global gold market."

"And that caused the price of gold to go up," I said.

"Exactly. Gold prices surged exponentially as John drained every major vault. Within hours, the price of gold had skyrocketed to unprecedented levels. Global investors, governments, and central banks scrambled to secure gold, but it was too late. John, with the Feds' own unlimited monetary firepower, beat them to the punch. There was none left to buy."

I shook my head.

"That's when John was killed."

"Yes," she said.

"I'm so sorry," said Colleen.

"I know. Thanks. Me, too."

Nat took a breath and sighed.

"Then the Federal Reserve sprang into action."

I nodded.

"I was there when all the suits arrived," I said. "Just like in '08, they hit the do-over button, right?"

"Right," Nat said. "To prevent the total collapse of the financial system, they initiated its emergency rescue plan. An unprecedented stimulus program to jump-start the US economy. By the end of the week, the immediate crisis had been averted. The dollar had stabilized. But the price of gold remained shockingly high."

"Why?" I said.

Nat smiled and turned toward the bar.

"Phil," she called over with a little wave of her hand.

A tall white-haired older man with a beard walked over.

"Phil, this is Mike Gannon, the man I was telling you about," Nat said. "Mike, this is Phil Molineux, a very good friend of John's."

I looked at the affable-looking old man. Then at Nat. She had a funny expression on her face.

"Is that right?" I said as we shook hands.

"Nice to meet you, Mike. I hear that you and John were good friends, too. Nat told me all about your exciting adventure with John this past spring."

"Oh, it was exciting, all right," I said.

"Phil's a writer, Mike," Nat said. "He's written several books about economics and finance. Brilliant, really. He can explain this stuff to anyone."

"I'll do my best," Phil said, smiling warmly.

102

Phil and I left the ladies behind and sat down at the bar.

"Before we start, Mike, I believe I owe you an apology."

"An apology to me?" I said. "For what?"

He patted me on the arm as he leaned in closer.

"For not charging that damned Tesla before I gave the fob to John."

"Oh!" I said, smiling. "You were . . ."

Molineux winked.

He was the contact with the software John had met at Jekyll Island.

"Guilty as charged," Molineux said.

We paused as the bartender came over. Phil ordered a Scotch, and when I was asked what I wanted, I smiled as I remembered the drink that John had bought me at Red's bar in Key West.

"I'll have a tequila sunrise," I said.

"To John," I said, lifting my glass when the bartender came back.

"To John," Phil agreed with a smile. "Now, what would you like to know, Mike?"

"Was it even worth it? What John did?" I said. "Despite the bailout, the banks are still failing, inflation's out of control, and everything seems on the brink. I mean, didn't John just create more of a disaster?"

"It does look like a disaster, doesn't it?" Phil said. "But don't worry. It's not the end. It's just the beginning."

"How?" I said.

"The Federal Reserve is about to collapse."

My eyes went wide.

"The gold reserves that the government holds and all of the gold that John bought with the funds from the Fed and the Criterion Group are about to be put to use in a way that no one expects," Phil said.

"A week from today, the US Treasury will announce a new gold standard. The gold will be distributed to a network of new state banks that we have ready to go. The government will hand over control to these state banks, and they will issue a new gold-backed currency that will stabilize everything. The Federal Reserve will no longer be in control. The money printing? Stopped. The instability? Over. The massive debt? Gone."

I let that sink in for a minute.

"How do you know this?"

"Because I just wrote the resignation speech for the president of the Fed," he said. "I've been in Washington working on the plan for the last three months."

"But a new system?" I asked. "Won't that cause more chaos? Bank runs or something?"

Phil raised his free hand, his expression serene.

"There will be chaos in the beginning, yes. But that's necessary. People need to feel the fall in order to embrace the rise. The current system has been built on the false premise that money can be printed without consequence. That's over now. Next week, the reset begins."

"You're saying that the markets, the banks, the entire financial system will just . . . change overnight?"

He nodded. "Yes," he said.

"That doesn't seem possible," I said.

"Well, Mike, consider all the wars, 9/11. One day, everything is fine. The next, the whole world has changed."

He had a point there.

"It's all set," Phil said. "The politicians are all on board, the Federal Reserve Board, the investment banks. It's all agreed. A week from this Monday, there will be a press conference where the Fed will announce its insolvency, and the shift to a new de-centralized, gold-backed transition will begin. Our country will be as good as gold once more. Pun intended."

"But how?" I cried.

"How what?" Phil said.

"How the hell did you get the politicians and the Fed and the bankers to *agree*?"

Phil smiled.

"It was pretty simple, actually. John's first target was the servers of the intelligence agencies and the tech giants. All of the top global law firms in New York City and Washington, DC, London, and Geneva were also instantly hacked. Cutting through their firewalls, the AI-powered system enabled John to collect all the incriminating emails, text messages, and video and JPEG files, which were transferred into an undisclosed encrypted vault."

"Blackmail," I said.

"Two weeks after the collapse, all the compromised individuals in DC and the Federal Reserve were sent text messages detailing bits of the evidence along with the instruction that if they put up any resistance to the new gold standard plan, all the files would be released on July Fourth this year. They were informed the whole thing was on a quantum-encrypted unstoppable dead man's switch set to release unless a worldwide announcement of a new US Treasury gold standard was implemented."

"He who holds the blackmail makes the rules," I said.

Phil smiled, his soft blue eyes twinkling.

"You'd be amazed at the cooperation our team has been getting."

I shook my head.

"You crashed the corrupt system, bought back all the gold with the stolen loot, then blackmailed the bums into creating a new gold-backed system all in one fell swoop. You really rooked them."

"Not me. It was John," he said. "He devised the whole plan after he discovered the chip. And he took it upon himself to execute it, though it cost him his life."

"If this works," I said, shaking my head, "John will be a hero, a true hero."

"Like Andrew Jackson," Phil said, "John may very well have beaten the bank yet again."

★ ★ ★ ★ ★